PARIS FOR TWO
TIL DEATH DO WE PART

PARIS FOR TWO
TIL DEATH DO WE PART

DOLORES MAGGIORE

SAPPHIRE BOOKS

SALINAS, CALIFORNIA

This and other Sapphire Books titles can be found at
www.sapphirebooks.com

Dedication

To my wife Terrie, for her belief in me and this work
and her ongoing patience.

Acknowledgments

To Chris Svendsen and Schileen of Sapphire Books, for championing this project and to all the warm, beautiful women writers in the Sapphire family. And to my editor, Tara Young, and my book designer, Lori Reynolds.

To my critique group in Portland: Kylie Schachte, Elena Wiesenthal, Susie Frank, Mary Rose, and especially Lori Ubell for suggesting I begin book number three with Pina in Paris. Without their support this work would not exist.

Another shout out to my beta readers/editors in Canada, Borrego Springs, New York, Hood River, and Portland. Thanks Kari Dehli, Pam Blake, Barbara Murphy, Shannon Perry, Debbie Dodds, and Ali Shaw of Indigo.

Finally to a wellspring of creativity, Portland's Literart Arts INCITE: Queer Writers Read and its founders, *the Kates*—Kate Carroll De Gutes and Kate Gray.

Chapter One

Shipboard

Black waters swirled around the stern of the ship. I hung my head low over the steel-cold railing, my stringy hair dripping the icy rain down the neck of my jacket. I'd left Katie at the pier ten days ago. Ten sunsets over briny waters. Black with the many fathoms beneath us. Black like my mood.

"Go," Katie had said. "Go and grow!" Now I was truly at sea, alone. This was the longest I'd been separated from her since that summer in 1959, two years ago—that summer marked by our evolution from just good summer friends to girlfriends and sleuths solving a murder. And only a few months later to lovers, when we got to Albert Academy. Together forever.

The ship entered the English Channel. I was way gone now. The early morning fog draped the Isles of Scilly—a bland British welcome. There was no turning back. I sighed at the bleakness of it all.

An albatross squawked. I barely lifted my head in its direction. A ship's mate approached.

"Miss, are you ill?" he asked, trying to see my face. "You seem troubled. Do you need help?" He continued to bother me with his questions. God, maybe he thought I was going to throw myself into the sea.

"No, thank you. Just writing a poem in my head,"

I mumbled, waving him off.

Ha! Yes, I was deeply troubled, but not to that degree, and certainly, if I ever was that depressed, I wouldn't choose to end it all in the water—not before dawn. Besides, there would be no dawn in this soup.

The pease porridge parted for just a second, long enough for me to spot something large and rolling in the water—oil barrels, several oil barrels. The ship lurched, engines roared, alarm bells sounded. I flew across the deck, skidding on the slick spray, propelled toward the lifeboat slip where the chain used to be. There was nothing between me, the slip, and falling over the brink of the ship. I had no words, no concrete thoughts, except a flash of death cutting short my eighteen years.

This was not the first time my life had flashed before my eyes. For a split second, I relived the cutting, penetrating bodily sensations of the gruesome attack and murder that haunted my dreams and the real one Katie and I had helped to solve two summers before. My body jerked as if it were happening—now, again, to me.

I opened my eyes. I was flat on the deck, wet but safe, stopped from meeting my briny doom by see-through plastic barriers blocking the lifeboat stations. The same mate as before perched over me. Was his grin sardonic?

"You said you were not troubled." He raised his eyebrows and strutted off.

I dug my nails into the heel of each hand and pushed myself up. Fine. I was fine. My past had nothing to do with this. I slipped; that was all.

A metallic clanging drew me back to the mate's receding figure and the lock and chain dangling from his pocket. I blinked. Gone. Imagined?

❧❧❧❧

Thank God for good coffee on Italian ships. I went below to get a caffe latte at the bar since I was in no shape to take a seat in the dining room. I had no idea how close I had actually come to disaster or why even I thought that. The ship had lurched; that was all! Everything had resumed its air of normalcy.

There was the normal array of students and professors. They had the normal conversations about normal intellectual subjects in English, Italian, French, and German. They were all American and European. All normal. We all had the same initial destination: Le Havre, France.

The crossing of the Atlantic had taken ten days. Our Italian ship, the *Aurelia,* was small, three hundred people plus the crew. We had become familiar, dancing together at bars, sipping espresso and wine at one of the smaller bistros.

This was European life, an introduction to my senior trimester in Paris. Maybe my mood was also part of a role: morose, beat existential, queer poetess. I'd heard that was fitting for Paris in 1961.

Actually, underneath my blasé, pseudo-intellectual mask, being off on my own away from Albert Academy to study at the Institut Catholique in the heart of the bohemian 6th arrondissement—that somewhat excited me. *Somewhat* because the real benefit was an escape from the pressure my folks, Katie, and my instructors were putting on me to choose a path, get on with my life, and apply to colleges. I was doing none of those things.

The only thing missing was Katie—and maybe some Librium for my anxiety. Missing now ten days and ten nights. Every night, I heard the ship's bells ring out over long, long hours while the vibrations of the engines rumbled and clanged under my meager stateroom. For ten nights, I'd roamed the ship's corridors searching for the galley, searching for sustenance, searching for something solid to hold on to.

All I wanted to embrace was Katie and my life with her. *That* filled me up. I'd be nothing without her. I struggled with this feeling of emptiness. What would my mind and body do to fill it? No way could I imagine college apart from her.

After those forays around the ship, I always returned to my solitary bunk to dream of Katie's phantom touch. I would have to wait four months until January to hold Katie again.

Waiting. As a kid, I had spent seven summers vacationing with my folks and Katie and her family in Maine, waiting cluelessly for my real feelings for Katie to spring to life. When they did, no phantom feelings there. So four months, four months to feel her next to me and to share my bed with her.

My dreams with Katie alternated with nightmares of a reaper letting my life ooze out through his fingers. At other times, I was dressed as the reaper cutting short my own life.

❧❧❧❧

I had to stop thinking of Katie. *Here*, here I was *now*—in the bar—on the ship. *Now*.

I took a sip of my second espresso as a butter-yellow stain spread across the bar's porthole in the corner of my eye. I lifted my gaze toward it in the hopes of lifting my mood. Maybe I would catch the sunrise. Instead, I found myself almost eye-to-eye with a sweet leprechaun-like man seated across the table. He was dressed in a black soutane and wore rimless glasses. A smile crept over his face as he pointed to the thin, somewhat dirty white collar peeking out from his black top. His green eyes twinkled behind bottle-gray lenses. He was a priest unlike any I had ever met.

He stood, bowed with a flourish, and extended his arthritic hand. "*Mes salutations, mademoiselle. Joseph Sablé, Père Sablé.*"

His smile was infectious. My whole face responded. I suddenly felt alive.

"*Enchantée*," I mustered up, unsure of what the protocol was for meeting a priest with impish, sprite-like qualities.

"I have been watching you," Père Sablé fired off in French. "You have many gifts, I know." As he sat, he touched the side of his thin Gallic nose and removed his glasses. Still studying me, he breathed on his glasses and rubbed them dry on his soutane.

"*Merci, Père*," I responded. What did he know?

"*Ah, mon Dieu!* You think I'm just flirting. I can assure you I am not. I have known many, many students. *You* are special."

He squirmed about in his bent-wire bistro chair to reach into his pants pocket. He pulled out his business card and a holy picture of Saint Sebastian, martyr. "The little people, eh? They still know best."

I thought he was referring to himself. He only stood about five-foot-three.

He explained, "Ah. How do you call them in English, djinns—*ah non*, genies? Ah, yes, the little people…But here, take this. I think Saint Sebastian is important for you."

Huh? My father's name was Sebastian. I had no time to ask since Père Sablé was already standing again, bowing, and shuffling off. His soutane danced around his sabots, mule-like leather slippers. He turned around, flashing me one last smile, and said, "You *will* see me!"

"*Ciao*," I said, waving goodbye.

I laughed, a bit more upbeat. I flipped his card over and over as I finished my second espresso. I noticed the title under his name: *Professeur de français, Institut Catholique.*

⁂

Docking at Le Havre later that day was a sailor's ballet, a maritime opera. Ropes unfurled and flew through the air while tanned, muscular arms slipped knots around nautical bitts. Chants of "*Bien, par ici*" rang out, answered by "*Fais gaffe*" and "*Zut! Alors.*" An aroma of seaweed, rotting fish, and wine permeated the fog rolling in.

After I had taken care of my papers and luggage, I spotted my first bit of French manna for sale for one franc or *mille balles*: a crunchy baguette of French Bayonne ham and butter—pure, rich butter. The sandwich, along with sheer piss and vinegar on my part, got me on the train to Paris. The passing farmland of Normandy and the clickety-clack of the train lulled me to sleep most of the four-hour ride to Saint-Lazare station in Paris.

Getting off the train, people formed a frenetic ant-like queue to find the Métro. I remembered all the instructions Mademoiselle Lesage, my former professor, had given me about buying a *carnet* and not just a ticket. I had memorized the route to Alésia station.

I switched my leaden suitcase from hand to hand as I took in a deep breath. I would arrive at my room at the Foyer St. Joseph de Cluny in a few blocks.

When I saw it, the cement block wall and the iron grille put me off. This did look like a convent boarding house. There was a sign with instructions for after-hours entry—after 8:00 p.m.

I felt tears rimming my eyes when a torpedo of a human clothed in black and white sped in my direction. A nun made a straight trajectory to the heavy locked gate—and me. When the gate opened, flowing sleeves covering short stubby arms draped themselves over my suitcase. A voice sang out, "*Venez*, come."

Before I knew it, the woman had clutched me to her ample breasts and given me a heartfelt Gallic welcome. Mère Paul, I thought, based on the description Mademoiselle Lesage had given me. She escorted me to an austere building whose wrought-iron stairs led to my corner room. Mère Paul deposited me at my door, thrust the massive key in my hand, and disappeared almost in a puff.

Inside, I decided I would investigate my room later. I collapsed fully clothed on the bare mattress.

Chapter Two

Cassia

A metallic scraping screeched to a halt. A window slammed against its casement as a gauzy curtain whipped in and out with the chilling gust. An electrical storm lit up the room. I startled awake to blackness and tumbled off the bed in search of a light switch.

The bare electric bulb introduced me to my stark eighteenth-century room with its tall opened windows, blowing and banging against each other.

So, there was my *chamber*, which reminded me that I had to pee. A quick glance told me that my room was equipped with a *lavabo* (sink) but not a *toilette*. The old enamel bidet would work well as a chamber pot. At this point, I really lacked the guts and the energy to work the intermittent lights down the stairs to the outdoor WC.

With a sigh of relief, I plopped back down on my bed. I really felt jumpy—not quite homesick yet. Not afraid of storms, in general—but…that weird thing on the boat…that creep of a sailor…Man! I needed sleep.

I snorted, thinking about the priest and the nun. Definitely far out, but friendly spirits.

Oh, merde—I decided I would now adopt French mannerisms and curses! I just wanted a cool French experience, no drama, nothing creepy, well…not boring, but *normal*.

I started to space out, back to Katie and the last two years at Albert. That was natural. Katie was my norm. Well, I thought of us as typical—as typical as… uh…the local chapter of the Daughters of Bilitis, the lesbian group in Andover we lied about our age to join; as ordinary as Doc and Joe, Katie's parents in Faggots for Freedom, their nickname for the Mattachine Society in Boston.

I just wanted normal. Everything just the way it was. I wrinkled my face. What was I doing in Paris? Besides the fact that Katie made me come. She liked that her girlfriend was going to live in Paris.

Normal? And what part of normal was I choosing to forget? As if I could ever forget Headmistress Craney and my death wish. Ha! I would have rather died—I even thought I would when she cornered me… threatened me, breathing down my neck, her clothes in my bed…her hands, her tongue all over my…

I felt the icy perspiration on my forehead. If I didn't pinch myself or start breathing deeply…images from the summer before Albert, before Craney, impressions of the bones, lurid flashbacks, dreams of rape and murder. I had to stop. We had solved that murder way before Craney even crossed our path when we arrived at Albert in September. I had to stop connecting the two.

Blackout. I shut my mind down. I had to. I blew out a huge breath and leaned back on the scratchy pillow. I did my breathing exercises. Slow. Rhythmic. In, out. Craney was over. Gone, vanished like the ghoul she was, driven out two years ago now.

I yawned. And I was dead asleep again, at sea, swirled about in a maelstrom with eerie northern lights illuminating translucent sea creatures staring at me through neon green eyes. They were rocking me back and forth—me, a mere toy for their water sports.

"*Réveille-toi! Réveille-toi! Ça va?*"

"*Oh, merde!*" I shrieked. And then, "*Oh, merde!*" again when I knew I had to apologize to this person—she was real, I think, a real French person—for cursing. "*Je suis desolée,*" I managed to say sorry before tumbling out of bed.

She laughed. This pixie-like creature smiled. She smiled with her eyes, her mouth, and every strand of her short, lush blond hair danced in a smile. Her eyebrows, too, seemed to smile. "*Je suis Cassia.*" She laughed again. Cassia extended her hand. I thought she wanted to shake hands—how French! I tried to do a formal introduction, mumbling instead, "Pina, Pina, Pina!" from where I still lay on the floor. She snickered in a burst of warmth and complicity as she pulled me up.

"I am Pina," I babbled. "I don't usually hang out on the floor."

"*Dommage,*" she said and repeated in English, "What a shame."

We finally shook hands. I thought I heard a bell and the fluttering of wings. Cassia wore her blond, shiny hair in a short artichoke cut, and her outfit was hardly a maillot-type swimsuit, but she could have played Tinker Bell.

I snapped out of my Peter Pan references to laugh with her. She guffawed and shook me by the shoulder in a playful move. "*Mais non*, I like you better on your feet."

She looked me over from head to toe, all five feet of me.

"Come, I will help you to bed," Cassia said.

I gawked at her until I realized I had translated her suggestion wrong. Very wrong.

She flipped open the package of rough muslin sheets lying at the foot of the bed and showed me how to tuck in the sheets French style, all the while chattering in fast, heavily accented French. She was from Bastia, Corsica, she explained, and bumped me out of the way with her hip to finish my corner tuck for me.

I admired her work—as well as her hips nicely accentuated by her fuchsia knit wool dress.

"*Voilà*," she exclaimed, patting the bed. "It is ready, like you. You are sleepy, yes?"

"*Oui*. I'm tired from the ship."

"This room is special, alive with noises! Wait, you will hear the old lady next door, the old goat I call her. She tinkles all night long. And that fireplace, it howls, too, but good for cooking. Speaking of cooking, I will take you to the dining room. Come!"

We descended the stairs arm in arm, breaking step only to punch the timed light switch. We took an intermittent semi-dusk stroll. Maybe I would like this French adventure.

Chapter Three

French Table Manners/French Kissing

Cassia and I rattled our way down the outdoor iron stairs. She jumped the last few steps to the ground and held out her hand for me.

The dining hall, located in the building across the courtyard, was convent spartan and lacked the historic charm of the medieval-like refectory at Albert. Girls and nuns, a few in black and white religious habits, stood. Mère Paul presided over the head of the main table arranged in a cross formation with five other tables.

"Bless us, O Lord, and these, thy gifts…" Mère Paul's deep resonant syllables intoned the grace prayer. I quickly swallowed the olive I had already swiped.

We sat in a collective scraping of chairs. Cassia introduced me to the four others at the table—girls with long, unwashed, bowl-type haircuts, maybe novices— two wearing frowns and those typically French smoke- gray glasses.

I let out a soft sigh. Cassia tapped my leg under the table. Under her breath, she mumbled in English, "Dull table tonight," and gave me a signal to hurry and finish.

Unaccustomed to such huge leaves of lettuce, I attempted some furious fork-and-knife work, resting my knife after each cut and replacing my hand in my lap. Cassia became my French etiquette coach. She whispered in my ear, "In France, one doesn't cut lettuce." She shrugged with an impish grin.

Man! All I wanted was to get the heck out of there, and I turned to gape at Cassia, whose eyes shot wide open. A huge hand grasped my right shoulder as black fabric fluttered in my face. That deep, resonant voice asked, "*What* are you doing in your lap?" Mère Paul was scarlet, perspiring, and breathing heavily.

"*Rien!* Nothing." I gasped.

She pulled my hand onto the table. "One keeps one's hands on the table in France." She blew out a huge breath and floated away.

I froze. I started to drift away. No, I couldn't faint. But that swish of black, that long habit, the drape of the sleeve…I put my head down as old visions of Albert Headmistress Craney flickered on and off in my mind.

Cassia did a quick pan of my body. She slipped our napkins into the holders, excused us, and all but enfolded me in her protective French arm hold.

"*Qu'est-ce qu'il y a?*" She inquired what had happened once we were outside.

I opened my mouth to explain. Nothing came out. I felt my legs buckle, my stomach turn. My heart was in my throat, choking me, my left arm paralyzed, my chest knotted in an old, familiar constriction. I started breathing deeply now so it wouldn't go full-blown. I was not dying, and I wouldn't allow myself to really panic, not any more than this.

I hadn't had an episode this extreme in ages. Two years to be exact. And I was having none of this attack now. I did a series of deep breaths again. I pressed my eyes tight and willed the words, syllable by syllable, out of my mouth. "I'll explain, but what I'm thinking just can't be."

Cassia's eyebrows shot up. She glanced right and then left, gaze dancing with concern, as well as curiosity. "I like this intrigue, but I like you better on your feet." With that, she zoomed us up the stairs and navigated us deftly through darkened doorways to our room.

Cassia pushed me onto my bed. She made a very French pout with an added shrug. "Eh? Worried about Mère Paul? Harmless." She spoke with her hands mimicking eating salad to explain that Mère Paul and the others would teach me French table manners. She giggled. "In America, you cut salad, and you play with yourself at table?"

I exploded in laughter. "Play with myself?"

She shrugged. "What do I know? I just met you. But something bad happened. Yes?"

I gave Cassia the short version of Craney: "Once upon a time, there was an old witch who wore a black academic gown—who had it in for me. Mère Paul's black outfit made me think of her." I gritted my teeth, afraid I'd go on.

"And?" Cassia opened her eyes, two thirsty orbs ready to drink in all the juicy details. "More, more." She clapped her hands.

"No! It's ancient history. Besides, she's gone." Wasn't she?

"Gone...dead?"

"Don't think so, but she wouldn't dare..."

I only occasionally got the willies these past two years when Craney wandered through my dreams, leering at me, trapping me in the bathroom... The newness of everything here and that weird nowhere feeling on the long haul at sea, seeing nothing but dark, roiling, cold waters, no land, nothing to hold on to—jeez, I was breaking into another sweat even now—all that left my nerves kind of raw.

"*Oh, zut!* End of story?"

"*Oui. La fin.* End of drama." I yawned, thinking of my first day of classes the next day.

"*Excuse-moi.* I think you are tired, but wait. First your French kisses. In Corsica, four times." She kissed me on one cheek, squished past my nose to the other cheek, and kept up this nose-to-nose ballet another two pas de deux.

Oh, Lord! I just wanted to sleep.

Cassia flitted to her bed. I thought I heard fluttering and a bell again.

"See! Hear her tinkle? It's the old goat peeing already!"

Chapter Four

Night Noises

Ping! Ping! Pee and porcelain. The old goat next door must have peed in her pot at least five times in two hours. Almost midnight...I was hearing bells, church bells, tinker bells. I even dreamed of Christmas. Hmm, maybe Katie could come before February.

Each time I fell asleep and started to dream of Katie, of Cassia, of school bells, the old lady goat peed again. I was just about settling into a lusty dream of Katie with bells on her toes when louder bells sounded.

I laughed in my half sleep, but then I heard the gong-like sound again, along with a rumbling vibration, followed by metallic bongs.

"*Au feu!*" shouted Cassia.

I didn't understand. I yelled, "*Merde!*" but Cassia repeated the word *fire* again and dragged me out the door and down the stairs. This was real—no drill.

Red lights flashed in the courtyard, emergency lights blinking on and off from inside the main building. Short two-tone blasts—French sirens reminiscent of war movies—pierced the night, punctuating the French girls' breathy exclamations: "*Mon Dieu!*" and "*Maman!*" whispered across the courtyard gardens.

We stood there, just outside the door to our building, half-naked in the autumn chill, stars lighting our silhouettes. No emergency directions. No one in charge. No flames.

A thin wisp of smoke funneled out of the kitchen door at the far end of the courtyard. A rotten-egg stench wafted across the grounds, thick and dank. Still no flames. No fire engines. Just contained confusion.

And then the air was still. Emergency flashers extinguished, and pitch regained the night. Voices hushed. Stars illuminated. The central floodlights soon bathed the courtyard in their sickly yellow glow.

I crossed the courtyard and leaned against the stucco of the main building to get a better look. A door adjacent to me thrust open, bringing me face-to-face with a woman—I had no other descriptor for the sight before me other than *bull dagger*. She was, as my father would have described her, built like a brick outhouse—but *outhouse* was not the word my father used. Her short, very short, buzzed grayish head complemented her piercing blue eyes that immediately sought mine.

"Ah, mon enfant..."

Who was this big, strong woman, and why was she calling me her child? And why did she grasp my shoulder that way, a grasp I recognized?

She moved me gently to the side, whispering that there was no danger. It was then I recognized her, out of her habit, in her nightshirt—Mère Paul.

Still clutching my shoulder, she quickly told all of us there was no fire. "Just the devil blowing smoke, as they say." She laughed. "But who is this devil?"

"Someone has set off a stink bomb. *Crétin!* Go back to bed, all of you. I am sorry for this disturbance. You are safe. Now scoot out of the courtyard!"

She turned to me. "Stay!" Her clutch gave me no choice, and I somehow doubted her facile explanation.

There was something bizarre about all this.

"My child, you must not be scared. I will teach you. At dinner, I was not angry with you, just with an old fool who still haunts me from the war. Sometimes, she gets in my head, and I go crazy. I rule this convent, not that witch!"

Her piercing blue eyes begged acknowledgment in mine. I smiled weakly, weary and bleary-eyed. "*Oui, Mère.*"

"I take care of you, don't worry." Warmth seemed to radiate from her, from her whole compact presence. She smiled, patting me on the back. "Go, *ma petite. Bonne nuit.*"

This time, I believed Mère Paul was as harmless as Cassia had said. Yet I stood there a second shaking my head. I found this whole mid-night scene unbelievable. A smoke bomb, an old, haunting spirit, the war.

By the time I mounted all the steps, I knew I had not been dreaming. I was wide awake. As I approached my room, I heard the old goat peeing and Cassia—who seemed to remain unfazed by strikes, power outages, and fires that did not materialize—already gently snoring. All else was still.

Sleep? Heck no. Write to Katie? Yup! That was what I had to do. This was her specialty: calming me in the middle of the night, usually with one soothing glance from the deep aquamarine oceans of her eyes.

I took out her picture, eased myself between the scratchy sheets, and propped her on the block of stationery. God, I ached for her. "Oh, Katie…"

No other words came. Not at first. My head nodded over the paper. I kissed her photograph and imagined the thoughts flowing from my head directly to the paper or through my eyes to hers.

I must have fallen asleep, but when I woke with ballpoint ink all over my arm, I was holding something I had actually written.

Craney—I am not afraid! I haven't really worried about her for two years. She's gone. For sure. Maybe I'm just homesick, a stranger in a sort of strange land. Like I worried about fitting in at Albert. Tonight, Mère Paul, the bull dagger (yeah!) head of this place, told me there are always old devils blowing smoke. Now I know what she meant. It's the old devil of fear inside of me. Just something old when I have to face something new—without you.

Send me some dreams, my sweet. I do feel your eyes on me now, on and in every part of me, flashing warm and safe sensations all over. I love you, Katie.

At this point, there was a huge squiggle of ballpoint ink. I must have really conked out. Well, something worked in that letter—Katie's magic—because now I felt calm and safe. I liked Mother Paul, and Craney was absolutely gone, gone, gone! *And* I knew that night I would probably sleep for a few hours before I had to get up.

Chapter Five

Catacombs and Construction Sites

Yellow. A yellow haze filtered into the room. I had forgotten to lower the metal shades and close the shutters. I thought about the French word *jaunâtre* and those French suffixes meaning "-ish." So it was really yellowish haze that coated the windows and crept across the floor. My blackish mood had lifted somewhat. I would walk all the way to my first day of class.

Wow! It was October 4. I'd almost forgotten my birthday, my eighteenth. Here without Katie, it didn't mean that much to me. Besides, we had celebrated with my first legal cocktail at the Exeter Inn a few nights before I left. Eighteen…so I couldn't vote yet, but Albert considered us adults. They trained us that way; they demanded that we act like *tomorrow's women*: independent, competent, ready to take our place on the world stage.

Well, here I was on the Paris wing of that stage. And I was about to make my entrance *en scène*.

Too early to eat. I would treat myself to a croissant en route. Wearing the only article of clothing I considered artsy, my mother's rustish suede Eisenhower jacket, I walked up Rue du Père Corentin to Avenue René Coty. I lusted after the lean look—a leanness that my short, muscular body would never possess—of the French girls wearing body-hugging, jewel-necked cashmere or fine-knit sweaters and hip-clinging skirts. Their shoes were clunky, made for walking.

I drifted along, spellbound by the aroma of butter and eggs baking and fish fresh from briny waters. Early morning sounds of unloading crates of fruit and piled baskets of seaweed and oysters were lyrical movements squishing and seeping. I was drifting off in my head when I focused on a familiar Parisian feature. I laughed at the sign for the catacombs. My French catacomb project at Albert two years ago came to mind.

I walked down memory lane for a second, smiling, thinking of all those bones and tunnels that Katie and I had made out of papier-mâché.

As I approached Boulevard Raspail and the short cuts that went over to the student quarter, I looked at signs with unfamiliar words. "*Chantier*" written on a boarded-up fence in between "*Anarchie*" and "*DeGaulle=Dégout*." A whole new world opened before my eyes: a construction site for a new building. Fascinated by the dance of brown, taut bodies walking up girders and operating cranes, I peered deep into the excavation and wondered what ancient beings had walked there. I leaned over quite a bit, squinting at a pottery shard. A man's voice cried out at me, "*Attention au crâne!*" I tried to shrug French style. He continued to yell, tapping his head.

So what? He thought I was crazy. Crane? Oh, right, cranium—the guy was telling me I should have a hard hat. Crane? Craney…I shivered. No! I wasn't going to do this. Craney was ancient history. I was alive and safe. I had to bury this chapter once and for all.

No sooner had I repeated this to myself and

marched away from the construction site than I heard a loud whistle, a huge commotion—a girder crashing to the ground from the crane's dangling cables. I looked back up. A body suspended—falling?—close to me. Too close.

Sirens blared, echoing up and down the narrow streets. I ran and finally slumped against a building a block away, out of breath, and allowed myself to slide to the ground. I sat there, my mind racing. Was there a net? Safety mats? Those guys did this all the time, didn't they? I mean, they didn't die… There must have been another safety cord, no?

My forehead was wet ice, clammy. My gut heaved. I dug my nails into my palms. If I could feel my sharp nails, really feel them, I would not faint. And there was nothing in my stomach to throw up.

I rose to a squat and watched the Parisian flow: rusty black mopeds, rickety Deux Chevaux, their side windows flapping, men in lush turtlenecks and berets, stylish women whose jackets flared just at the hips. Not-so-little boys wore long shorts and high socks and carried rectangular wooden pencil cases. A body remained suspended in my memory. Should I go back? Did I really see that?

I stood and walked, feverishly naming all the makes of French cars, repeating the names of all the new shops, and mumbling all the French expletives I knew. Finally, I entered a *boulangerie* and bought an almond croissant. I allowed the buttery paste to squish through my teeth, the better to release the almond essence. Petal-like pastry flakes scattered all about my face in the morning breeze.

Could I block out the questions screaming in my head? What the heck had just happened? Did it have anything to do with me, and why was I allowing dead spirits to haunt me? And did I actually know he was dead? Did I really see this? Maybe my jangled nerves and lack of sleep…

I arrived at the Institut and sat on a step. I painted a blank screen inside my forehead and practiced deep breathing. I settled down now, thinking in black and white. Okay, so I was nervous. Why? My French was good. I saw cuties checking me out…some sweetie with a real pixie haircut, a nonchalant scarf knotted around her neck, and the sexiest dimples—on a moped no less—actually fingered my suede jacket and pronounced it *chouette*! I had to believe I, too, was just too *cool*! With that, I blew out a huge breath.

Chapter Six

Père Sablé

Once I had convinced myself that both my jacket and I were cool, I held my head high—in time to see Père Sablé roll up to the curb on his ancient moped carrying a black leather folder and a crushed baguette under his arm. He dismounted, gave me a wink, and marched off to the side door of the Institut. Turning back, he smiled at me and tapped his watch, a Mickey Mouse watch.

I managed to get a front-row seat right beneath the teacher's desk on a raised platform. I really lucked out: upon entering the room in a swish of his flowing black garb, Père Sablé immediately took to the podium-like desk and began to orate.

He spouted famous lines from seventeenth-century classic French plays. He was at the top of his game when he cited the "go, run, fly, and avenge us" speech from *Le Cid* by Corneille. The class continued to cheer as he bowed.

Père Sablé stopped abruptly as a look of sadness or fear crossed his face. The silence in the room was deafening. After a minute or two, the only sound was an occasional squeak of a chair as someone shifted uncomfortably.

"You." He pointed a lazy finger to a gaunt student with a short, shapeless French-style crew cut. "Would you risk losing a loved one to keep your honor?"

The student rose from his seat to answer but clearly froze. Père Sablé strode down the student's aisle. The student blanched.

"Aha! Just as I suspected, you have no answer. Yet this is what Don Diego demands of his son, Don Rodrigo—avenge me, kill my enemy, your lover Chimène's father, and claim your *self*!"

A hand shot up. A voice cried out, "Revenge?"

Another voice hissed, "Self-respect at the price of a life and his love life?"

"*Vive la révolution!*" sang out a girl dressed in a red beret, black turtleneck, and black slacks, clearly an anarchist.

This clever priest was forcing us to think. His eyes flashed bright emerald green, wide and grinning. He laughed, delighted with what he called "this brief demonstration."

"You will see. I will teach you about war and how not to lose yourself in the battle."

The class applauded and cried for an encore.

I felt myself choking up. This quirky priest reminded me of home. I pretended to brush a hair from my face as I wiped a tear dry. This minuscule man was so much like my father, citing famous lines, acting out the pathos of a scene for family and friends.

I startled when he boomed, "Boring!" to no one in particular. "Students say the classics are passé. I will show you passion and excitement and current-day drama."

Soon, he yawned and dismissed us early, saying he was too hungry to teach any more today. He grabbed the baguette he had carried in and caught me by the arm before I got out the door.

"Come have brunch with me!"

I followed him to the end of the hall, where we slipped through a narrow passageway. He asked me to hold the baguette as he scouted for the key in his pants pocket. Then he opened the heavily paneled door, revealing a stone spiral stairway.

"Come!" he said. "This is my tower. I show it to you so you know where to come."

"I don't understand." His vagueness intrigued me.

He perched on a step, broke off a piece of bread, and passed me the loaf.

I wondered if he was a bit…eccentric. He seemed to read my thoughts and pulled an exasperated face.

"I will teach you French history and your own personal history this way. Here in this staircase in this tower, priests and nuns hid when the revolutionaries tried to kill them. This is true! You must pay close attention to towers."

"Oh?" I didn't recall that from my French civilization courses. I munched on some crusty bread because I really didn't know what to say.

"Your teacher back home at the Albert Academy, Mademoiselle Lesage, I know her. She told me to look out for you. So, I offer you this peaceful spot if you ever need it. You come to get the key from me."

How could this be? Shoot! What did she tell him about me?

"You know Mademoiselle Lesage?" I tried to keep the doubt out of my voice.

"Yes, I know her, but when she was very young and, now, when she returns to see her family. You see, her parents and I go way back, to the Résistance during the war. You will see—in France, so much goes back to the war. And the Résistance. Ah! But I do go on. Sorry. I am old. So, you like Mademoiselle, eh?"

"Wow! She's the best. But...she didn't tell me about you."

With a twinkle in his eye, he said, "She wanted me to be a surprise. You say a jack-in-box?"

I laughed. By now, I didn't think he was crazy.

"Come." He led me by the hand to the roof.

"*Magnifique!*" I burst out. What a show. Tons of steeples—Saint-Séverin and Saint-Sulpice were the closest—along with the domes of the Sorbonne and the Panthéon. Splashes of blue in rivers and fountains, roofs in verdigris and gold, flashes of shade and sun. Grizzly gargoyles—some stonewashed recently, others blackened with the soot of ages—grinned eerily, hanging from the cornices of churches. And in the hazy distance, La Tour Eiffel and Notre-Dame, and ant-like people and cars swarming around the Place de la Concorde and the Arc de Triomphe. All of that and the vapors of garlicky wine sauces rising up on waves of accordion music. And this smiling, guardian angel by my side!

"Wow! It's really magical. *Merci, mon père!*"

"*Oui.* It is *magique.* But you must listen. Let me know if there is a problem. Mademoiselle Lesage said sometimes trouble finds you—and sometimes you have dreams...dreams about trouble to come. Find me, and we will make magic to help you." He clapped his hands twice and started down the shallow steps. "Be careful not to fall. There is this cord—no handrails when this was built. Pay close attention."

I took hold of the cord and nodded my thanks to him. When we emerged into the hallway, it seemed like we had re-entered the twentieth century. And here in this century, there were already two teachers, a nun and a priest, who wanted to teach me something and who already knew who I was. And trouble? *Merde!* I just wanted to have fun—no melodrama, no trouble. Ah, yes, but if there was a problem, I could always get the key to the tower.

Chapter Seven

Trouble

After my magical visit with Père Sablé, I floated down the hallway to my art class. Magic awaited me there, too.

The prof spoke little. Instead, she patted her projector, saying it would do all the necessary talking with its slides.

The slide she projected was Manet's *Le déjeuner sur l'herbe*, where properly garbed nineteenth-century men dined with a buxom naked woman in nature. My mind traveled to Katie and the Maine woods, where we'd vacationed right before going off to Albert. When could we go back there—and picnic au naturel?

Man, I couldn't believe I was imagining that. I mean, Katie and I almost skinny-dipped one night with our panties on, but shoot, totally naked? I couldn't risk thinking about her naked body, not now, not in class.

After class, I crossed the Luxembourg Gardens on my way home and thought about what a great place it was for a picnic with wine and cheese between classes, but Katie and nudes would definitely be missing. I sat on a wooden bench and watched model boats adrift on the pond. I felt one with them, just drifting. Kind of at sea, alone. I lost myself again in the mini ripples brought on by the autumn breeze as a few falling leaves brushed by my cheek. Where was I going? In life?

Alone? I reached up to dry a tear.

I had to distract myself from this hollow, this loneliness burrowing in my chest. My heart beat slowly, empty and alone. Damn! I let out a huge, bitter breath. It might be easier if there were no Katie to miss. I bit my tongue.

The Métro with its rubber tires and wafts of garlic and sweat would definitely change the monochromatic images flashing through my mind. Lots of local color to feast my eyes on there. Besides, I could always dream of Katie later.

I got a corner seat at the far end of the car so I could people watch. I focused on a tall guy with a light brown crew cut who wore small round, wire-rimmed glasses. His old suit, shiny from wear, was definitely out of style by a good ten years. The dark undertaker-type, striped jacket, cut way too long and tightly buttoned all the way up, revealed the frayed collar of a once-white shirt and a loosely knotted, soiled black tie. He stood reading. I imagined it was a communist tract until I saw the title *La nausée*. Of course. Sartre.

My mind wandered back to Père Sablé's class. Give up one's love to claim oneself? I frowned, and my insides cramped and wrinkled the entire length and width of my guts. Katie had asked me something like that once, about losing your identity when you fall in love.

My stomach roiled. I really didn't want to think about that conversation. That and the other one, the one about college. Both of these had caused really, really tense scenes between Katie and me. Why wouldn't people just let me be in the here and now?

I sighed. I began to study the pretty teenager with the long ponytail. She swung her hair back and forth, smiling at no one and everyone. Taking a pencil from her pocket, she wrote feverishly on typically French blue-and-white-checked graph paper. She lifted her head, licked the point of her pencil, and wrote another few words. At the top of her page, in large letters, she wrote, "*Mes pensées.*"

I wanted to read what her thoughts were, but she got off at the next stop, and a worker took her seat. His blue cotton workman's jacket gave up the odor of smoke and hard-earned sweat. His watery gaze seemed to fall on the tall full-breasted woman sitting opposite him. Then he lowered his gaze, staring instead at the short chubby nun fingering her rosary beads. I was curious about the kind of hard work he did and about his home life, but we had arrived at my stop.

Exhausted from my Métro ride, I mounted the stairs to my room, pushing the first of the intermittent light buttons. A few steps brightened as I grabbed the rickety handrail. The dim light flickered and went off. My hand patted every centimeter of nearby wall and flushed out the button. Light, finally! I continued two steps, when the light crackled and went black again. As I pitched forward toward a dubious switch, something crunched as the handrail rattled in my hand and plaster particles clattered to the floor. The screw riveting the rail to the wall loosened and gave way.

I scrambled to keep my balance, groping in the dark for a stair, a molding, a lip of a step, any hold possible. My hand encountered something, a bony, gauzy object—an ankle covered by a cotton stocking inside a mud-encrusted brittle leather shoe. *That* ankle... I blinked, and Craney's ankle stepped over me. I bit my lip to stop this flashback.

I managed to look up and peer beneath a long

black dress reeking of urine. Before me stood a stooped person carrying a chamber pot, slopping a foul liquid.

"You're in my way," she croaked.

With that, she stepped over me. I had just met the old goat.

If urine were luminescent, its gaseous state would have left a glowing trail. I almost gagged.

And the lights? And this old goat? What or who was messing with my head? God, was *Gaslight* the name of that film with Bergman that Katie dragged me to at the vintage cinema?

Scraping myself off the steps, I felt a sharp pain as I lifted my hand. I shrieked. An inch-long splinter had pierced my finger. I started to wail, giving in to the blackness and my sense of being nowhere. I lay on worn, dirty steps on a blackened staircase from where to where, what to what? I wasn't home with Katie; I wasn't homey in the room upstairs with—how to think of her?—my roommate.

As if on cue, a narrow beam of light bore down on me. I was fully spooked. By now, I anticipated an interrogation by my captor, whoever it was. Then I heard the bell, her bell.

"Whatever are you doing?" she asked as if I were scrubbing the stairs with my tears. "Why are you sitting here crying in the dark?"

"I didn't plan on the dark or on crying," I said with a touch of sarcasm that may or may not have translated well into French.

She turned the flashlight directly on my eyes, blinding me, and must have read fright in them. "Oh, you know, you must not be so afraid of the dark—"

I started to bare my teeth.

"We have many outages and stop-and-go strikes."

"Normal," I muttered.

Cassia helped me up, explaining that the only reason she was on the stairs was to go down to look for some matches. She said she had a surprise for me that "needed fire."

She went to take me by the hand, and I screamed again as the splinter wedged in farther. With that, both of us slipped down another few steps. I managed to grab the flashlight before it cascaded the full length of the staircase. It was then I noticed the little bell on Cassia's tennis shoes.

Chapter Eight

Surprises

When we got back to the room, I wanted to crawl under the covers. Cassia, however, was flitting around, mumbling about matches to "make fire surprises." The last thing I needed was a surprise of any sort, but I had to extinguish Cassia's immediate passion for burning.

"In my closet." I tossed the words out lazily from my bed.

Cassia rubbed her hands together, ready to uncover *les secrets profonds* of my wardrobe. She stopped short. "And why do you have matches?" She stood there tapping her foot, judging from the sound.

I jumped up and stepped in front of her, gritting my teeth. "I confess, Cassia. In my foul mood, I pictured me smoking French cigarettes, the image of a sulky expat, and somehow that calmed me. I threw the pack of Gauloises and matches up in my closet to hide them. Here, I'll get them."

"*Sacré bleu!* You must not have the *cafard*." She sighed.

I didn't know what cockroaches had to do with my bad mood and rolled my eyes at her. Cassia guffawed and informed me of the slang meaning for *cafard*. No! I was not depressed—just clinically anxious.

Cassia chirped on and on about the evils of

smoking and depression while I climbed on a chair to retrieve the matches and toss them to her. As I stepped down, my foot caught in something. By now, I throbbed with fatigue *and* crankiness.

"What the hell?" I whipped the bundle out from underfoot—a black robe—and slumped to the floor in a puddle of massive sobs. "*Pute!* Is it an academic gown? Were you in my closet? What the hell is this?" I held up the shroud-like garment in Cassia's face.

"I…*mais non*. Never. It…it is a nun's gown?"

"Fuuuuck! It's got to be Craney's." I pawed over the frigging gown and found the initials M.M.C. "Look," I screamed at Cassia. "Her initials!"

Cassia blanched. In a whisper, she formed the word, "Who?"

Craney had not yet become a household word for Cassia. I had only told her the Cliffs Notes version of the Mary Margaret Craney saga to explain my explosion over Mère Paul grabbing me.

I barely breathed. "Craney."

Cassia tore the gown from my grasp. She raised her hand and cut her gaze at me, shouting, "*Non!* I will fix this. You will see." Forming a halting smile, she went to pat my shoulder but bolted from the room with neither a word nor a gesture.

I sat. I didn't stir. I had to compose myself. Had I ever looked on the floor of my closet? No one had been in the room except Cassia and me. God, I needed my pills, the evil pink ones I thought I had finished with forever.

Cassia returned. She gave me a glass of water, approaching me on tiptoes, no sounds, no words, no fancy gestures. Her mouth formed a soft smile. "Marie Madeleine de la Croix, M.M.C., the name of the sister who used to live here. In your bed, in your closet. Her gown…Now, okay?"

Her tenderness caressed me, a mother's soothing after a skinned knee. I felt the tears releasing, but I couldn't sob. Not now. I held my head. "Sorry. I thought…"

"*Oui*. But you think too much. Some things are easy. They can be. I will help make them this way for you, yes?"

Cassia bent down to hug me. I kept shaking my head at the drama I had created. Cassia tsked to quiet me and offered her hand to pull me off the floor. I stood and brushed myself off, ready to breathe a normal breath again. Rubbing my fingers, I thought I noticed a small flurry of cat hairs drifting to the floor. Cat fur—not ermine? Not *the* ermine from Craney's academic gown?

Cassia's cheery voice broke the draw of the new impending drama.

"So, I make surprise for you! We are better now, *non*? Please, the gown, it is true, it belonged to this nun. No worries. Mère Paul promised."

Back in bed, I rolled my eyes and completely covered my head with the blanket again, this time in shame. I shut my eyes to block out any flashes of Craney's ermine academic gown. I tried to relax my legs, but my feet instinctively searched the edges of the bedclothes as if sweeping out the gown she had hidden in my bed two years before. In an instant, I relived the scene of Craney standing in front of me, too close. Commanding me to caress the ermine trim and to dress her in the gown I had just returned.

The fireplace guard clanged, waking me from my flashback. Bricks sounded as if they were crumbling.

Bottles clinked together. Metal wires jangled.

I opened one eye and lifted the covers. Under the flue, Cassia was assembling three empty champagne bottles with a candle in the middle. She tenderly placed a flaky pastry stuffed with béchamel sauce and cheese in a tin on top, and with a great flourish, lit the match, touched it to the candlewick, and then started to clap.

"In a few minutes, I will present you with a wonderful French treat. I went to the special delicatessen to cheer you up."

I had to admit I was impressed by her French Girl Scout skills and touched by her kindness.

The candle's flame cast a cool glow through the green bottles. The smell of melting cheese and the buttery, flaky pastry were working wonders on my nose and my mood. I emerged from my cocoon to marvel at this scene when Cassia handed me a special glass.

"From my parents. Taste!" She beamed with joy, waiting for me to sample this pale yellow liquid.

I was about to take a sip when a tiny frothy fizz sprayed my upper lip. This was real champagne in real flutes! I smelled toasted cookies and grapefruit essence, and the taste was so crisp and light and—

"Eh?"

"Oh, my God, I've never had anything so good!"

"Wait. Wait to drink it with the *vol-au-vent* pastry." Cassia clapped her hands and served me the pastry.

I was a little tipsy and started telling Cassia a tiny bit about missing Katie and my fantasy about Manet's naked picnic painting. I must have waxed eloquent about the passion Katie and I had for the outdoors and our roaming in the woods. I wanted her to understand just how playful Katie and I were.

"Cassia," I said, "you know, my sweet Katie, she was like Jane, and I was Tarzan." I hiccoughed. "Tee-hee, no, Tarzana." I pounded my breasts.

"Ah, *oui*, like the movie, but I think Tarzan does not have breasts. Ah, this is why you say Tarzana." Cassia almost grazed my breast and winked. "You and me, we could make a movie like the people in Manet's painting. Eh?"

What? Uh-oh! Was she really asking me to go on a naked picnic? Nah. She couldn't be coming on to me. But I did just imply I was a lesbian. Then again, she was really cute, and I was flattered. Well, maybe I was more than flattered, but...

She interrupted my thoughts, saying, "I think there are things you don't say..."

I nodded. "Yes, I don't know how to say all that in French yet. I will soon enough, I'm sure." I lied to buy myself some time. I wasn't quite sure how much I should risk, especially with the champagne talking.

"*Eh, bien*. You will find the words, I am sure." She giggled.

This was France, right? But Cassia seemed a bit of a fairytale character. I hadn't figured her out and certainly didn't have the energy tonight.

I decided not to go down to dinner, claiming exhaustion. Cassia would be out of the room for an hour and a half. Some silence. Some peace.

No sooner had I wished her *bon appétit* than she skipped out the door and down the stairs. Minutes later, she waltzed back in, humming. She sailed the blue tissue-thin envelope of an airmail letter across the bed to me. She calmly asked, "From Katie?" She burst out giggling and darted from the room. Ah, peace and a *letter* from Katie.

I held it up to my nose. I searched for the vaguest whiff of her Canoe cologne, her Noxzema, bread, bacon, *anything* that said, "I'm really here, flesh and blood with you." My tears flowed. I gulped when I saw the paper swell and wither with wetness. I quickly shook the envelope and took out not one but three sheets, front and back.

Holding my head in my hands, I sighed with the sheer joy, knowing that for the next twenty, maybe thirty or forty minutes, I would be with Katie.

I felt the warmth of the tissue-thin sheets. Katie had held them. Her hands had smoothed over them. I would almost hear her speak these words.

My darling Pina,

I waited to write until I knew where you'd be when you received this letter. I can almost see you in your corner room, perched on your bed, folded up in your favorite Pendleton blanket, white stripe, red stripe, green, the Hudson Bay one you brought back from Maine. Do you, does it still smell of pine needles? My resin girl!

I miss you so much. I've been rereading letters, looking at photos of us in Maine, at Albert, here at my folks' place at Thanksgiving. I'm home on first trimester break. It won't be the same without you. My father and Joe send their love.

And us? I can't wait till January. At first I thought I could swing Christmas, but my senior project is due then. But you, my sweetie, what are you going to do for Thanksgiving? Are you putting on your blasé "I don't care about the small stuff" face? Oh, honey, it is a big deal. We can call you if you'd like.

Everyone from Albert misses you. And I even got

a letter from Dorotea, and Joe said he thought your first-year roommate Alda had signaled Fifi that she's in the witness protection program.

My bed also misses you. It seems so empty…cold…and…

Big blotches told me Katie was crying. There were a few sentences I couldn't read and then something about "pay close attention." Something else about "on the day of your…a package…and in it this poem…"

And then Katie copied the bad poem. This was tripe, pure, unadulterated crap!

> May your Paris tour
> Escort you to yet a world more
> With girls and ladies galore
> With **lascivious affairs** to adore
> So you'll go no more a roving
>
> Than you're currently proving
> Be not she who *trips* a port-a-call
> Fall not, dearie, to flirtations or more
> There's **danger** for you, don't ignore
> On train or bus or plane
> At quay's, catacomb's, sewer's shore
> At water's door,
> From towering heights all the more!
> Beware, Beware, Beware!

Shoot! I knew that line about roving. Oh, Christ. "We'll go no more a roving." I did know this line. It was Craney. She was back. It was the friggin' poem she recited to me on Halloween two years ago. That Byron poem about love and lusting after youth.

This was a clear threat. I wasn't crazy. Didn't Katie understand? Why did she send this to me? I finally skipped ahead in Katie's letter. I just wanted to hear her words.

I thought I should tell you. Doc thinks maybe some Albert underclass students wanted to pull a prank. It does feel slimy. Or maybe someone's trying to spook me into thinking you'll have a French escapade.

Oh, sweetie, I trust you. I don't want anyone but you.

I wish I could give you a real kiss. Just imagining your lips on mine, all over…

I'm holding you and this letter close to my heart.

Your Katie

P.S. I forgot to ask about Paris. Ugly, isn't it?

A prank? What, was she kidding? I pulled the blanket over my head and whimpered. Suddenly, I sat up. Trouble wrinkled my forehead. What? *Trouble.* I grabbed for the pages lost somewhere between the sheet and blanket. They sailed to the floor.

I scrambled after them and stopped dead. Shutting my eyes tight, I combed through my knotted hair with my fingers. Craney was back; she was warning me. And man, that sailor business on the boat—was that her, too? And all that garbage about lots of ladies and sex. Damn! Did she know something about Katie? "F-u-c-k," I screamed. Why did Katie send this?

I was doing it again. I was making mountains, moving earth, landscaping hills. Piling, pounding, and heaping up imaginary strata of molehills. Psychological mountains.

Merde! All I wanted was to lose myself in Katie,

in the kisses of the letter, not slimy poetry and affairs. I picked up the letter and attempted to reread it through my tears. I crumpled it and tossed it in the bone-cold fireplace.

Why tell me about the poem? And this crap about cheating? Man, why couldn't I just get some Parisian downtime?

I curled myself into a ball, punched my pillow into something almost cuddly, and tried to sleep. Tossing and turning, I awoke in a cold sweat.

In my early evening nightmares, I felt the old swish of Craney's black academic robe up my arm and past my cheek. The lingering smell of her menthol inhaler trailed in its wake. I was reliving the horror of my first year at Albert Academy.

Chapter Nine

Down the Chimney/Out of the Closet

When I finally slept without Craney slithering through my dreams, Katie slipped into my dream and spooned with me in the scratchy muslin sheets. As I reached back to stroke her long pageboy, my hand glided over smooth, cool fabric. I tried to untie the kerchief hiding her hair, calling her my "bubuska granny," but the scarf stayed in place. I finally turned to face Katie and peered into her deep aquamarine eyes—now sunken into a hooded skeleton.

When Cassia tiptoed into the room, I sat up, yelling, "*Merde!* Can't you be quiet?" As soon as I realized it was Cassia, I lowered my head and attempted apologies.

"*Non! Desolée,*" she said. "I did wake you."

"No, listen. I've been awake on and off the whole evening. I'm angry, too angry. Sorry."

I rubbed my eyes, feeling all the more heat. I really was angry—about my dream, at Katie. And shoot! Why was Craney coming up now? She had run for her life and her dignity after the newspaper articles Joe and I wrote. The authorities said she was nowhere to be found.

Cassia interrupted my thoughts. She sat on the edge of my bed and placed her hand on my shoulder. In a soft voice, she asked, "But why? I made you nice treat. And I have special plans for us."

I patted her hand and thanked her again for the wonderful pastry.

"Don't you want to know where we are going?" Her smile seemed to dance as she rocked her head from side to side.

"Okay. Yeah." I sighed.

"I take you to the Quai d'Orsay. We go to the sewers."

I screamed no and grabbed her wrist. "What do you know? Did you read the letter?" I bared my teeth.

Cassia's other hand flew to her forehead. She shrugged off my grasp.

"What? Did I read a letter? What do I know? I, uh…I…Pina, this is folly. Stop!"

I took several deep breaths. I shut my eyes tight. I chose my words, one by one. "I just received a letter with a warning about accidents and the sewers and *quais*."

Cassia tilted her head. She stared at her hand and rubbed her chin as if teasing out the reasoning behind this. She summarized, "I don't understand."

She softened her gaze. I read pity there for this crazy American.

I had to do a better job at explaining. Actually, *what* was there to explain? A bad poem? No, a threat. Sewers and *quais* and catacombs were part of Paris. What was the warning—something about tripping? Something specific about water and boats. I wasn't going to lose it, but I knew it was Craney, and I'd have to explain to Cassia.

I bit my lip and tried to reassure Cassia that I really was sane. I decided I'd start my horror stories slowly by telling her the dream about Katie in a skeleton costume. She giggled and all but bounced up and down on the bed.

"Why, yes! In a few weeks, it is Halloween. We will dress up like the Americans do, yes?"

I laughed a strained laugh. I remembered Katie dressing up as a skeleton and scaring the heck out of Alda and me at Albert. I blew out several deep breaths and apologized profusely to Cassia, agreeing to talk about the sewer trip in the morning. But in my gut, I knew. Craney was back. I would tell Cassia the story in the morning. Now I just needed to sleep.

After the Corsican good night ritual, Cassia got ready for bed and shut off the lights. I threw my head back on the pillow and imagined sheep to count. My body remained hot and throbbing. Streams of anger and fear still coursed through my veins.

The night passed slowly. Springs in Cassia's and my old-fashioned mattresses creaked, testimony to our tossing and turning. I didn't recall any more dreams. Caffeine from the numerous coffees I had downed earlier joined the river of anger flowing through me, adding to the St. Vitus's dance my body was performing. I heard the rain on the flashings above the balcony and chimney. A light metallic dance, until the breeze blew more intensely. Wind whipped down the flue; the night guard rattled and clanged and screeched shut. Something pitter-pattered or fluttered—perhaps a mouse.

Dawn eased through the blind and shutters. Cassia and I took zombie-like steps around the room. The circles under her eyes were as concentric and deep as mine, and we only grunted when we accidentally got in each other's way.

I felt guilty that I had crumpled Katie's letter.

Besides, I did want to show it to Cassia. Remembering the rain, I lifted the fireplace guard and retrieved the soggy pages of Katie's letter still wadded up and the bottles from our cook-in, and stared at slices of wood scattered all over the slate floor of the fireplace. Those weren't there before. I picked up a piece, noticing a smudged-ink mark against a chalk white background. I grabbed another and another, equally smudged. A few had remained relatively dry. When I squinted into the dark hearth, I noticed more and more of these curve-topped rectangles. Each was marked "R.I.P." Each read, "PINA," smeared in what had been bold black letters.

Cold air blew down from the chimney. I sat on the floor surrounded by miniature tombstones. I fell back on my elbows in front of the fireplace and scrambled to find one gravestone without my name. None. I let out a piercing shriek.

Cassia appeared at my side and immediately pulled a wooden stone from my fist.

"*Nom de Dieu!*" Cassia took God's name and instantaneously blessed herself. "What does this mean?"

I cleared my throat and attempted to speak—to no avail. Tears flowed as I let myself collapse flat out on the wood floor. Cassia helped prop me up and patted my eyes dry with a corner of her shirt.

"Shush. Take your time," she cooed.

I crab-walked over to the balled-up letter and clutched it in my hands. "Read," I muttered.

Cassia squinted. I extended my index finger to point to the poem. "Where it talks about catacombs and sewers," I said.

"Halloween, *oui*?"

"But...but..." I had to tell Cassia about Craney,

and fast. "My name, it's on the tombstones. Someone has dropped these down the chimney on purpose, someone who knows me and knows about my catacomb project at Albert."

"Impossible!" Cassia squinted at me again and sighed with her whole slender torso. Her face was a map of question marks. "What evil person could know you are here?"

"Right. Not here. And the only person who would do this is supposedly out of commission."

"Yesterday you called her 'the witch,' yes? She is not dead, eh? But out of commission…Come." Cassia helped me off the floor and onto the bed. "We will find the witch."

Clearly, she had to make French sense out of this. "These tombstones could be meant for somebody else. The word *PINA* has smeared. Maybe it was *PIONNE* or *PIPAT*—slang words for *pipi* or a person from Polytechnique or…or…"

"*Merde*! Cassia, this witch Craney is evil. She followed me all over, appearing from behind closed curtains, slithering past me in the hall. She gave me gifts, left packages at my door, hid her clothes in my bed."

I chewed my lip. I dug my nails into my jaw. Anything to block out that old image of Craney pushing me with her entire body toward her black canopy bed. All black. And white…the white polar bear skin dead center. I snapped myself back out of this footage.

"Worse. It got worse and worse." I paused, unsure of Cassia's grasp of my terror.

I tried to read Cassia's look. Was it just concern for me or fear of me, the lunatic roommate?

"*Cassia*. She tried to abuse me! There, I've said

it." I was shaking so hard, the words almost rattled as they tumbled out of my mouth.

"Abuse? You mean like sex?"

"Yes, damn it!" I was angry, really angry.

"Listen. You've got to know. I'm *gouine*, a queer. Katie—the Katie in the letter—she's my girlfriend."

"*Oui...amie—*"

"No. *Gouine*, lesbian girlfriend." I grit my teeth. I had to make her understand and almost didn't stop myself from shaking her by the shoulders.

"Cassia, Katie is...she's special. We've known each other a long, long time. *Tu comprends?* We were just nine, summer pals running in the woods, playing at girl detectives at an old deserted boys camp." I took a breath, softening a moment, losing myself as all those sweet memories came rushing in.

"We discovered clues in those broken-down cabins, clues to an old, unknown murder—clues that we were more than just good friends. We fell in love, without knowing what was happening, even in the middle of all that horror. Two years ago, two beautiful years. And then a few months later, there was Albert Academy—together!"

My chest tightened again. My words poured out. I spat out *Craney*. "And then there was Craney. She knew what I was. And I found out what she was—a lecher."

I rocked almost dangerously now as I turned my face to sneak a look at Cassia. Oh, God. Would she bolt, leave the room? Would she tell?

I felt like terror had wedged my eyes wide open. I convulsed in sobs as I whispered, "Craney...tried to seduce me, and when I didn't reciprocate, she tried to blackmail me. She stalked me, you understand *stalk*?

She followed me and leered at me, her tongue almost hanging out." I choked on my words and stopped several times to breathe deeply. "She was about to rape me! I got away. If I didn't become her sex slave, she threatened, she would tell my parents I was a queer. You understand…they would have thrown me in a mental ward, given me shock treatments to fry my brain. Thrown me out of school, church, my home!" I coughed, reaching for her hand. "Please, I'm not crazy. I haven't thought about this for almost two years. But she's here." I shook my head like a Bobo doll. "So, if you want a new roommate"—I tried to shake myself alert and chase the panic—"just say so!" I sighed and flopped back down, arms crossed, head high, but drenched in tears and sweat.

Cassia stood straight up, cleared her face of any emotion, and pursed her lips in silence for two minutes. Neither of us spoke.

Then without warning, she clapped and clapped and bent over with laughter. I stared at her, my mouth hanging open. What the heck?

She ran to my side and slapped me jubilantly on the back. "*You*, you are okay. Now I know a real Parisian queer! In Corsica, we are backward, no queers, no rock and roll, only rocks and rural old goats and fuddy-duddies! *You*, you are *chouette*!"

"Huh?" There was that word again. I was just too *cool*. Man, what had I just done? Totally lost my mind, almost frothed at the mouth. Told a perfect stranger, well almost, I was a lesbian. Funny. It made my Craney-phobia go away for a whole ten minutes.

I smiled at Cassia. "*Merci*." But I wondered if anyone but Katie and our Albert roommates Alda and Dorotea could really ever get Craney and the dread, like acid in the veins, that she instilled in me.

Cassia shrugged and grinned a Sylvester grin. "*De rien!*" she answered. "But we will make inquiries about this Craney. You call your Katie—by the way, where is her picture? I must see her. But for now, you don't worry. It was a Halloween trick, yes? Who knows, maybe meant for the old goat's chimney."

I blew out a whole windstorm and hugged Cassia four times. "*Merci*, Cassia. Good idea to call Katie. I will."

"Yes, and then we will go to the sewers, no?"

"Um." I could do this. I had to. "Yeah." I nodded. "We will."

Chapter Ten

Katie's Voice

Cassia's cheerleading motivated me to roll myself out of bed and into the shower, toward my mission for the day: find the local post office to call Katie. Even the cold shower—when I ran out of centimes to feed the heater—wasn't enough to dissuade me from my goal: Katie.

Katie. The thought of hearing her voice, of being *alone* with her in a booth inside the PTT office, inspired me to race through the gray drizzle. Paris in the early fog refreshed me. I could sift through my fuzzy thoughts, Craney, the sewers, the letter... Katie would definitely clear up the rest of the thick confusion in my head.

After I signed up for a transatlantic connection at the post office, I had to wait for my call to come through. All my feelings of longing for Katie—and other feelings—ran through my mind and body. Hmm. Not all good and loving. That kink in my nervous system caused me to sweat despite my cheap French deodorant. Butterflies started to tango in my stomach when the clerk called me over to booth four.

I slammed myself in the booth so quickly that I caught my jacket, which prevented me from picking up the receiver. I heard the operator tell Katie I was not on the line. I shouted, "*Non!*" and started sobbing. God. I had to cool it.

Katie's voice! I thought I heard it. She was there! Sort of in the flesh.

Katie spoke softly and sweetly. "Hi, my love," she cooed through some crackle on the line.

I slumped down on the bench and held my hand to my heart. "I love you," I bawled.

"Me too!"

"I miss you." I managed to form the words without choking on sobs.

We reduced our beginning conversation to monosyllabic sighs and variations on "I miss you/love you/yeah/me too!" Lightning-like crackles brought me back to my present surroundings—a felt-lined, black tobacco-reeking, two-foot-by-two-foot cubicle with a ticking timer. I had other important things besides love to say to Katie.

"Katie, the letter—"

"Oh, good." She sighed.

"Huh? No, you've got to explain...*sweetie*." I tried to soften my tone by tagging on *sweetie* at the end, but it didn't do the job.

"What? I don't get it. What's up?"

"Katie, *honey*, the poem!"

"Yeah? What about it?" Katie cleared her throat, but the lilt was gone from her voice when she continued. "Well, I had to let you know. God, Pina, you sound really cranky. What happened to 'Oh, Katie, I love you sooo much?' The poem? It's got to be a prank."

"No, Katie. It's scary. It's a warning. About tripping at all those places in Paris. And...and that thing about all those women and me and *roving*..."

"I know. That sounded familiar. But I really think it was somebody's bad prank."

"Prank! Katie, weird things *are* happening. That roving line? Definitely Craney."

"Pin, stop! You're doing it. Honey, you're in a new place, alone, and your anxiety…"

"I know, but you're not listening to me. I can't joke about…well, you know, when things make me relive two years ago and Craney. And…and last night, tombstones fell from my chimney with my name on them. Well, maybe my name."

"Oh, honey, take a breath." Katie sighed.

I could almost feel her pat me on the shoulder across the line, across the waves, across the transatlantic divide. "Katie! *Please!*" I started to lose control of my volume.

"Okay. So maybe, just maybe. Shoot, Pina, I don't know. What do you want me to do?"

"*Not* have an affair, damn it!" Man. What else could *roving* mean?

"What!"

I took several deep breaths. This wasn't going the way I wanted. I'd try to start over. When I began again with "I love you," there was a loud crackle and deadness. Pure, empty, black space. I clicked the buttons, nothing. I stuck my head out of the booth and signaled the clerk, who threw me a bored look and mumbled, "*Un instant.*"

Katie's voice yelled out, "Why'd you hang up on me?" I could almost feel her tapping her foot.

"No, Katie. It's the phone system here. Listen, I do miss you, but you've got to do some research. Please. Is Craney around? Please ask Joe to investigate."

"Okay, okay, Pina, but—"

"No *buts*," I said, hand poised gavel-like.

A brief silence preceded Katie's casual question:

"Hey, how is Paris?"

"I'm kind of into it, but I miss you, and then I kind of lose my Paris obsession."

I was feeling hot all over, cranky—and scared. Katie didn't get it. I opened my mouth, and a whole bunch of crap came tumbling out.

"I can't always have you in my head."

"Well? Do you want to put me out of it?"

"I…uh…uh, no!"

Dead, black silence. Empty air. I signaled the clerk again. She shrugged.

Oh, merde! Now I really had to talk to Katie. I started to exit the booth. A crying jag took over. I retreated back inside and perched my legs up on the bench, hoping no one would attempt to dislodge me from this den. Trapped. Trapped with my frigging emotions.

What the hell was going on in my head? I *needed* Katie now, especially now. I was begging…and she couldn't hear me? She was the real one who sent me away, away to grow up. Not the parents and the teachers; they weren't the ones who mattered. And now I was convinced Craney was busy building booby traps all around me. I was just bound to trip into one. That was the bottom line.

I reminded myself I wasn't alone. There was Cassia. And…and what? No, no hot stuff. Yeah, Mère Paul and Père Sablé and the tower…

I heaved myself off the bench, took several deep breaths, and bolted from the booth. I knew I had to send an urgent postcard to Katie. I couldn't scribble "I love you; Forgive me" all over the back of the Folies Bergère or cancan dancers. Maybe the Eiffel Tower? No, she'd think I was just focused on Paris. Ah. They had this fold-up airmail stationery. You bought it already stamped. I could write it in a café.

It was still raining when I sat on the outdoor patio of a nearby café. I watched cloudy drops plop one by one from the overhead canvas awning and splash at my feet. My toes felt damp, my spirits, too. I ordered a Schweppes Indian Tonic and let the spray tickle my nose. I might perk up if I wrote the right thing to Katie. But what?

"Help?" I really did need help, and I had always counted on her in the past. I would make her understand I wasn't being clingy. It wasn't just my anxiety…I didn't think.

Dear Katie,
This has to be short because of the folded single sheet.

I crossed that out.

Oh, God, Katie. I screwed up. I love you so much. Please forgive me. I want you in my life. I was begging you to hear how scared I was, and you made me feel real clingy. Like you've been telling me—if I only color my world Katie color, then I don't leave room for any other shades or tints, and I become a one-note person. I know I'm lousing up my metaphors. I'm having a hard time saying I think I want all of you AND all the new experiences, too! But right now, I'm panicking. At times I do feel desperate. I'm not sleeping well, and my dreams are weird—well, weirder. I know that's no good, but I'm not really thinking straight.

It definitely is Craney. Remember the poem she recited to me? I know it in my gut, but I'll try to stay sane. I've met some good people who can help. But no one can replace you, sweetie. Please call or write real soon. I'm begging. I'd do it on my knees, but the puddles are getting deeper, and I just realized the awning leaks.

Love,
Your drowned Parisian Rat, Pina

I reread it, licked it shut, and kissed it. I couldn't resist printing "S.W.A.K." on the seal.

When I returned to post it, the clerk told me I had just missed a return call from Katie. She seemed to notice excitement filling my red-rimmed eyes and added that the cables were blocked again due to another daylong strike.

I wanted so badly to joke and slap myself upside the head. There was this voice in my mind telling me, "Doofus, get real. It's just anxiety." Right, what the good doctor used to call separation anxiety…and panic and…

God! I had to get out of my head. Besides, I needed to rush back to meet Cassia. We had a date with fate in the sewers.

Chapter Eleven

Aimer = To like or to love

Leaving the post office with a small dose of optimism, I grew even brighter when a slender ray of sunshine streaked through the clouds. I opened myself up to this pale yellow strip painting my route home. Paris, City of Lights, welcomed me, and I finally let her warm my heart and soul.

My worries about Katie still washed over me, but I trusted we would work it out. I actually skipped the last block to my foyer, looking forward to the sewer trip with Cassia. And Cassia was definitely cool.

"Well," demanded Cassia as she threw open the door to welcome me back to our room. "What did Katie say?"

I told Cassia how I had jumped the gun and didn't give Katie a real chance to explain.

Cassia playfully slapped me on the back. "Ah! She will forgive you. I know. *But* she is right. In your life, you have to leave space for other things and people—like me."

Cassia did a little cha-cha-cha step and bowed. "You, Pina, you also push me away."

I gritted my teeth. "Sorry. It's just that I'm frightened about Craney. If it's really her—and my senses tell me it is—she really would love to get back at me."

Cassia held her chin and rolled her eyes. She began to tap her foot. "Hmm. Someday, you will tell me all the details, but now, you promised… Before we go to the sewers, where is my picture of Katie? Show me your Katie, your *chérie*."

I dug into my wallet and flipped through the diary I kept by the side of my bed, pulling out my favorite shots of Katie. One was from two summers ago in Maine. I had caught Katie by surprise with her soft-eyed look of love. Her shiny hair fell just right, a relaxed pageboy over one shoulder. Her smile was penetrating. It always pierced my heart.

"That one, yes!" Cassia brought it over to the sun pouring through the windows. "She looks deep, right into me. I want this one. Yes!"

"But, Cassia, it's mine." I gave her the stink eye.

She ignored me and waltzed about by the side of her bed. "I will hang this one on the wall by my bed. And you, you paste that one, the funny student one, over there by your bed. I like prettiness on my walls. Eh? So now you've got Katie on your side and Katie on my side."

Cassia was smiling from ear to ear. I flopped down on my bed, scratching my head. This felt like the biblical story where the false mother wants to divide the kid in half.

"Ah, Cassia, wait. This feels a bit icky. Like you want Katie. You don't even like girls, I don't think. Do you?"

Cassia's tears drew me from my ruminations. Uh-oh. What the heck was going on?

"It's okay. We can talk about it." I would definitely chew on this, and we would definitely *talk* about this.

She sat on her bed and exclaimed, "Fuck!"

"Okay," I said. "What's happening?"

I really was not ready for another emotional roller-coaster ride, but I did have to room with her for six months. Besides, I kind of liked her.

"I am sorry! I, Cassia, I do not know liking and loving. My parents, *hein*? They are married, yes, but there is no love. My mother, she calls my father '*le baron*.' She makes fun of him, and he is a kind of goose. I don't know. Maybe my mother runs around in her Mercedes coupe on her trips to the Côte D'Azur. Who knows? They say my father, maybe he wears the horns, you know, cuckolded."

Cassia snorted loudly and dabbed at her eyes before letting out a body-shaking wail.

"I do not know people who talk about love, like you. You care what Katie thinks; you listen to her and take her advice, well sometimes. I think this is what love is like. And I am green with envy. I want people to love me, too. I don't even think my parents know what this is, for me even."

Cassia hung her head. Her chest heaved up and down. Tears like I'd never seen splashed soundlessly against the floor.

I went to Cassia's side and rubbed her neck and shoulders. I cooed, "I'm sorry." I smoothed her short choppy bangs from her face and rubbed her tears dry with my thumb.

"I like you!" I had to be careful to use the expression for like and not love—a tricky thing in French based on the proper placement of one adverb. "Come," I said, "we'll pin up Katie's photos."

Cassia clunked her head down on my breast. She looked up at me, doe-eyed. I read something more than gratitude there, so I quickly pulled her up so I could look for thumbtacks. I still felt a bit weird about this pinup thing, but my heart went out to Cassia—well, not that way.

As soon as we had attached the two photos, I immediately produced Cassia's coat so we could take her excursion to the sewers. I had a few thoughts I could definitely wash down the drain.

Chapter Twelve

The Paris Sewers

The now-hazy sun lit up the sidewalk on our walk to the Métro to visit the sewers. According to the song *Under Paris Skies*, the Parisian sun didn't stay happy for long. But for now, I was very happy with the sun and life.

I forgot about Cassia's tears, and I blocked out my fight with Katie. With each step I took, I discovered a new herbal scent, a novel musical melody or mechanical tone, flashes of whiffs and shades I had never experienced.

Cassia pulled me into a *pâtisserie* just to marvel at the shapes and colors of pastries: flaky and golden shells, multicolored creamy and fruity tartlets, red, burnt orange, saffron yellow. Chocolate lathered on or thickly banded, cascading over the sides of pound cake towers.

Accordion music flowed around corners and through alleyways. Pressurized steam escaped from espresso machines through open-sided cafés. A woman singing a Piaf song crooned from a window. Yes, Paris was seducing me, and I started to welcome her in.

I floated my way to the Métro at Cassia's side. Even the pungent *eau de M*étro scent of garlic and urine mixed with mildew didn't sour my appetite.

We jerked to a stop at Alma, the station for the

sewer tour. Cassia had to nudge me a few times to get us out of the Métro car before the doors closed.

I was in love with the whoosh of the car leaving the station, the dull foghorn signal for closing doors, the rushing blast of sunshine descending the Métro stairs. And then, magic! The sky, the bridge, the Seine. To the left and right of me, marvels: the Louvre, the Eiffel Tower, the old art deco d'Orsay train station.

Cassia laughed and laughed. She grabbed my face to make me focus.

"You have four months for your affair with Paris!" She was beaming.

I could see myself reflected in her eyes, smiling, smitten with Paris. All I could say was "Ah!" as she took me by the arm and swung me along.

"Here we are at the sewers. You will see the smells in the sewers are not so good. Get ready." She handed me her handkerchief. Hints of its lavender scent filled my nose.

"Where?" I looked around for a large entrance. A minuscule board announced "*Entrée*" in front of an open manhole. The stairs seemed to appear from out of nowhere and descended into darkness. As we climbed down the stairs to the sewer tour, Cassia placed a protective hand on my arm. I hadn't remembered the word *tripping* from the poem in Katie's letter until that moment.

Cassia was rambling on about waste floating in the streets in the Middle Ages and how the drinking water from the Seine was like swallowing "toilet water." Cassia's history lesson combined with the vapors of urine and feces and mold almost made me gag. I had to hold on to the handrail and Cassia to adjust to the ambience: near blackness, water sloshing, cavernous sounds echoing through miles of meandering underground channels.

"*Venez!*" The swarthy boatman urged us to step down into a kind of canal boat. He wiped his hand on his blue-and-white-striped boatneck before offering it to us. His too-long, old-fashioned denims, dripping with putrid water and dragging underfoot, didn't offer me much reassurance.

I felt the muscles in my face tighten. Cassia kept whispering I was fine, I was doing fine. I didn't usually like hankies, but I held that piece of flowered cloth smack up against my nose—as did most of the other passengers, all French-speaking, all decked out in tight-fitting designer suits and swaying crepe skirts and cowl-necked sweaters. All with the exception of a very American-looking girl about my age wearing a huge pullover with a pom-pom zipper. Under a sort of pillbox hat—weird for an eighteen-year-old girl—her hair puffed into a short, stiffly sprayed pageboy. Her voice carried, strident and loud in English. She tsked at an older French disabled veteran that *she* was next in line.

The canals were narrow with smaller channels jutting off at right angles. On either side, enamel signs marked the names of the streets above. We floated by familiar names: Rue de Rivoli, Champs-Élysées, Champs de Mars. Sometimes, the boatmen had to get out and walk on a ledge to pull the boat along. A guide in an official blue but crumpled jacket and greased-back dark hair narrated interesting bits of history: some from literature, others from the annals of famous crimes. Some definitely bogus.

"*Messieurs dames*, Victor Hugo was so smart to place Jean Valjean here in these sewers. But the *pauvre bossu* could not hear anything you folks hear today. You know, he was *tout à fait sourd!*" The boatman, who looked more and more like a derelict, waxed eloquent about Valjean's being hunchbacked and hard of hearing. He stooped over, even putting his dirty fingers in his ear, to mimic him. Too bad he confused *Les Misérables* with *The Hunchback of Notre Dame.*

"Cassia, did you see his filthy finger? And he screwed up his Hugo novels."

"*Dégoûtant!* Don't let him touch you with those digits!" Cassia crawled her fingers up my neck.

"Gross," I whispered as I swatted at her hand.

"*Et toi*, are you my Esméralda, my gypsy girl?" Cassia all but frothed at the mouth.

"Shush, Cassia, people are looking."

"Okay, okay. But what is *that* smell?" Cassia snorted and pointed her nose in the direction of the American. "Her *parfum* smells like dirty panties!"

By now I'd grown accustomed to the smells—all smells—and to Cassia's ramblings. I half listened to the boring guide, fascinated more by the exclamations of wonder and disgust expressed by the French tourists, and more and more intrigued by the American girl. Yuck! That was Evening in Paris she was wearing.

Why the heck was she here? She spoke no French, judging from her loud New York English.

Cassia slit her gaze at me. "What is she saying?"

"Shush!" The noise of sloshing water and the echo of the guide made it hard to hear. I strained to catch bits and pieces of the complaints the American made to the French guy sitting next to her as she fanned herself with her *Mademoiselle* magazine. I cringed, creeped out that she might recognize me as her "fellow American."

"No, I don't like this tour, *and* I don't like you! And no, I won't have coffee with you." she screeched.

"Oh, but you are so *belle*. You must be an American movie star, *non*? Or Italian, a real Gina Lollobrigida! You are Gina, yes? *Non, non*, no, you are Ina. *C'est ça!* And where, *ma chère*, do you reside?" This Romeo was a real smooth operator.

How dumb could she be? This guy was definitely hitting on her. He was so obvious, asking stupid questions about her curfew and where she lived.

Cassia whispered to me, "Psst! Pay attention to me. You like her?" She made an ugly face.

"God, no!" I rolled my eyes.

Cassia stifled a laugh. She put her finger to her lips and feigned innocence. We pantomimed the flirtation scene going on behind us, turning occasionally to sneak a glimpse of the Romeo's progress.

"Oh, American girl, *fille de mes rêves*, my dream girl, I want to kiss you, smooch, smooch!" Cassia nuzzled closer to me.

"Ah." I sighed. "Romeo, Romeo, you are sooo sleazy, you drip oil on me..." I fluttered my lashes at Cassia. "Please, kiss my patoot."

"*Hein? Mon cul?*"

"Yeah, a cute word for *butt*."

Cassia leaned her head against my shoulder and spoke just above a whisper. "You are so bad."

I strained to understand the slang word she used, thinking she called me malicious, but after a great deal of sign language—so we wouldn't disturb the guide—I learned the great word *maligne*. Now I was *chouette* and *maligne*. Now I was cool and cunning.

I leaned over to poke Cassia, who almost jumped. She turned to give me the evil eye and tickled me.

"Shush, we hear about the famous jewel heist."

Whatever the guide had been saying about the theft for the previous five minutes was totally lost on us. We tuned back just in time to hear: "Even in *Jackie Gleason Show en Amérique*, Norton, a poor plumber, dresses up as Pierre Brioschi, designer of the sewers. Even these *Américains* know about our sewers."

"Well, this American thinks they stink." Gina Lollobrigida—my name for the American girl in back— was on a roll. "You stink. Ever hear of deodorant, buster? And stop calling me Pina. I told you my name is Tina!"

"Ah, *non*! You must be Pina. You study. Your family is Italian…You know the saying, 'What's in a name?' Pina, Tina, Gina, all the same to me—"

I pulled on Cassia's sleeve. "I think I heard my name. This guy just called the American Pina."

"How can you hear? That woman with the pinched prune face is making such a fuss about the guide's story of the naked couple. According to the guide, the police found them stranded '*en flagrant délit*' after their sexual play in the sewer. Who called who Mina?"

"*Merde*, Cassia. The Romeo called the American *Pina*."

"Ah, and now you want to be Juliet for this Romeo?" Cassia cast a lewd look at me.

Shoot. She didn't get what was going on.

"Cassia, Listen."

We heard some rustling from behind us. I glanced back to catch the Romeo sneak his arm around Gina Lollobrigida. She bristled when his hand grazed her breast. "Stop! You keep saying, 'Pina, Pina, Pina. Dang it! If you're going to paw me, bozo, at least get my name straight. It's Tina to you!"

"Oh, f-u-c-k—oops, can I whisper that word, Pina?" Cassia frowned. "I heard him. Is he stupid, or do you think—"

I covered my eyes. That spinning in my head and the static noise… This tour was just an innocent tourist trap, no? The hokey guide, the weird echoes… Maybe this whole thing was a spoof, staged for gullible sightseers…

The action in the back of the boat produced more muffled sound effects. I visualized bodies squirming, dry groping, wet kisses, heavy breathing. On edge, I tingled with disgust on one hand and morbid curiosity on the other—*and* the droning noise in my head: *Pina*, why did he call her Pina?

I sobered up when I heard a loud splash and furious screams of "Help!" and "You bastard!"

Cassia and I turned completely around to see the American in the murky water behind the boat. The boatmen immediately threw a life preserver and clambered along the ledge to reach the floundering girl. When they pulled her out, she shook with fear and disgust. She continued her angry litany through bouts of dry heaving.

She slumped over in a heap as projectile bile spewed over the bank and her brown and white saddle shoes. Yellow-blotched brown. The cascade continued with confetti-size bits of cheese and olives coating the whites of her shoes. Her legs skittered about. No, she couldn't attempt to stand, could she? She wouldn't…

Water poured off the stretched-out sleeve of her sweater as she raised her hand to swipe at her mouth. She stared at her hand now holding a palm full of regurgitated lunch juices and without thinking, ran it through her matted pageboy.

I moved my head in Cassia's direction. Both of us sat there openmouthed and ashen.

"Where's the Romeo?" I mumbled.

"*Oui.* He's gone," she said, biting her lip.

We finally managed to swivel our heads around. He was nowhere in sight.

"We must say something, no?"

"Yeah. Sounds like no one speaks English well enough to understand."

By now, boatmen were escorting other passengers out and focusing their attention on the American. She sat covered with blankets, waiting for emergency vehicles to arrive. She continued to ramble in English.

I explained to the boatmen that I spoke English and approached the girl slowly. I bent down by her side and forced a smile. "I'm American. My name is Pina."

Her eyes stared straight ahead, fixed. She gasped for breath, managing to squeeze out, "I hate this wretched country!"

"Uh…maybe I can help."

"You…you are Pina?"

I ignored her question; I had to. I had too many of my own, and I didn't want to end up like her, retching on the side of the *quai.* "What happened? Do you know?"

"Pina?" She blinked mechanically. "When the boat slowed down, we were supposed to get off. He told me. It was over, right?"

"Huh? When? The tour wasn't over." I needed to just stick to the facts. I pinched myself.

"No?" She blanched, her face contorted, her eyes wide.

"Breathe in and out." My chest almost did it for

her—I knew this anxiety exercise well.

Somebody passed me a paper bag, encouraging me to continue. Cassia, whose English wasn't great but who understood, translated for the boatmen still signaling with whistles and walkie-talkies for emergency help.

After breathing in the bag for a while, the girl closed her eyes. The staccato jerking of her body told me she was reliving the whole scene like a looping filmstrip.

"Can you talk now?" I placed my hand lightly on her shoulder.

"I thought I tripped getting out of the boat. But… but…"

"What?" I dug my nails into my palm, trying to stay focused. I was beginning to flash on the poem Katie sent, on the words *tripping* and *quais* from her letter.

"He pushed me. I'm sure. Where is the bastard? Where…" She started flailing her arms and twisting around.

"Shush. They will find him, I'm sure. My friend and I can also describe him."

I glanced over at Cassia. She was chatting with the police—now on the scene—explaining the conversation I had just had with Tina. She described Romeo and agreed to identify him when he was found.

Before the police could get to her side, Tina yelled to me, "He did it, the bastard did it on purpose. He knew who I was, an Italian American student from New York. The name got him—he insisted I was Pina—but he knew ahead of time about the rest. He insisted I was you. It was a setup, damn it!" Her eyes seemed to be pleading with me. "Help me, please. It could have been you…"

"I'll tell the cop. I promise we'll help get him." We had to get him, for her and for me.

I needed to get out of there immediately. I pulled Cassia aside, muttering through my clenched teeth, "We've got to go."

"Pina, you are white." She tucked in her chin and stared at me. "You going to faint?"

"Now!" I snapped.

She quickly gave our names to the cops, saying we were witnesses and would cooperate. Emergency services had finally arrived and were checking Tina out. I overheard English, so I knew Tina could explain the whole story, her story. I had heard all the explanation I needed. "It could have been you," she'd said.

Chapter Thirteen

Discovering Cognac and Corsican Wine

Finally above ground, I could breathe. The late afternoon rush-hour traffic rolled by thick and loud. Horns blared, brakes squealed, sirens shrieked. The Paris soundtrack kept me focused.

I grabbed Cassia by the arm and navigated, weaving her through the crowds in the direction of the student quarter.

She sneaked a look at me out of the corner of her eye and mumbled, "Ça *va pas!*"

Pouting, Cassia was telling me to cut it out. She hadn't heard the details of Tina's story. She continued to grumble, "*Folle, cinglée, fanatique, malade, bizarre...*" *Merde!* How many different ways would she call me deranged?

"*Ecoute.*" I stopped short and spun her around. "*That* was meant for me!"

"*Hein?*"

"Tina told me the guy knew she was an Italian American student and argued that her name couldn't be *Tina* with a *T.* Cassia, he was sent for me."

"*Mon Dieu!* For sure?"

"Yes. Tina said he called her Pina—you heard him—and she kept on repeating, 'He did it on purpose.'"

"Hmm! We must stop here," Cassia said, gesturing to a very French hole-in-the-wall, Bar de

Nevers. "We will have a cognac to digest this."

We entered the dark minuscule café. Not a soul, with the exception of the couple necking at a table tucked away in a corner. Cassia bit her lip as she ordered a *double poney* of cognac.

"*Bois! Un, deux, trois, tout!*"

I had never drunk so much alcohol—and all at once! Cassia smiled softly and reached for my hand.

"Now, slowly explain," she said, her bright green eyes starting to sparkle.

I closed my eyes and took a deep breath. Definitely less shaky.

I looked up into shimmering lights. Wow! I had never really noticed Cassia's eyes. Green. Like the glistening through the tall bottle of Chartreuse liquor set against the chipped mirror behind the bar. Ooh là là! And the yellow lights and Cassia's blond hair… Was I drunk? I giggled.

"What? You silly…" Cassia's voice rang out like a knife on a crystal glass. A ray of light leaking through the boarded-up window highlighted Cassia's streaky golden pixie bangs.

"You are tipsy, eh?" Cassia reached across the table and mussed my long straggly hair. "But please, tell me your crazy—oh, no, I mean your Craney story. Then, you can make goo-goo eyes at me all you want!"

"Huh?" I blinked to clear my head. "Soo." My mouth felt like cotton. My tongue weighed a ton.

"This is how Craney works. Creepy. I know she's behind it. That guy was there for me! That…that poem Katie sent—remember it said something about tripping and boats and quays."

I started to lick my glass and saw Cassia signal the *garçon* and point to our glasses.

I tried to follow the *garçon* with my gaze. The fog of fragrant Gauloises smoke and the gloom of the darkened bar swallowed up the white apron strings swaying across his bottom. A backlit haze enveloped the formerly necking couple, now dancing a grind across the sawdust on the tile floor.

"*Eh oh!*" Cassia snapped her fingers at me.

I jerked myself back to the table and Cassia. What was she saying?

"More! I desire more—about Craney. More about you, you crazy American!"

"*Oh, merde!*" I smacked the table with my fist to shake off the creepiness of a whole-body Craney flashback. I remembered I had been telling Cassia about the poem.

Cassia shot me the hairy eyeball and grabbed my hand. "Pina, we must have more!" She pointed to her heart and the newly arrived cognac.

"Not the cognac. The whole poem...Craney recited that to me two years ago. I can hear Craney's voice oozing the lyrics out to me. The bitch! Where the..."

"Fu-ck?" suggested Cassia.

"Yes, damn it! Where the hell is she? She's got to be here."

Cassia sipped slowly as she warmed the funny little glass in the palm of her hand.

"Okay, okay, Pina. I believe you now. Give me a minute to think...*Oui*, I've got it now. Did you recognize the guy in the sewer? Ah, but he was not American, maybe Sardinian with a strong accent or from the Corsican underground."

"No, I didn't know him. He had to be Craney's hired thug." I took a drop of the cognac, which almost evaporated in fumes. My face flushed hot with alcohol and angry steam, and my knees throbbed, burning and rubbery. I don't know why, but I began to hum, "*On ne sait jamais,*" along with Charles Aznavour on the radio.

"Yes, you are so right to sing 'We never know'! But I think you should stop inhaling your cognac and tell me more about Craney."

The way Cassia pronounced *Craney* made me think of the construction site and the man who fell almost on top of me. I blew out a long breath. I tried to cut to the chase on the Craney saga. That proved nearly impossible, what with the cognac. I had to hold up my head and form each consonant and vowel deliberately, kind of like doing gymnastics with my jaw muscles in French.

"Craney…she touched me. Well, not *there* or *there*, but it felt like she was *there*. Know what I mean?" I pointed to Cassia's *down there* with a quivering index finger. I took a huge gulp.

"Fug!" Cassia slurred, but she wore a smile I could only interpret as pride in her appropriate use of the f-word.

"Was she punished?" Cassia licked her chops to hear the juicy details and, she hoped, the positive ending of the story.

"Well…with a little help from my friends—my mother was so cool, she even accepted Katie and me as a couple—and Katie's folks, we had her banned!"

"Banned, like she had to run out of town?" Cassia almost danced in her seat, moving every part of her inebriated body to Jerry Lee Lewis's *Great Balls of Fire* pulsing from the radio. She actually rocked the bent-wood chair on the tile floor.

Cassia poked me hard. "You teach me. I feel—how you say?—backward, naïve. People, they love you. I want that, too." My pixie Cassia with the tinkling bells on her pointy Moroccan shoes let a sly grin ease its way across her face. She yanked me to my feet. "Dance!" She giggled.

I swung her Lindy style. My hand slipped to her hips. I throbbed with the beat and the drink. Her arms positioned to mimic the Twist, I moved her hips rhythmically with both hands.

I was breathing heavily. Too much dance? Too much wine? Too much Cassia?

The *garçon* sauntered over to the table, shaking to the beat and flapping the apron he wore around his waist. I sat back down dripping wet, but Cassia continued to move across the floor. Her dance steps and gyrations were flamboyant and suggestive. I couldn't resist drumming on the marble table. A few newly arrived patrons cheered her on and sent over some wine. Cries of "*bis*" rang out in the cave-like bar as they asked for more—dance steps and wine.

Cassia plopped herself down, bleary-eyed but radiant. I started to sip my wine, telling her how Jerry Lee Lewis married his thirteen-year-old cousin. I also mentioned the Bay of Pigs, the Berlin Wall, and my mother's heart attack and blubbered that I thought I was going to die.

"You die a lot." Cassia smirked, flashing a shit-eating grin.

"Huh? No." I hiccoughed.

I leaned over to tickle her. She pitched forward across the table in a convulsive jump.

"I get you back." She giggled and pinched my cheek.

My cheek burned with her touch. How much had I had to drink?

"Schweppes," I called over to the waiter wiping a dirty rag across a nearby table. "*Douze* Schweppes!"

He walked over in a cloud of Gauloises smoke. "*Douze?*" He wiggled all ten fingers and then held up two more.

Cassia corrected me. "*Non, deux*—two. Not *douze*—twelve. Your wine math stinks!"

Guzzling our Schweppes, we giggled, fizz spritzing our noses.

"Listen. I give you French vowel lessons!" Cassia announced in a loud voice.

She stood, clapped her hands in the direction of the bored barman, scratching himself under his apron, and the patrons who were clearly amused. Someone flashed a lighter at her and cried, "*Allez!*"

Cassia drank quickly. More than half a bottle. A low, rumbling sound began to make its way out of Cassia's throat.

"*A.*" She burped—a simple, dry burp.

"*E.*" She opened her mouth again. An acute *e* rolled out, almost a hiccough.

In quick succession the vowels *i*, *o*, and *u* poured out. Cassia was slowing down. A patron shouted, "Eh? The last vowel in French?"

Cassia constricted her chest, swallowed, and belched out. "*Igrec!*" *Y* in French.

Applause rang out. I was afraid I'd wet my pants. Patrons pumped Cassia's hands. People stomped the floor in appreciation. Cassia cried tears of joy, her fondest wish—to be appreciated, special—granted!

Her smile was beautiful. She beamed at me. "Thank you. You make me special!"

I patted her hand. "*You* were wonderful."

I stopped laughing. I stopped drinking. Suddenly, I was sober. A huge lightbulb went off in my head. Really frightening things like my mother's heart attack and the almost war over the Bay of Pigs had happened just before I sailed for France. *And* a really frightening thing had just brought us out of the sewers and into this bar. Enough. We had to talk about Craney—and now!

I shook Cassia's arm. I raised my voice, urging her to straighten up.

"Listen, Cassia, you've got to help. The tombstones, the sewer *accident*, they are very real."

The *garçon* had sent over some coffees, which Cassia all but chugalugged.

"Okay. I stop my teasing. Pina, you are right: the sewer accident…very *bizarre*."

"You don't say…" I grimaced.

"*Oui*, it could have been you. Come, we must go home," Cassia said, trying to stand. She began to wobble, giggling. The barman nudged the *garçon*, who strode over to Cassia's side. He informed us that we had entertained the clientele so much that the barman and patrons wanted to send us home in a taxi.

I breathed a sigh of relief and helped support Cassia to the backseat of the cab. Safe inside, I practiced the deep, trance-like concentration my therapist had taught me years before and tried to visualize a peaceful and sane solution to the Craney problem. Within minutes, I was asleep, but I was not aware of any answers or dreams when I awoke at our doorstep.

We stared at the gate to our boarding house. We were no longer totally smashed, but we were still too vague, our breath too colorful, to meet up with anybody in the courtyard and certainly not at dinner.

Cassia took the lead, sneaking around corners and assuming positions straight out of Interpol. Her stealth maneuvers got us up the two flights of stairs unseen—and unsmelled.

"*Très bien!*" She flashed a thumbs-up. "Now we must eat."

"But—"

"*Ah, non!* I have good Corsican cheese and sausage," Cassia said, pulling out a box from under her bed.

Pushing our beds closer together so we could use hers as a table, we unwrapped the stinky cheese. I almost gagged when I saw the little worms, but Cassia assured me that was *très normal*! "All good Corsican cheeses have the little wiggly things."

She jumped off my bed and ran to her dresser. "I almost forgot the *pièce de résistance*!"

I looked up expecting to see her magically produce escargots, but she stood waving a bottle of Sciaccarellu red wine, complaining, "It is only a half bottle—but *attention*, it is very heady!" She guffawed as she plopped back down next to me on my bed.

"Just a sip," I said, cutting a round of sausage. I knew we had to start making plans about Craney. I had to keep a clear head, but I took two swigs just the same.

"Eh? You like? Here, you must have some wine with this cheese." She giggled and smeared the crumbly, aged cheese across my lips.

"I like, I like," I mumbled, licking my lips. "Righto, just another sippy."

I handed the bottle back to Cassia, who shook it. Empty. She tee-heed and fell back on the bed. Out cold.

Squinting up at the window, I realized it was already dusk. I yawned and got up to switch on a light. I didn't quite make the scramble across to the other side of the bed. My pillow was sooo comfortable, and I forgot whatever it was I had wanted to do.

⁂

Dreams of Corsica, of huge wheels of wormy cheese, and stuffed sausages swirled in my head. Cassia was stomping grapes next to an old shack, a kind of shepherd's hut. Katie appeared swinging an ax, whacking the thatch out of the hut. Whack, whack, whack, whack!

I blinked to get a better look at Katie to try to understand why she seemed so angry. I couldn't see her in the dark and only then realized I was in my room and someone was knocking at the door, yelling, "*Livraison Spéciale!*"

I rolled over to jerk myself out of bed. I turned to look at what my hand had smacked. Cassia? What? In my bed? Flushed with shame, I looked at the pattern the sheets made and the contortions of Cassia's body. Did we? Could I have?

I heard the knock again. I swung my head back and forth between the bed and the door. I took several deep breaths.

Numb with guilt, I stumbled the rest of the way out of bed to open the door. Someone apologized for the early hour and handed me a special delivery letter.

I was in hell, flashing on the scene I had just

left—damned ecstasy between the sheets. But it was a heavenly act I couldn't remember. And Cassia, would she remember? And now? I was in heaven with the afterglow of the wine and finally a letter from Katie. I was panting for Katie's words. I would let the other sleeping dog lie as I made my way ever so quietly back into the room.

My sweet, sweet Pina,

Oh, God, I am so sorry. I love you—miss you so much. I was wrong, really wrong, about sending you the poem. I didn't mean to get you all worked up. Maybe I was trying to convince you *and* me that it was nothing.

And Paris? I'm kind of jealous. I hate to admit that, but...

What the heck did you mean by tombstones falling through your chimney? Maybe I didn't get you right. Because, I mean, you'd be dead.

I know I'm babbling, Pina, but you've got to know, you must, I am loyal to you. I could never think of being with anyone else, not even in flirting! Sweetie, I only want you.

I was so upset that you were pissed at me. Please send me a telegram if the phones are bad. Tell me quick, I really need to know we're okay.

Your darling, Katie

The letter shook in my hands. I sobbed and kissed the pages. I would go to the Western Union office as soon as it opened. I'd telegraph her how much I loved her, but also the news about Craney. Right, my plan...

I grabbed the edge of the sheet to dry my eyes when I spotted Cassia—in my bed. I had gotten lost in the letter and forgotten about her. What was Cassia doing here?

My stomach reacted faster than my head. I ran on tiptoes to the bidet. I couldn't vomit, but I was sick trying to remember what had gone on between Cassia and me. A million fuzzy, lurid thoughts went through my mind. Two remained: get out of there without waking Cassia and telegraph Katie.

I grabbed my clothes and my wallet and headed to the shower downstairs. The cold water didn't help the fog in my mind. I remembered dreams about Cassia stomping grapes with a white see-through, gauzy, sack-like dress hitched way up to her thighs. And I could still feel the cheese she smeared on my lips. The rest? Ah, man! We couldn't have…I wouldn't have…

I'd just ask her. Shoot! No, I couldn't think. I'd see how she acted, but for now, I had to get to the telegraph office.

⚜ ⚜ ⚜ ⚜

The Western Union office reeked of stale cigarettes and urine. I swallowed hard not to throw up; I had to get out of there fast. The telegraph form was small. I could only write the most important stuff besides "I'm yours alone." At least, I thought I was. *Merde!*

Craney at it again—Proof—Man pushed wrong person instead of me off boat—Get Joe, Alda, Dorotea involved—Craney in Paris? —love only you.

I wrote. I sent it. I did it. *That* was done. Now back to Cassia. Was I done for?

Chapter Fourteen

Consequences

Paris was only just waking up. Metal blinds barricading shop windows rose upward in a rumble while carts rattled down sidewalks packed with crates of eggs and baskets of oysters and mussels draped in seaweed for freshness. Buttery flake pastry released its fragrance to funnel out bakery doors and mingle with diesel fumes and the seafood's salty scent. Paris was going about its daily business. I dreaded facing mine.

I dragged my feet getting back to my room, fooling myself that I was merely drugged with the sights, sounds, and smells of Paris. My anxiety over confronting Cassia about our night of sex under the influence—if it even happened—prevented any aroma besides the stink of raw fear from intoxicating me.

As I neared my boarding house, my eyes started to burn, and my throat tightened. Fear's partner was rearing its angry head, or was that red shame creeping up my neck?

Merde! That meant trouble. I couldn't storm into my room, guns ablaze, targeting Cassia in an unexplained fit of shame, guilt, and anger at Cassia, at myself. And was it Cassia who had seduced me or...? Ah, jeez!

I was awake now, for real—and sober, stone-cold

sober. Last night, man, I'd never been plastered like that. I'd have to stop drinking wine as if I had been raised like Cassia on a diet of a drop or two of wine at meals.

Hmm! When I'd gone to turn on the light, Cassia was already asleep. Oh, shoot! I remembered now. Her nightgown had slipped off her shoulder, and her breast was…Wow! It was full and round and creamy white, and her nipple was huge and rosy.

I covered my face. Did I really see all that? I felt my cheeks. I was roasting.

I slowed down on my way upstairs to my room to try to recall something, anything. A fog draped everything from the previous night, but hanging out here on the stairs, I could feel my underpants stick to me. Shoot!

Okay, okay, so I got turned on. Now. That didn't mean…what? That I did something last night? Well, maybe not a whole lot. Maybe just looked—or touched a little bit?

And Katie? And now? So I had an active imagination. Shoot! Damn! I was hot just thinking about her. Cassia, not Katie. I mean, Cassia was cute. Well, more than cute, but I wouldn't have, would I?

I shook my head. I was all over the place. I couldn't tell if the heat screaming off my body was shame, lust, or anger. And at whom?

Right. I'd just have to wait and see. Anyway, I could only stay for an hour at most since I had class, and I had to see Père Sablé. What could happen in an hour?

I cracked the door a smidge. Cassia was awake. She was doing what she called her morning calisthenics in her bra and underpants. I opened the door wide and slipped into the room behind her as she continued to do jumping jacks and deep knee bends.

"*Salut*," she said, all breathy as her tight, perky breasts rose and fell in her very French skimpy bra. Her undies were equally brief.

I reminded myself of my plan to avoid the growing evidence—my body's automatic arousal system—that I may have succumbed to Cassia's pixie charm, not to mention her delightful, sprite-like physique and the wine!

"*Bonjour*," I answered. I sat at my desk with my back to her and busied myself with my books.

"*Eh oh!*" Cassia stopped her exercise and tapped me on the shoulder. "You do not mention last night?" She fluttered her lashes.

"Uh…" I froze.

If I said thank you, what would that mean? As I pondered this, Cassia wandered around my desk area and stopped in front of Katie's photo as if mesmerized by it.

"*Ooh là là!* You are so lucky to have her." Cassia made a smooching sound with her thumb and index finger to her lips. "And she is so lucky to have you!" She wore a look that all but undressed me.

But who was disrobing whom? Was she flirting? Yeah, for sure, but did she know what she was doing? What had gone on overnight? Maybe I was offering myself up for her to remove one teensy article of clothing after another. Her look was scorching.

My face was fuchsia, for sure. She stood so close to me, still in her bra and panties. I was certain she could feel the heat of my fluster. That was it. I was just uncomfortable. She wasn't my type. Her hair was blond; she was very thin; I loved Katie.

So, I couldn't have, but she? I had to know.

"Ah, Cassia…" I stalled, trying to locate my courage. I got up from my desk and put some space between us.

As if just noticing my malaise and her lack of clothing, she said, "Oops!" and quickly put on a robe. "I am sorry. You Americans are so modest. I forgot. But what were you saying?"

Ah, man! Did she just wink?

"What did you mean about last night?" I asked in rapid French, head down, again casually flipping through my books.

"Oh! Have you forgotten the cheese, the sausage, the wine? And that I will help you with Mère Paul?" Cassia's shoulders sagged. Every spark of enthusiasm extinguished. She looked down; her lips quivered as she asked, "You do not like it? Or maybe"—she raised her tear-rimmed eyes to mine—"you do not like me?"

"I do, I do, and thank you," I said, forcing a smile. Shoot! I had hurt her. "Cassia, listen, thank you. You are so generous—"

"But?"

Damn! I couldn't do this now. Maybe I didn't have to know what happened. Maybe I didn't want to know.

"Ah…but I have to go to school, and I want Père Sablé to help me figure out this sewer business. I am very—how do you say…?"

"*Crispée?*"

"Yes. Tense!"

I sneaked a quick glance at Cassia. Her jaw relaxed, and her emerald green eyes sparkled again. She placed her hand ever so gently on my arm. A tingle ran from that spot up my arm and found its way down and up the length of my spine.

"I would never do anything to hurt you, and I will tell Mère Paul. We will take care of your problems."

I hurried to pack my books and tossed another "*Merci*" over my shoulder. As I approached the door to leave, Cassia attempted to kiss my cheeks. I pulled back, apologizing. "I really am too—"

"*Oui, je sais, crispée!*"

Running down the stairs, I tried to weigh the arguments for and against Cassia having seduced me. She was very sexy; maybe she did. But her behavior just now? Was it normal? Had it always been like this— what word—alluring, irresistible, maddening? I didn't know. Maybe the real question was, did I seduce her? And did I still want to? God! Just get to class!

Chapter Fifteen

Help!

My racing thoughts sped me to the Métro station. The train, also in express mode, took a mere ten minutes to arrive at Saint-Placide. The smoked-earth smell of chestnuts roasting on charcoal wafted down the Métro stairs, scrambling all my crazy thoughts save one: bite into this soft, nutty-flavored kernel of warmth and wholesomeness. I purchased some from the old guy on the corner and frantically peeled their scorching fibers, trying to occupy my hands and mind on the four-block walk to school.

Every rustling movement of my clothes released the lingering essence of charcoal and chestnuts as I slid into a desk in Père Sablé's nineteenth-century novel class, stirring up a longing for Thanksgiving, which I wouldn't be celebrating this year. While he lectured about *Madame Bovary* and the dreary realism of the life of a country doctor's wife—before her affairs—I longed for some of that boredom. My faraway look must have betrayed me. Père Sablé narrowed his small dark eyes at me, pushing his wire-framed glasses up to his forehead. Sunlight bounced off his lenses, highlighting the crown of his salt-and-pepper buzzed hair.

"Mademoiselle Mazzini," he called. "See me!"

As students filed out, Père Sablé took my arm and escorted me to the tower stairs. He fished his key from his deep pocket and signaled with his hand for me to enter and take a seat on the step.

Pulling bits of tobacco out of his mouth from the Gauloise he had just lit, he stared at me in silence. I declined the cigarette he extended to me and looked up into his soft gaze when he said, "This is not boredom I see. Tell me."

I shook my head and rubbed my chin in what was becoming my favorite cool French gesture. This time, though, I was not playing a role, nor was I cool.

"*Aidez-moi*," I begged.

"*Et comment?*" Père Sablé wanted me to spell out exactly how he could help.

I elaborated all the details of the sewer story. He nodded in understanding and patted my hand, explaining that Mademoiselle Lesage had told him about Craney's former pursuit of me. I smiled when he agreed she could look guilty of this latest incident.

I closed my eyes as my whole body went limp with relief. Finally, someone understood.

The next few moments passed in silence as my eyes fixed a soft gaze on this mystery man. He had taken the time to speak with Mademoiselle Lesage. So he knew all about me *and* Craney. And probably Katie, and…he really cared about me—still.

A loud slap of his hand on the step brought me back to the present.

"*Ça y est. On y va!*" Père Sablé grabbed me by the hand.

"*Où?*" I should have known where he was taking me when he saluted.

Mumbling something about case updates and police, he had brought us outside the school to the corner of Rues d'Assas and Vaugirard in no time flat.

We stood in front of his moped.

"*Allez-y!*" Père Sablé handed me a helmet and pointed out the back fender to me.

I flopped gracelessly on the rusty old contraption and held on to him as the machine sputtered and whined into motion. We zoomed along the Boulevard Saint-Germain and turned left onto the Boulevard Saint-Michel. Bookstores and small cafés zipped by while bearded and beret-wearing students flashed thumbs-up to me. If I hadn't focused on my balance on the moped, my shifting emotions would have had me careening all over the place until I landed on my *derrière* in the gutter.

Finally, we crossed over the river to the Île de la Cité where Notre-Dame's towers filled the sky. We had arrived at the police station. Père Sablé said he'd do the talking.

Appearing small and wiry, even in his baggy cassock, he stood up to the "*flics*," as he called them, and insisted upon getting an immediate update of the case. The officer and Père Sablé disappeared into a small adjoining room and emerged a moment later flashing photos presumed to be of the sewer Romeo for me to identify.

Père Sablé sat opposite me, grim and still. His gaze seemed to encourage me to go back in my mind to the sewer incident even if remembering caused me to twitch. I read comfort and hope in that look.

I took a deep breath when he said "*doucement*," slowly. The Romeo-thug appeared even darker in the black and white photos. His deep Mediterranean complexion emphasized his glassy stare and the whites of his bulging eyes in this austere police picture. His left eye followed me, I imagined, as I turned my head away for a moment of relief.

Turning back to the glossy print of this typically hoody-looking creep with his long greasy sideburns and the dangling hairs of his Brylcreemed pompadour, I flashed on his hand creeping up Tina's neck and back. The sounds of sucking kisses still turned my stomach.

"*Oui!* That's him!" I shouted through clenched teeth.

I turned left and right, looking for the WC. I had to leave the room that minute. Père Sablé spread his hands around his expanding chest to urge me to breathe deeply and pointed to a door off to the left.

After a drink of cool water, I returned. I gave a thumbs-up to Père Sablé, whose gentle look was all the comforting I needed.

The cop and Père Sablé secluded themselves once again behind closed doors. When Père Sablé re-emerged, he wore a cunning smile. He clapped me on the shoulder, saying, "*Oui,* you did it."

I raised my eyebrow. "Eh?"

"You identified him, yes? They got him already, and there is a story, of course."

"Please, *je vous prie,* tell me quickly," I urged.

"*D'accord!*" He nodded, explaining that the culprit was hired in Corsica. "An old witch, a true witch, paid the thug to get back at a girl. This girl—supposedly *you*—she had seduced the husband of the woman who hired the witch. The witch wanted the girl drowned, but the lucky bastard couldn't do it. Besides, the name Tina, instead of Pina, confused him."

"What? I didn't have any affair! This is *merde!*"

"*Attention!* You are, after all, in the police station in the presence of a priest." He smiled a devilish smile. "But yes, this is—how you say in English?—a *horsey manoor* story the witch told him. *Eh, bien*, this *sorcier*, she chose a real *crétin* for her hoodlum."

"Hmm," I mumbled. "And this witch... Do they know what she looked like?" I bit my lip, hoping she was young and blonde and wearing a Chanel suit. Like no witch I knew. Not even any witchy person I knew...

"*Eh, non.* Just an old lady in black, tall and skinny with bony fingers in a black hood." He scratched his crew cut. "Like many Corsican old ladies, but they are often round, you know, short and puffy."

I sighed way too loudly hearing the description, which fit Craney to a tee—I think. It just had to be her. Heads shot up. I felt like a hundred pairs of eyes were studying first me and then Père Sablé, as if he were upsetting me—which he was, just not like that.

"Let's go," I said.

"*Oui, allons au café à côté.*"

Of course there was a café right next to the police station. Père Sablé grew silent—darkly silent—as he drank his café express. Finally, he groused, "Drink up. Too bad it is not cognac."

I started to gag. There was no way he could know about my binge with Cassia. He screwed up his face and peered more closely at me, mumbling, "Many disturbing thoughts..."

I held my breath, reading fear in his eyes. He looked away.

"The thugs, they know all about you, all right! Corsica...hmm. They traced you through your roommate. Cassia, she is from Bastia, the main city, and her father is mayor, they say. I know this, the police know this. We will share with him this dossier. Yes?"

"Yes, of course. But—" I stammered.

"*Oui.* There is more. I can only tell a piece

because, you know, the confession, my lips, they are sealed. But…*une personne*, she left my confessional, running. I just see a black gown. I had to poke my head out because I smell burning. Then I go back, and I see something. Burned crucifix. This *personne* warned in bad, bad French, '*Gare à vous, mon prêtre!*'—Watch out, priest!"

"*Mon Dieu!*" I choked on my coffee.

"*Oui*, you can pray to God."

"And you think—"

"There is a connection. I will work on this and talk with Mère Paul. From here on, you will see lots of priests and nuns around you. Not to worry—maybe police, maybe real priests. We will solve this *mystère*. Now back home to safety for you."

❧❧❧❧

I rolled my eyes internally. Back home…safety. *Oh, yeah?* The moped's rough start jerked me into the present, and my arms instinctively grasped my savior's waist.

Driving at breakneck speed, even for a moped, he shouted that La Toussaint was coming up, and it might provide a welcome break for me. I scrunched up my face, trying to figure out why the French holy days honoring the dead, All Saints and All Souls Day, would give me some relief. And I certainly would not dress or undress myself for Halloween with Cassia.

"*Alors*, when home is not where the heart is, then you must take a holiday with your days off," he yelled back to me, turning his head almost completely around to check for—understanding, tears, or what, I didn't know.

My God, was this priest psychic? And what did he mean about days off?

"*Ma chère enfant*, you have free days for Toussaint. Go!" Again, he swiveled his head.

"Oh? *Oui!*" I quickly responded before he totally took his gaze off the road. "*Chouette!* I could get away and go visit a friend!"

"*Bien!* It is decided. You go away, *but* you must make sure you tell me where."

As we reached the curb in front of the foyer, Père Sablé giggled. "You know, Mère Paul, she is the spitting image of a witch. Do not misunderstand"—pursing his lips, he nodded—"a good witch!" He winked again and quoted the famous play *Le Cid*, "*Va, cours, vole et nous venge!*"

Of course. I would go, run, and avenge us! I was already feeling better.

Chapter Sixteen

Somewhere Safe

As I pushed open the gate to the foyer, I pondered where to go…anywhere away from Cassia and here. But for now, I had to climb the stairs to my room.

Two steps at a time…would I be safe? Two more steps…safer here with Cassia? Or…? One step…where? One last step. I stood in front of my door.

I tried to take my emotional pulse. Breathe, slow down, breathe again. Was Cassia really a risk? I would just be strong and clear with her. But what if I had been the seductress—if anything even happened? Well, I'd just be clear with myself. No flirting. No lingering looks.

Katie? No, I couldn't go back home to see her for my four-day vacation. Hmm. I sighed, sick and tired of my own obsessing. I would wait and see and write a long letter to Katie or call her. Maybe she could send me some of my old pills, the ones for anxiety.

The thought of Katie's voice sobered me up. I straightened my jacket and ran my hand through my windblown hair. God, I needed a haircut, a French one.

Cassia was propped up in bed reading a textbook when I peeked in. I settled my face, put on a calm mask, and walked in—hardly breathing to avoid disturbing her.

"*Ah, te voilà! Ça va?*"

"Yes, fine. Well…" I hesitated.

I bent down to pick up a dirty sock and shove it in my laundry bag next to the sink. I could tell her the basics of what happened. I blushed thinking I should tell her the rest of the story, the drunken night story.

"But really? And Père Sablé and the police? Did you go?" she said, jumping off the bed to embrace me.

"Cassia, slow down and sit back down! Please." I softened my tone. "Yes. The police had already caught the guy and confirmed everything we'd suspected."

I joked when I said he was her compatriot, "a Corsican bandit."

"*Vraiment?*"

I looked up from the laundry I had started to fold.

"Yes, truly, he is Corsican and hired by Craney."

"Oh! *Mon Dieu!*"

Cassia got up and softly touched my arm, saying, "*Mon père—*"

I flinched, cutting her off. "Precisely. Your father can help big-time. The police and Père Sablé will call him."

"*Moi aussi*, I will call him right now."

"Hold on. I'll go downstairs with you to check my mail."

Cassia vanished almost immediately into the convent's inner hive of cells, looking for Queen Bee—Cassia's nickname for Mère Paul since she was always buzzing around. I thought of her as a torpedo, while Père Sablé called her a good witch.

I stood in front of the slatted mail cubbies on the far wall of the dining room. My box was on the second row, dead center. Neat. A letter, a skinny envelope with very European-style handwriting. From Dorotea in Heidelberg.

I flashed on the good days at Albert Academy two years ago. Dorotea, Katie's former roommate, turned out to be a wonderfully crazy friend. We hadn't seen each other in about a year and a half, but we spoke and wrote often.

As I stood there mooning over the "easy" days at Albert—which were hardly safe and mellow—a postman came in, waving another special delivery letter.

"*Pour vous, mademoiselle. Comme vous êtes spéciale!*"

Wow! I did feel special, especially now with this letter from Katie.

My heart skipped beats. I couldn't wait to get upstairs to read Katie's letter. For the moment, all was warm and cozy and secure. Things were back under control. Or were they? There was the slight problem of honesty and guilt and…

I looked up at the clock. Two o'clock. Plenty of time to read these and write back. The badly formed figure on the crucifix hanging next to the clock seemed to smile down on me. I laughed. Magical thinking maybe, but I did feel protected.

Back up in my bed with my mother's maroon and pink crocheted throw covering my knees, I propped up my legs and tore open Katie's letter.

My dear Pina,

It's been so long since I've seen you and felt you next to me. Two weeks *is* a long time! I feel your breath on my neck, your thigh touching mine, your wispy hair tickling my shoulders. I'm afraid to go on—I'll be crying and/or excited, and I won't be able to do anything about it.

I glanced around my room, twitching. I was quite aroused until my gaze drifted back to Katie's letter and the word *bad* in bold, capital letters:

BAD news. I called Dad and Joe, who immediately did a thorough investigation. He asked Headmistress Emily Whitfield about your current file and records from Paris. Missing. Dad and Joe think someone tampered with the locks and stole the addresses of your foyer and your school. Dad has already hired a private detective.

Joe also went to all the local Andover inns. The manager of the Exeter said a recent guest looked familiar. They identified her as Craney.

This is disgusting, I know. I started to panic and beg Dad to get you to come home, but I know that wouldn't be fair to you or good for you. Mademoiselle Lesage told him she had been in contact with friends of her family in France, the nun at your foyer and the priest at your school. She said they were "well connected." Is there a French mafia?

They also talked about your roommate, Cassia, saying she was somehow very special. What's she like? She better not be sexy.

Merde! Katie just had to ask about Cassia.

Sweetheart, please, please be careful. The sewer thing. God, that was the first thing I should have asked you about. I was sick to my stomach when I thought of someone falling, no, being pushed into the water—and that someone was supposed to be you.

My father said Joe and his father, Fifi, are in touch with the French cops. Seems like everyone's in on it.

I'd just be…Please let's talk by phone. I need to hear your voice. Dad says to send you his love. This is weird, maybe, but he said not to tell your parents because of your mom's blood pressure and heart, I guess. Are you okay with that? Or really, Pin, should you come home? My folks don't think it's necessary. They say you'll be safe, but please tell me what you need.

I love you. I can't think straight enough to tell you about school or what I'm reading or my science project up for a National Science Foundation Award. I just want you. Call me, like now.

All my love, your Katie

I laid my head back on my pillow and stared at the tin ceiling tiles through my tears. Tossing off the throw, I fanned myself with Katie's letter. Yeah! She finally got that I was scared, and now all those people were taking action, but…

I got what I wanted, didn't I? She certainly was concerned. And now if I told her about Cassia—although what was there to tell?—she'd have even more to be concerned about.

Aw, man! Katie had to go and ask *that* question, the other thing I was too chicken to think about. Did I want to go home?

Screw this! I tossed the letter aside and checked out the age-old soot on the ceiling again. No answers there. No, I just couldn't go home. Home…

I squeezed my eyes shut and clenched my teeth.

I could feel a string of expletives brewing, effervescing from my gut to my mouth, when the doorknob rattled. I opened my mouth, but nothing emptied out except, "Oh!"

Mère Paul stood in the doorway. Framed by the blackness of the stairwell, she appeared angelic, hovering with the white wings of her coif headpiece. No, not angelic, witchy good. I needed a spell.

"*Puis-je entrer?*" she asked.

"Yes, come in," I answered, pulling myself together.

Scrambling off the bed, I pulled out my desk chair for her. Mère Paul motioned for me to sit at the foot of my bed. She nodded at me with a slow, wise look and reached across to pat my hand.

"*Mon enfant.*" She cleared her throat. "I have chatted with Cassia, but more importantly with Père Sablé. I will not let anyone get to you, no tombstones, no baths in the sewers. No, none of that." She paused to catch her breath.

I blotted escaping tears. "*Merci, merci.*"

Red-cheeked, she seemed to be building a head of steam again. "Tonight, I will patrol. *Oui*, I will do surveillance tonight, and tomorrow, I will have the chimneys screened. No one harms my girls!"

Mère Paul slammed her hand on my desk and stood, saying, "You will be safe." She pursed her lips and looked deep into my eyes. "Your Père Sablé and I go way back in the Résistance. I know about fear and sleepless nights and things you're not sure you really see."

I thanked her profusely. I stood, hand on my heart, moved to tears, good tears, that she had told me of her past. She really was a human torpedo.

"*Merde! Oh! Excusez-moi.* I forgot. Père Sablé said to tell you about the crucifix. You know our fire, here in the kitchen? Many hours later, I found this—"

Mère Paul pulled out a burned crucifix. The brass Jesus was still mostly intact. I blanched when I flashed on the scorched crucifix Père Sablé had found outside his confessional.

"This," Mère Paul said, holding up the remnants of the crucifix, "this is evil. This is war! That night, someone threw this burning cross into the kitchen. Someone has declared war on Père Sablé and me!"

She whipped around and marched to the door, almost toppling Cassia as she breezed in, eyes glowing, humming *Alouette.* Cassia's glee hit me like a victory parade in the streets of Paris after the liberation. Boy, I needed a breather. Her bubbly face gradually donned a mask of pure befuddlement as Mère Paul rumbled out the door and down the stairs.

My distraction had vanished. Cassia reappeared.

"*Hein?*" She turned to me.

"Oh, boy…" I sat myself down on the edge of my bed again. "Do you know about the crucifix?"

"Crucifix? Now you want to talk religion?"

I explained very briefly since she was impatient to tell me about her father and the good news.

"*Mon père,*" Cassia said, "he is on to this mystery. He has spoken with the police in Paris and Père Sablé and his police in Bastia."

"*Merci.*" I sat there slowly rubbing my hand back and forth on the chenille bedspread for comfort.

"Ah, but there is more. Word travels fast in Corsica, and my father has already learned a lot."

I chewed on my lip. "Uh-huh."

"Yes. A scrawny, ugly person dressed like an old

Corsican widow all in black, she was in Bastia, but—"

"What?" I gestured to Cassia to speed up her story.

"She hired a taxi to go all the way to the other end of Corsica, to Bonifacio, and got a ferry across to Sardinia." Cassia smiled as if she had told me Craney was dead in the water.

"And? So what? I mean, that's great that your dad could get all that info, but what does it mean?"

Cassia stared at me as if I were dense, which maybe after all these details from Père Sablé, Katie, Mère Paul, and now from her, maybe I was braindead.

"This," she said, "means Craney has left France for Sardinia and is either going to the Italian mainland or Africa. Ta-da!" She beamed.

"Oh."

"Oh?"

"Well, yes, that's good. I'm thinking…"

"No thank-you?" Cassia's eyes twinkled. Was she just desperate to be liked? Or…

"Oh, Cassia, yes, thank you so much. I'm just so tired, and I should tell my Italian friends Alda and Fifi. They have connections."

Cassia tilted her head and smiled at me. She knelt in front of me and put her hand on my knee. "Scared? You can sleep with me if it helps." She tried to catch my eye.

I jumped up. Right, there was that Cassia problem again. "No, no, I've got to read this letter." I scooted around in the covers, looking to retrieve Dorotea's letter. "Please, I need time for this." I waved the thin blue envelope at Cassia.

Chapter Seventeen

Toussaint Vacation

I closed my eyes and held Dorotea's letter against my forehead. I had to pause between communications from such diverse personalities as Cassia and Dorotea. In an instant, all the warmth I felt toward Dorotea rushed in, filling me with hope. Although she had decided to continue her studies in Heidelberg and not the U.S., she returned to Germany a very different person from the milkmaid-type character I first knew at Albert. She was now a very good friend.

Hello there,
My good friend, I miss you and worry about you. Katie told me that Craney is here again. Perhaps I can help. I hate who my father was in 1940, and that's why he stays in Argentina, but...he does have ways to find out about evil. I think he helps the American feds. I question him about Craney.

Four months with no Katie...Pina, you asked my opinion: you must stay in Europe. You need this time to grow—away from America, away from Katie. You will become the global citizen: the best of America, the best of Italia, and the best of Europe.

You will come to visit, yes? I will keep you safe. Here the *studentenwohnheim* is most secure, and I find you a room on my floor. *Jawohl?* Come soon because I have good surprise for you!

I do not treat Craney lightly, but I know the solution is logical and will come.

Many kisses, your D

D's letter was so loving and real, I didn't feel as alone. I reached over to shut out the light. I stifled a sigh and rubbed my eyes dry. Cassia's soft snoring calmed me. I could almost imagine my old cat Choux snuggling into the crook of my arm as sleep crept over me.

❧ ❧ ❧ ❧

A beam of light tracked across my wall, startling me. And then, pitch. After a few deep breaths, I went to the window. In the courtyard below, a dark, squarish figure pivoted around. I heard a thwack-thwack somewhere overhead. Rocks against something solid. Not wood. Cement.

I squinted through the shutters. Yes, the human torpedo. Mère Paul without her habit, with a…a… Holy crap! A flashlight and a slingshot, bombarding bats away from the chimneys.

Man! I was having a great night. Warmed by D's letter and protected by Mère Paul's patrol! So secure and unaccustomed! I was wide awake.

Raiding my stash of peanuts from the closet, I strategically planned each chew in order not to wake sleeping beauty in the next bed. Ruminating in this way helped me. I really did need to get away for a few days. D and Heidelberg would fill me up with heartwarming German *Gemütlichkeit*—that hokey folksiness—

wurst and bier. I could already feel D's nurturing and supportive arm and schnapps!

I would call Katie in the morning and send a telegram to D to tell them I was going to Heidelberg for a few days. I also had to let Cassia know I'd be leaving the next afternoon so she could inform Mère Paul, who would tell Père Sablé.

When I almost choked on a peanut, I realized my sweet plans had lulled me to sleep. I shut the light off and drifted.

❧ ❧ ❧ ❧

My dream was black. Dark in feeling, dark in shade. Black curtains draped the walls of the poorly lit room. A black canopy bed occupied the center of the room, its blackness broken only by the white polar bear skin dead center. I went to exit the room and felt blocked. Craney was plastered against my front, dressed in her ermine-decorated black academic gown. She picked me up as if I were just air, empty air, and tossed me on the white bearskin, which immediately came alive, as did the ermine collar around Craney's neck. From her waist, Craney drew out a black leather cat-o'-nine-tails and lashed it out. She whipped every object surrounding me, teasing the beasts to anger. Her eyes flew wide open, focusing on me. The only sound besides the gnashing of the animals' teeth was the lick and whack of her whip.

In my dream, I screamed out. In my room, I was mute. I bolted upright, dream sitting. I still heard noise, not dream noise.

Overhead banging broke the dream spell. Startled awake, Cassia and I stumbled to the windows to see workmen rigged out with ropes, installing chimney spark guards.

I caught my breath. My dream...a Craney flashback. Luckily, I hadn't screamed out loud. I couldn't tell Cassia, not now when I needed to keep her at arm's length.

"See?" She stifled a yawn. "You are safe from things falling out of the skies!"

Her smile was so open and caring, I hated to tell her I'd be leaving for a few days. Or did I have to leave?

It was already past seven. I washed and dressed in silence—into my new teal jewel-necked sweater and cream and lilac pleated skirt. Cassia raised an eyebrow and whistled. "Chic!"

I swallowed hard. "*Merci*, Cassia! *Ecoute*, I have to go away for a few days—Toussaint holy day, you know."

She stared at me. "You go to honor your dead?"

"No." I scratched my head for the right words. "My friend D needs me, and she is not dead."

"Oh." Her lower lip quivered as she asked, "Are you angry with me?"

"No, but..." I didn't want to have *that* talk with her now. Maybe I was angry with myself because...I didn't trust myself. Damn. "Look, I need to see this old friend. I just need to relax for a few days, you know, get away—"

"From me? Since that day we drink so much? What wrong do I do? Tell me. I do not know." Was it anger or something else that pulled her face into broken pieces?

Oh, merde! Not this, not now. I couldn't do this.

"Oh, it's an American thing," I bullshitted and held my breath, hoping that would explain just about anything.

"I didn't think you were so…so…superficial."

I had to take a big gulp on that one. What the hell did she mean? I didn't intend to…My eyebrows shot up, and damn, she answered my unspoken question.

"You, you pretend to come close to me. I get ideas you like me and then…"

Oh, hell! "I do like you." I brushed some imaginary lint off my sweater.

"No. I think you just tease."

Cassia's cow-eyed look told me all I needed to know. She was in love with me. She blinked her long lashes, her smile softened, her lips parted. She reached out for me.

I melted. Sweet sensations burst out, tingling in all the wrong—and right—places. Shit.

"No." My tone was crisply brittle. My thrust, pushing her away, nearly a karate slam.

She crumbled. She cried. Her chest heaved in great sobs. I stood torn between regret, shame, anger, and a burning desire to comfort her—and me.

"No, no, Cassia." I patted her arm and tried to come up with a story, a plausible and calming one, for her and for me.

"You see," I stalled, "I don't want to start having these attacks. I get really crazy, like my heart pounds out of my chest and is killing me that very instant. And I faint and…and…" I took a deep breath to calm myself. "I, uh…I get overstressed."

Cassia turned into my arms and hugged me tight. She sniffled and patted me on the back. Her recovery was swift and dignified. My shame and cowardice overwhelming.

"*Oui!* You must let your friend take care of you,

and when you come back, I will be here." She pulled back and smoothed my hair behind my ears. She nodded. "You will be okay, okay?"

"Yes. Thank you." I blew out a huge breath. Was it just Cassia's need, or did *I* really want to be taken care of?

I felt guilty as hell. Guilty for leaving. Guilty for wondering about staying. She watched as I threw a few things into my suitcase and said she'd inform Mère Paul of my departure. I said I'd bring her back a souvenir and pecked her quickly on both cheeks—twice. I felt her tear on my lips as she pulled me close again.

❧ ❧ ❧ ❧

Suitcase in hand, I grabbed a few crusts of baguette from the breakfast table, excused myself, and exited the foyer to go to the post office.

I lucked out. I was third in line for transatlantic calls. In the meantime, I rushed off a telegram to D at Western Union, saying I would see her in about eight hours.

My call to Katie came through in booth two. Her voice, her sweet voice was there: real, mellow, repeating over and over: "Darling, darling Pina."

Heat ran through me, through every cell of me. My cheeks burned, and my body throbbed with wanting. Wanting Katie.

"Katie, oh Katie, I just adore you."

"Ah, me too." The phone almost scorched my hand.

"Did you get my letter?" Katie asked, all breathy.

"Yes. Listen, I do want to stay."

"I respect that, but either way…"

"God, I love you. I know you think I need to be here and not in your arms all the time."

"*Mmm!* Say more about you in my arms—"

"Stop, Katie! It's hard enough. You don't want them to arrest me for phone booth lewdness."

"Wow! It's as if you were right here and I could touch you. Ha!" Katie laughed.

"Listen, about staying here… You're right. I am scared, but there are a lot of good people involved in this now, not just in Paris."

"Phew! That feels better. And Dorotea?"

"That's why I'm calling. I'm going to Heidelberg for four days. It's a holiday here."

"Oh?"

"Yeah. Want to come?" I joked.

"Right. Like we get four days for All Saints Day."

"Yeah, for Halloween."

"So, when…are you going?" Katie yawned as if she didn't really care about my answer. She was hiding something—I could tell.

"What? What are you cooking up?"

Katie yawned again. "It's late here."

"Shoot! I gotta go. This is costing me a fortune, and the train, I don't know the schedule."

"That's right, run off. Seriously, you sound okay. Sure you're not bluffing?"

"I'm okay for now. Cassia's father thinks Craney's in southern Italy or Africa. And D's father—"

"In Argentina?"

"Yeah. He's got FBI connections. Okay? Listen, I'll call you from Germany."

"Why? Oh…I mean good!" Katie sounded like she was choking on a laugh.

"Yeah. Good! God, you're weird."

"I love you, too. I do really. I'm kissing you goodbye."

I made kissing sounds and hummed our old Buddy Holly theme song *Maybe Baby* and the line about love coming my way.

I hung up. As soon as I regained my composure and my legs, and paid, I rushed off for the Métro and the Gare de l'Est.

Chapter Eighteen

Arriving in Germany

I stood looking at the schedule board at the Gare de l'Est. Trains coming and going at all hours, except mine, which didn't leave until 3:55 p.m. *Merde!* I wouldn't arrive in Heidelberg until 9:00 p.m.

The station's aromas of cigarette smoke, garlic, and sweat blended with burned coal didn't encourage me to hang out there. A few sleazy-looking characters making smooching noises as they undressed me with penetrating dark eyes also discouraged my parking myself for any length of time, even in the WC for dames.

I had about three hours to kill and decided to go out to get something to eat. The skies had just opened, releasing a torrent of unfriendly, pelting rain, but I spotted the Café en Face, just opposite the station, a great place to people watch—out of the downpour and away from the perverts.

I nursed my espresso and *baguette au jambon* and allowed the rain outside to rinse away my psychological muck. My breathing slowed, my neck swiveled freely, and my gaze softened. I felt safe for the first time in a long while.

My mind started to wander. I pictured myself slumped in a Degas absinthe painting, just without the booze. People passed by outside in the rain. Today, even the freakish and the stylish, men, women, in-betweens—people just seemed like too much trouble, as if even their gorgeous faces asked something of me.

I buried my head in Ionesco's play *Le rhinocéros.* Ha! Sometimes it seemed my life was onstage in this theater of the absurd. I felt infected by eerie metaphors for the Nazi malady taking over the world in the thirties and forties. More and more people could still change into Nazi rhinos with double horns. I shut the book. I forced myself to focus on my coffee, the pressurized sounds emanating from coffee machines, the clink of glass on marble, and the scraping of chairs against tile.

But thoughts of the war led to Mère Paul and Père Sablé. Did they lapse into an affair at their Resistance hideout, secreted away with goats and guns as their sole compatriots fighting for freedom? *Merde!* I had to get out of my fantasy world.

I collected myself and crossed over to the station without getting too wet. Since I had a nonreserved, second-class ticket on the cheap train, I boarded right away to find a seat in an empty nonsmoking compartment.

I slid over to the window and tossed my things into the spaces next to me. Still feeling antisocial, I tried to make my immediate surroundings and myself less than desirable. Messing up my straggly, uncoiffed hair still more, I spread out my books and papers and dared to put my feet up on the opposite bench. In a final act of "I dare you to sit here," I placed a copy of Trotsky's *Dictatorship vs. Democracy* on the seat next to my feet. Maybe I could keep the compartment all to myself.

As the train rumbled to life and the whistle blew, I admired my strategic setting. I was alone. A split second of guilt washed over me: This wasn't who I was, but…For today, no more demands on me: I was taking all the space.

A few dreary suburbs sped by, factories and houses made even bleaker by the gray rain and the soot the train sprayed. I soon tired of the sleepy places and nondescript churches. I craved some color, some vibrant life, just not the kind that asked for help or concern.

Vibrant? Yes. I had just the thing to pick me up. Alda, my old roommate. I would write to her and have Katie or Joe send it. Alda, my larger-than-life friend, who just might be able to do some sleuthing for me if I knew where they had relocated her. Hmm! Italy, I thought. Neat. Alda was exactly the person I needed and where I needed her to stake out Craney.

I started my letter with one of Alda's favorite expressions:

Ciccia bella,

I miss you. I miss your stories. I hope you're settled someplace safe. I heard you might be in Italy.

Maybe you know that I'm studying in Paris. What you probably don't know is that Craney is back and has tracked me down. Some weird and dangerous things have already happened, but I'm okay. This time, it's not just the psychological games and toying with me like two years ago. According to the authorities, she's out for blood, and I'm scared.

I'm on my way to see Dorotea—D's good, kind of a beatnik now, definitely cool—in Heidelberg. I need some fun and maybe some of D's protectiveness. Now don't get ideas about "protection"; besides, I know your dad has cleaned up his act, along with Joe's dad,

Fifi. I really am so glad that some of us can redeem our mistakes.

If you are in Italy, can you keep an ear to the ground for Craney? And…it would be so unreal to come and see you.

Baci, Baci, Baci,
Pina

I reread my letter and worried it was boring. I was falling asleep. Still alone in my compartment, I got up to shut off the heat and crack the upper transom of the window. *Merde!* That only let the smoke and sounds of whistles and sirens waft in. I slammed it, flicked the light switch, and stretched out on the brown vinyl seat. I remembered to flip the lock on the door, and I held my trusty heavy flashlight-as-weapon by my side.

The rocking rhythm of the train's clickety-clack along with the stale air in the compartment put me to sleep. I stirred, opened my eyes, and double-checked the lock.

My dream featured my Sicilian grandmother, who spoke of *stregas* and explained that there were good witches, like Mère Paul, and bad witches. Unlike her usual fare, this was not a very enlightening Grandma dream.

In the dream, I clearly visualized Mère Paul's habit, her black robe and white coif, her hands dug deeply into her side pockets. She strode about, rolling her butchy shoulders from side to side. She formed a fierce fist and menaced some unseen enemy while her other hand whipped out a crucifix from her pocket and brandished it at the same nemesis.

My black and white dream switched to Technicolor when the compartment door reverberated with a sharp crack and forceful thump. I could see the dark golden glow of the oak door and the sickly tan of the train's interior. The smeared glass of the door intermittently illuminated by trackside floodlights flashed flickering images of a black hooded robe, a bony nose in an ashen oblong face, smirking dark eyes, and a shrieking mouth distorted and plastered against it. A white hand seemingly drained of blood smashed a partially burned crucifix against the pane as the Jesus figure slithered down and out of the picture.

Craney! I startled awake and grabbed my flashlight. Lunging for the door, I swung at the now-blackened glass. I tried every setting on the flashlight, straight beam, flicker, blinking light, to see beyond the door and to mimic the earlier flashing light. Nothing!

Armed with my raised flashlight, I ventured into the hallway. Nothing but snoring, flatulence, and the metallic grinding of cars cutting tight curves. I returned to my compartment and took a swig of the miniature bottle of cognac I had purchased for Dorotea.

I needed to distract myself or put myself to sleep. Should I read more of *Le rhinocéros*? Did ground rhino horn really act like an aphrodisiac? Fantasizing about rubbing some on Katie. Where? Her forehead? Her—? I risked lapsing into an erotic dream.

I fell asleep again and dreamed. Nothing erotic, though, unless submission to authority proved arousing. In my dream, there were rousing speeches and double entendres—and men in uniform and jackboots.

I slowly emerged from my dreams. I licked my lips to test my taste buds. As I nibbled on some *saucisson* and grapes, I all but bit my tongue as the figure of a German soldier appeared, rapping at the door, demanding, "*Hieraus!*"

The uniform was shouting, "*Reisepass*," as the conductor sang out, "*Saarbrücken.*"

Merde! I craved those flipping anxiety pills. No raid, no arrests! It was only the German border. I had to get out and show my passport.

Settled once again, I chugalugged a package of Smarties. I decided not to read anything too intellectually stimulating and located a copy of *MAD Magazine*. Between Smarties and satire, I spent the last few remaining hours of the trip in relative calm.

After a dwarfed cup of train coffee, I managed to keep my eyes wide open until the train eased into the station. There I was, 9:05 p.m. at Heidelberg Hauptbahnhof. No D, no Craney, no rhino. No worries, other than to find more Smarties and a taxi to get to D's dorm.

Chapter Nineteen

D's *Willkommen*

Sinking back into the plush seats of the Mercedes taxi from the station, I savored the nubby grain of the leather seats, the light musk fragrance, and the comfort of the ride.

We passed by fields, cleared and burned for a winter crop, still smoldering in the evening breeze. Four-story, yellow-brick, student-housing towers framed the fields and stood like night sentinels over the missing crops.

* * *

I located D's building but had to guess at her floor. There was no welcoming party; maybe my telegram hadn't arrived. Starting my search from the bottom up, I heard deep-throated laughter from the first-floor kitchen and greeted smiling faces gathered there. None of them D's. I managed to leave without the beer so sweetly offered but also without any clue about D's room number.

As I started the trek down the darkened third-floor hallway, a door opened, depositing D directly in my path.

"*Achtung liebe! Was machst du da?*"

"I wrote I was coming—"

D swaddled me in her fierce embrace, muting any further explanation for my presence in the hall.

"*Ich bin ganz froh. Wie schön.*" She danced with this delight—and with me still wrapped in her arms.

"*Schnell, schnell, komme* into my room."

I collapsed on D's bed, looking around and smiling at so many of her little knickknacks, which used to Germanize her room at Albert two years before. I almost bawled when I saw the framed photo of D and Alda and Katie and me from Thanksgiving 1959.

D leaned over to me as I jumped up to hug her again. We danced about, laughing.

"Schnapps," she said, running to her desk to produce a bottle of homemade *Eierlikör*.

"Oh, God, you are amazing, D. My favorite, German eggnog."

We sat back and sipped in silence. D studied my face from several different angles.

"This is not good that you are here?"

"Well, it is good to be here..."

"But..." D tilted her head and threw me a sidelong glance.

My old friend D had matured—in grace, intelligence, and sensitivity. What she lost in country girl awkwardness, she gained in fitness and subtlety. She could always read me, and right now, she had just about finished speed-reading my whole story.

"So. *Was ist los?* Tell me all that is bothering you." She nodded for me to go on and took my hand.

"Everything?" I smirked.

"It's almost eleven p.m. Too late..." D stuck out her lower lip and pouted for effect.

"Okay. *Craney.* There, you've got it."

"Ah? Only that! We can fix that, *nicht wahr?*"

"Yeah, right!" I rolled my eyes and sighed.

"*Morgen*. Tomorrow, we have cakes and *Schlag*. That makes everything better."

"You know I love whipped cream, but come on."

"No, my dear, I do take you serious, but not so late at night. Craney is not a new story. She will last until tomorrow. Besides, we have to put you to bed. Hmm…you trust me to sleep here in one bed tonight? I will not eat you, Pina, I promise."

I laughed, remembering how grossed out she was at first that I was a lesbian. "Bite, D, bite! I won't bite you, either."

We climbed in at opposite ends of the bed, bundled under plump down comforters. The *Eierlikör* was working its magic: We fell asleep immediately. No rhinos, no bites, no worries.

※ ※ ※ ※

I turned over in bed, still sort of asleep, and rubbed my nose. There were different aromas in the room this morning. Not croissants and chicory coffee. More like mushrooms and wet leaves and apples and cinnamon and…fish? I opened my eyes, blinking to focus on my strange surroundings. Posters of castles, not French, and coasters advertising beer, German. As my mind cleared to reveal recent memories of my train trip and arrival the night before, I spotted the tray bearing sweet and savory goodies, dark bread, ham and *Lachs*, and a bowl of whipped cream.

D had already gone out to get us breakfast. I stretched and sat back to take this in. Safe, here in Germany, warm and cozy, and spoiled by D. I looked around, getting my bearings. No D—until the door eased open and a flame preceded D entering with a cake, singing "Happy Birthday to You."

"But my birthday—"

"I know. This is belated. So, let's eat and drink."

In addition to coffee, D served festive and bubbly *Sekt* and toasted to the time "we cooked Craney's goat." Still somewhat groggy, I didn't react to the *Craney* word, other than to smile at D's mixed American metaphor and to swish a blob of whipped cream across her face.

"You, you will pay for that, Pina! There!" D flicked some cream back at me.

"Whoa. Better to eat it, huh?"

I sat up cross-legged on the bed as D piled my plate high with spice cake and cream, *Apfelstrudel*, ham and pickles on black bread, and pretzels with mustard. She had a strategy in mind—fill my mouth so I would have to listen.

"You know," she started softly, patting my knee, "you always believed it was your mother and Katie's father, Doc, and Joe who saved you from Craney. I have always called you *Dummkopf*. You are no dummy. You just don't want to see how strong you are."

I mumbled through the crunchy pieces of pretzel, "Thanks, D. You know damn well that without Doc's help, they would have wired me up in shock therapy for lesbianism, or Craney would have bound me as her youngest sex slave—"

"No, you listen. You were the star. You stood up to Craney. Stood up for who you were, *and* you had the guts to tell your mom and me that you were a lesbian. Me, the country girl who thought lesbians sucked blood."

I started to tap my ring finger on the tray.

"*Liebe*, Pina, you can stand up again…to Craney or the boogeyman or—"

I flashed back on Albert. It had taught us a lot about how to be in the world. Profs and rules trained us to be smart preppies, independent, perhaps before our time, autonomous. Katie and I had entered as sixteen-year-old goofy sophomores, accelerated two years in one, and emerged in this, our senior year, as tomorrow's women. So the school motto had promised. But my self-image hadn't always kept up.

"Yeah, yeah. I know. It's my head. I've got to shut it off." I blew out a huge breath. "You're right, you're right, you're right. But…man, that's so hard."

"*Ja.* I will go to *Herr Doktor* and get you a pill. *Gut?*"

"Yeah, I guess."

We ate some more in silence, save for the sound of busy chewing. A sharp knock at the door interrupted the silence.

"*Telefon!*" a male voice called out.

D wiped her hands and left the room.

The door whooshed shut, and silence took over. Except for the voice in my head.

D was right. I didn't want to hear all the blather going on up there, but…I got up to stare out the window: blackened fields, blackbirds, cars, black and white. I blinked slowly and then again.

Somehow, these things were calming, real, and concrete. I could see them. Almost touch them. Yeah. I needed that, to be a bit more black and white. Right now, my head was all over the place.

If I could stop. Focus. Look at solid things.

I watched a crow perch on a nearby wire. Smart, crows were smart. Maybe I could trust that the authorities—Je-sus, how I hated that word—would take care of the outside stuff. They did say Craney was guilty of other similar crimes. Then I would do the inside job. Yeah, I would handle the crazy thoughts.

The door whooshed open, and D bounced in, giggling. I stared at her.

"*Nah?*" she said, inquiring what my problem was.

"Well, you're almost dancing with joy. What the heck happened?"

"*Oh nichts.*" She shrugged it off as nothing, casually surveying what was left of the food. She bopped her head to some internal music that only she heard and took lazy swipes from the liquefying cream in the bowl.

"Come on, D, you're ten feet off the ground."

"What? This is vacation. No need to be so serious. All you can think about is Craney? Your Doc, your confessor, your momma will help. You, my dear, can play. Here, have some more bubbly stuff."

"How much booze have we already had? Wait, what the heck? You mean a priest?"

"Uh, wasn't there a priest you talked to at Albert?"

I blinked hard, trying to clear my head and remember. What priest? I didn't know any priests. I started to take another slurp and stopped. "Oh. Père Sablé? Wha? In Paris?"

"What? Huh?" D stood there, her mouth hanging open, her eyes seemingly searching for answers all over the inside of her cranium. "*Ich verstehe nicht…*I misunderstood, just now."

My mind wandered back to the phone call again. Something was off, but I wanted to say more about Craney. Tell D that this time Craney was out for blood. A hard thing while she was dancing and licking cream off her hand. My own thoughts loosened; my words slurred. What had I been saying?

"I hafta work this out. I hafta stand up, do this." Right…What I'd give for a big break. From my head. Just let it all go.

"*Ja, ja.* Time enough for worry, for old age. Up, get yourself dressed. I show you something beautiful of Heidelberg. I will bring you where philosophers and ghosts go."

Chapter Twenty

Philosophers and Ghosts

Our bus ride from the dorm was uneventful, and with the help of the bottle of champagne we had just finished, I started to nod off.

D tugged at my sleeve to get off just after the Heiliggeistkirche, the Church of the Holy Ghost, near the Old Bridge over the Neckar River. The sun, playing hide-and-seek on the ripples of the river, and the low-hanging fog calmed me.

"See what I told you? I can feel you just go easy," said D, taking my arm.

"I'm good, so good."

"Wait. We will go up many, many steps. Then you will see. Nothing more in your pretty head, nothing but pictures of fairytale castles, kitsch, and more *Kuchen*. Yes, I promise cake or ice cream at the end. No Craney."

Huffing hard, I stopped occasionally to sit on a bench. D was right. My head held nothing but thoughts of food and jousting contests and knights and damsels and the fairytale castle looming large before my eyes.

D gave me some Ritter chocolate and a detailed history of the Schloss Hohenzollern, the castle rising up from the horizon on the south side of the river. I begged off the history lesson, merely fascinated by the gentle ping of heavy mist on pebbles at our feet and the cloud threatening to envelop the brick Renaissance castle.

At a juncture in the road, we jogged left and then right to enter onto the Philosophenweg, a walking path draped in foliage, flowers, shrubs, and monuments. The romantic atmosphere of this quiet walk permeated my whole being. With every step, a certain lightness, a flash, coursed through my torso, my limbs, my eyes, and the crown of my head, transporting me away to idyllic places.

D's smile lingered on me. "Yes, you've got the philosopher's spirit. This is good. You will bring, uh… your loved one here—in your mind, that is."

I stopped to sit on a bench while D went off to a nearby ice cream vendor. She gave me an ice cream bar and said we would speak just a few words about Craney.

I was at D's mercy. She could call the shots for now. I let myself go.

"I will talk to my father. He has connections with the BIF."

"Oh? Oh. The FBI."

"*Ja.* We will know where Craney is heading now. We take control, but tonight we make reservations at the station."

"What?" D's sudden change of topic threw me. "Where are we going? You want to get rid of me already?"

"No. Remember, it is holiday. We should get reservations for your return in advance." D looked around, not meeting my gaze.

"Yeah, that makes sense." I tried to catch D's eye, but she was looking everywhere but at me.

She stood up straight, nodded, and took my arm. We walked in silence down to the bus. We had seen enough philosophers and ghosts.

On the bus, D kept checking her watch. She was obsessed with being on time. Four p.m. I joshed that we must be late for something. She laughed and said there were never enough hours in a day to sample all the goodies that life had to offer.

Without warning, D all but pulled me out of my seat. "*Hier!* We must get off here. Here we find the best wurst."

D began to fidget again, checking her watch. She pushed me gently onto a bench.

"Wait. I will get you a bratwurst sausage, yes?"

I nodded and watched her return with only one.

"You eat." She handed me the perfectly grilled, smoky sausage. "I cannot. I must go in the post office for news." Almost out of breath, she walked as if she were late.

I got busy eating the sausage. I rubbed my feet on the dark gray cobbles. Who had walked or ridden on horseback over these stones? I leaned back, sniffing the air, smells so different from the flavors of Paris: blond tobacco, not the almost marijuana-like musk of Gauloises; and sausages, some ginger scented, others with clove and fennel.

Where was D? Now it was my turn to check my watch. Twenty minutes had passed. I left my bench to go to the doorway that had swallowed D up earlier.

D sat ensconced in a phone booth in the post office. When I leaned closer to the glass door, D's expression changed—and her composure along with it. She was clearly speaking Ting German, a singsong yet guttural German, complete with fake laughter and precious exclamations.

I tapped my watch. D waved me away, still grinning, but cracked the door an iota.

"*Schnell.* Go! Meet me in the student *Kneipe* on Plock Street."

"Huh? What's a *Kneipe*?" I was already tapping my foot.

"The bar. Get yourself a beer. I come *schnell*. Go."

I walked several blocks to find Plock and the only student pub on the street. By now, I was dying of thirst and felt pissy enough with D that I ordered a half liter Of Dunkel Bräu.

Just like the beer, everything here was dark. Old wooden panels, dark-stained oak tables, somberly varnished floor, warped in spots from centuries of shuffling feet. The cedar-fresh smell of sawdust on the floor mixed with the pervasive fermenting odor of cabbage and hoppy beer confirmed what I read on the chalkboard: sauerkraut was a specialty here.

Cigarette smoke and the dim lighting revealed a few tables of students wearing student caps. They played cards and laughed big, hearty guffaws. They banged their steins on the table to signal to ante up.

Backlit by the sun stealing in from the street, D entered, bustling over to my table.

"Really, I am so sorry. It was so long. My father—"

"Yeah, yeah." I cut her off, tired of waiting, tired of her direction, and something else…

"Yes, I speak to my father." D repeatedly blinked her eyes.

I slit my eyes at her, confused about how easily she could communicate with her father in Argentina, banished there for his involvement in the war. Before I could probe, she grabbed my arm and leaned in to whisper, "The news is Craney heads to northern Italy. People are watching. But—"

"But what? Is it safe or not?" I breathed out so

loudly, the folks at the next table turned to glare—folks I certainly hadn't noticed before.

D's icy frown melted into a broad grin as she tugged on my sleeve, whispering, "Look."

It was my turn to stare. Sitting there in this historic pub were a knight rigged out in full armor and a buxom lady complete with flowing veil and daring bodice. I almost choked on a laugh when D slapped my hand.

"Shush! They are re-enactors of German history! *Klasse.* Real good." D flashed them a thumbs-up.

"I don't believe this place." I giggled, shaking my head.

"Shush. This is normal. Ignore them. We continue as I was saying…Craney has not hurt you directly. You have no proof for them to arrest her. Well, maybe in France."

"What? The guy in France confessed."

"*Jawohl.* But they could not identify Craney in Corsica."

"So what?" I winced and immediately bit my tongue to apologize.

"*Ja. Das stinkt.* If Craney threatens or touches you directly, then the local police can take her."

"She-it!" I fumed.

"But wait! Katie's dad's *friend*, Joe—he can investigate and prove she is a fugitive?"

I chewed on my lip, shrugged, and swallowed a huge gulp of beer to wash down my frustration.

"Come, give me sips of your beer before you get *blau.*" She laughed. "We will go, *ja*? Enough of this *scheiße.*"

We paid and exited the pub. I was fuzzy. Didn't have a clue where we were going; the black beer was no help, either. D was in command; I followed—in the dark.

Chapter Twenty-one

Dreams Come True

D was directing us back to the dorm—and ordering me back to bed.

My dreams came fast and furious. Good dreams. Katie dreams. She was kissing my neck—soft, warm, wet kisses—and nuzzling my ear. I stretched my neck, moaned for more, and uncurled my torso so tingles went farther and deeper. I longed for more and harder and searched for her full, open mouth. Reaching my hand out to clasp softness and warmth, I opened my eyes and lost myself in the oceans of those light blue eyes. I shook myself fully awake and stared at a furry cat.

D arrived a few minutes later, bustling as usual. "Ah, you've met Herr Katz. He likes the girls."

I smiled. D sneaked another look at her watch.

"Come. We must go."

"Right now?" I yawned but followed her command.

She fussed with my hair, pushing it back behind my ears, and straightened my button-down collar. "*Ja*, you are presentable now."

❧❧❧❧

We arrived at the station somewhat groggy. The

ride through farmlands and the more modern part of town had been rather boring. D flashed a peek at her watch and positioned me at the head of some tracks.

"Stay *da*. I will get the reservation."

I felt like a child with a history of wandering off, surprised that she didn't tap some lady on the shoulder to keep an eye on me. D rushed off into the crowd, which swallowed her up.

Bored, I studied people, women with frumpy felt hats, men in lederhosen. I fantasized about their journeys and towns of origins. I compared locomotives and attempted to understand the barked announcements from the loudspeaker.

Smells wafted by, some good, others reminiscent of the seemingly ever-present sauerkraut. A chime rang out from the PA system. I made out the word *verspätung*—something about lateness. Faces turned toward the track I stood by and swiveled back toward the schedule board where different numbers clicked into position next to the train arriving from Frankfurt. A few minutes later, a train groaned into the station and belched its way to the end of the tracks.

Chancing to turn around, I caught a streak of D and then nothing. When I looked back, the newly arrived train was spewing forth tired travelers. I yawned, tired of waiting for "Momma D," when another nurturing hug encircled me.

My skin tingled the way only Katie's nearness could excite me. The scent of pine and crystalline waterfalls transported me to Maine, to wild and natural spots. I knew immediately I was crazy. This couldn't be. Katie's cologne, her billowing magenta scarf. Katie's touch…I blindly found her lips and kissed her passionately. To hell with discretion! I cried, I danced,

I held her face in my hands.

"Pina, Pina, Pina," she mumbled between kisses and sniffles.

"Katie, Katie, Katie." I was equally articulate.

We stood there embracing for four whole minutes. The crowd parted, and D strode through, arms outstretched, grinning widely. None of us could say an intelligent word for several minutes until D clapped us on the shoulders and worked her way in between us. "Come, I take you home. *Ja*, so good, I kept the secret."

"You did." Katie rubbed D's shoulder. "You really did. We pulled it off. Hot damn!"

I laughed. "D, you almost gave it away a couple of times, but I thought you were just being strange."

"*Ja, ja.*"

"I don't know how you two managed to set this up so quickly, but wow."

I turned to look at Katie, still in shock that she was really here. But this wasn't just excitement and disbelief. My face flushed, my chest tightened. I thought of the last time my body had felt so tingly. Cassia. Oh, shoot. I had to do something quick before my mind and body took me back to the messed-up sheets, to Cassia's warm hand brushing my side, to the room and the doubts I'd left behind in Paris.

I stopped walking and stood in front of Katie, staring and savoring every feature—her long wavy, shiny hair; her deep-blue liquid eyes; her small, turned-up nose. We both burst out laughing, dumbstruck.

"Come, come, my little chickadees. I have food and a big bed for you two. *Ja*, you maybe want to sleep together and not with me?"

We giggled and hugged our blushing D.

"Dorotea, my dear, you sound like Alda, our sexy matchmaker." Katie gently pinched D's cheek.

My eyes lit up. I looked at Katie and imagined every inch of her under her clothes. We both blushed. She slipped her arm through mine and leaned against my shoulder during the entire bus ride to the dorm. As we stumbled back to D's room, stealing kisses in the darkened stairwell, Katie and I intermittently hugged D and ruffled her hair. She was truly our protective mother hen.

When D left to get food, Katie and I fell into each other's arms on D's bed. Katie's eyes bore deeply into mine. She kissed my ear with her whisper, "God, I've missed you."

Her hand barely brushed my breast as my body arched to meet hers. My eyes pleaded, "Wait," while the rest of me begged to yield. We ground to a disappointing halt when we heard D coughing in the hall. Flushed and bleary-eyed, we opened the door for D carrying two trays and a bottle of St. Michel red.

After toasting to our reunion, D escorted us to a vacant room across the hall and threw open the door in a grand flourish. Before us appeared a marvelously strange vision: a cross between a streetwalker's room in Fellini's *Nights of Cabiria* and a girl toddler's dream. Pink cherubim swung from gossamer silk threads across thin slats, jerry-rigging a canopy bed. Red velvet cloth draped the bed, while scarlet gauzy curtains waved across the windows. Pink hearts and red carnations abounded, scenting the room with cinnamon and clove. A candle's flame illuminated a glow-in-the-dark flickering heart, and a banner on the wall above the headboard read, "*Traume süss.*" I definitely envisioned sweet dreams.

Katie and I stifled giggles and hugged D, who—face flushed—threw kisses as she streaked from the room.

I looked at Katie, unclasped the suitcase from her hand, and eased her onto the bed. Staring at me, she licked her lips in an exaggerated sweep of her tongue as she caressed my ankles to remove my socks. Finished undressing my feet, she sat back up with a look of lascivious satisfaction, still staring into my eyes, and dove down to suck each toe while slithering her hand up my calf and beyond.

Her shirt buttons came undone easily, and I turned on top of her, my hand barely grazing her breast. Her lips met mine as she pulled my hips tight against hers. Her tongue danced on mine, releasing a flow of all the pent-up feelings and yearnings for her these past six weeks. I was liquid lava, molten and thick, pushing, moving, molding us together in its wake. We held each other up as our cries rocked us together. Our look was one, riveted, our pulse synchronized. Done, spent. We fell back as one on the pillows billowing with cupids and sensuous O'Keeffe-like blooms.

Chapter Twenty-two

Hard Talk

As I popped open one eye and then the other, I found Katie's soft face looking down at me. Propped up on her elbows, she blew lightly across my face. A feather escaped from the pillow and fluttered from my nose to my lips. Katie pinched it away with her lips, kissed my eyes, and scooped me into her arms—and onto her.

The next thing I knew, Katie was scuffing her way back into the room with two cups of coffee. We must have snoozed a bit. I took a sip and stared at her. It seemed all my problems had resolved themselves.

As if reading my mind, Katie spoke softly, asking me to tell her about Craney. I hesitated a minute and then a few more.

"What's wrong?" Katie smoothed my hair.

"It's hard to say."

"I don't get it. What has Craney done to you? Honey, you're the reason I'm here." Katie bent her head low to catch my eye.

"Well...she hired a thug to try to drown me in the sewers...And wooden tombstones with my name on them dropped down my chimney." I started to whimper.

"Pina—hold on, why are you crying?"

"And...and...a man fell from a crane. I sound

stupid." I started banging my fist on the mattress. "Katie, believe me—"

"Easy, Pin." Katie stroked my face and took a sip of her coffee. She took a deep breath and sat back in a chair opposite the bed.

"You're looking at me as if I'm making this up."

"Hmm." Katie put her cup on a table and took my hand. She wrinkled her brow and squeezed her eyes shut.

"What?" I flicked her hand away.

"Okay…what did the man falling have to do with you? Was there a warning?"

"Jeez, Katie, Cassia's father tracked down a potential suspect resembling the lady the thug from the sewers described."

"Okay, so that's really real." Katie sucked her lower lip and did that curly thing with her hair. "Got it. Craney is or was around. In Corsica. And there have been some strange coincidences, right?"

"Yeah. Like your damn poem." I gritted my teeth.

"Listen, don't be mad. I'm just trying to help keep your anxiety from popping the lid off your pressure cooker. You're kind of feeding your own fear—"

"Well, thank you, Dr. Katie McGuilvry! I suppose you'd say hysterical."

"Didn't say you were." Katie pulled in her chin and started again. "Look, I came here, I pulled strings to cram a lot of work into these six weeks you've been gone—and risked less than a four-point-oh."

"Big deal."

"Yeah, it is. You don't know how crazy you sounded on those phone calls. I do believe you're petrified."

"Hmm, yeah?"

"All I'm saying is Craney's presence is friggin' weird, and you are alone in a new place and scared. That's understandable. And that transatlantic boat ride made you kind of gaga—nothing solid outside, nothing but black water for eleven days. Your letter-a-day grew more and more, like, I don't know, frantic. Like each day you were away from land washed away more and more of your *you*."

"Huh?" I was sobbing now, becoming small, really small. And all I'd wanted was Katie? Ha. Here she was lecturing me now, just letting me have it. I raised my gaze to take a good look at her.

"You're saying I don't know who the hell I am?"

"Hold on. C'mere, darling." Katie leaned over and kissed my face.

"But?" I blew out a breath and prepared for the worst. "If I don't know who I am…"

"Look at me. I love you so much, *and* I can tell when you're growing scared and small. Come, kiss me and let's stop this. We're all here together, and we'll get to the bottom of this. Okay? You've got to know I'm with you. Because I am, and so is D."

I mumbled a quiet "yeah."

With that, Katie pushed me over, fluttered her hands all over my face, rubbed her nose with mine, and wiggled her whole body all over mine.

"C'mon, let's go to breakfast with D. You okay now?"

"Yeah, I'm better." I threw my head back. I had to lighten up. I reached up for Katie's pits and tickled her until she wriggled and rolled and writhed herself right onto the floor.

❧ ❧ ❧ ❧

We sat in the kitchen and looked down on fields and streams in the heavy fall mist. Pedestrians and cars moved in low gear on this lazy Saturday morning.

Katie and I quieted down after our difficult conversation earlier. D searched our faces and double-checking our composure, said we would eat before we said a single word about Craney.

After eating several of D's *Spiegeleier*, her "looking-glass eggs," we talked about D's plans to continue her studies in medicine. Katie announced for the first time that she had applied to Stanford and Berkeley and Vassar. She looked away from me as she said she was leaning toward Berkeley.

Wha? Since when? In the less than two months I'd been gone, she arranged all that? And when was she going to tell me? My shoulders sagged. I struggled to hold my head up. My eyes burned with anger. Or shame? I felt betrayed.

I gulped some coffee and stared out the window again. I revealed nothing of my plans. I didn't have any—no plans that would have meant separating from Katie for four years. My efforts to escape the pressure to choose a path and get on with my life might not go over well with both Katie and Dorotea working me over. I just wouldn't make it on my own. I didn't want to. Katie and I could move in together; we could make it. God, Katie and Dorotea together would definitely make me talk to a shrink. And I was friggin' scared I should.

Out of the corner of my eye, I caught Katie shake her head at D, who had started to question me about my future. Instead, D produced a letter from her father.

"He says he knows for a fact that international agents have gotten involved in tracking Craney."

I perked up, turning toward Dorotea and raising an eyebrow.

"He says agents are actually following Pina. What do you think of that, eh?"

"Didn't you see all those spooks yesterday?" My sarcasm seeped out.

"That's great. C'mon, Pina." Katie slapped my hand.

"See? There is something there. Otherwise, they wouldn't do that." I puffed myself up.

"*Jawohl. Ist* good. Yes, they must believe Craney has done this before to underage people."

I sat up straight. "What do you suppose they look like? Think we can spot them?"

"Who? Underage children?" Katie threw me a duh look.

"*Ja, ja.* You two…You can look for them on your walk. Okay?"

Katie and I decided on the same walk D and I had taken the day before. We would meet D later to go to Dilsberg, "a hilltop town to top all others," according to D. "It's like Venice; you 'See Venice and Die' it is so special."

❧ ❧ ❧ ❧

D had treated Katie and me to a taxi ride through old town and its monuments to Philosophenweg. It was still early, and the sun-lit dew brightened up even the most age-darkened monuments. Fog still draped the upper cornices of the gilded castle.

As we crossed the Neckar River in the taxi, Katie leaned her head back, holding my gaze.

"I go places with you," she whispered, gently touching my lips.

I started to say something silly, but she shushed me. "No. It's like you take me on journeys with your eyes, and then we float and swirl together. Like we're in a trance together."

Katie seemed to be writing poetry, her dreamy gaze riveted on me. I wanted to kiss her so badly. I ached for her touch now, especially after our talk that morning.

We left the taxi a few minutes later at the head of the nearly deserted trail. With every step I took, I brushed up against Katie, setting off an explosion of sparkling sensations rising up, searching for total release, for that one uncontrollable burst of corked-up tingles and bubbles and effervescent spritz.

Lingering, low-draping fog muted our steps and held us in its silence. Katie took my hand and brought it to her lips.

"This is why I love you. You see the poetry and joy and sparkle in it all. *That* you can never change!"

I turned to read her lips and bathe in her eyes. My face was scarlet, I'm sure, the flush I still felt when Katie said things like that to me. I reached around her waist and pulled her to me, looking for some secluded spot.

The remains of a shepherd's stone shelter stood in the distance, set off from the trail. D had pointed it out to me the day before when she slipped and told me to bring my loved one here.

Katie and I scrambled up to it. We peeked in through the warped door and threw Katie's coat on the bed of dry leaves. I clasped Katie to me and found her mouth and all of her waiting. We slumped to our soft, fragrant bed and lay wrapped in each other's arms and legs, already aroused, already merged as one. We kissed almost as an afterthought. Each toss of the head, each new glance, each shift of weight sent new shivers and waves. Over and over.

"Look at me," Katie murmured.

"I am, with my whole self," I whispered.

"I'm always with you—here, in Paris, always where you are. Trust me." Katie blew gently on my lips.

"I do."

We smelled of autumn, of oak and pine and mushrooms and earth. We were scented with each other, the way we'd always been in nature. We gave off a seasonal essence of love and passion. It seemed to expand as we grew and changed.

Back on the trail, we smiled a lot and oohed and ahhed over the river peeking through the shrubbery. In a shaded nook, Katie stopped and faced me.

"You don't have to be so afraid, you know. You really are strong. I think you forget."

This was a serious rest stop we were taking.

"You're right. I do forget that sometimes, but you help me remember." I went to kiss Katie, but she stopped me.

"No, listen, I can't always help you remember. And D's mothering, as sweet as it is—*occasionally*—is not always what you need."

"Uh-oh. Yeah...I just wanted to get a break." I plopped down on the path.

Katie stooped next to me. "Right, but...when you forget who you are, I don't. I know who you can be."

"Stop. And don't say a word about college. Not with all this crap with Craney."

"Okay...okay. But not everything is Craney. There, I've said all I'm going to say for now. So, tell me to get lost and then go back to loving me."

God, Katie could always tell when I had had enough. The river twinkled in sudden bursts through the openings in the lindens loosening their last leaves to careen down along the path. It was time to go back to meet D.

We had a sweet, quiet stroll across the river on the Old Bridge, walking arm in arm to meet D at the bratwurst stand. She arrived, bustling as usual, waving airmail letters.

"*Hallo!*" she announced, still several feet away.

"Hi," Katie and I responded.

D handed me a forwarded letter from my folks, on which Cassia had drawn a heart with "Hi" in the middle, as well as a letter to Katie. D was busy reading our reactions to mail from home. And checking her watch.

"Is there time for me to read this before we go to Dilsberg?" I flipped the envelope, which felt heavier than a typical airmail letter.

Katie looked up from her letter and nodded. "Yeah, for me, too."

"*Ja.* We go to Dilsberg tomorrow." D rubbed my shoulder. "Tomorrow is good. But let me see. Then tonight we must celebrate safety." D clapped her hands.

D had had news earlier from her father, who believed Craney was hiding out in Switzerland. Katie looked up from her own letter, which confirmed that Craney couldn't possibly make it here for several days—after Katie and I were back in Paris.

"Tonight, we eat *Maultaschen*, German ravioli, special from this area. Tomorrow, we go to our lovely Dilsberg. *Gut?*"

"Yup! I hear it's to die for!" I laughed, hugging both Katie and D.

Chapter Twenty-three

Towering Heights

On this sleepy, overcast Sunday morning, Katie and I were both slow to rise and even slower to eat the hefty apple-cinnamon hotcakes, German *Pfannkuchen*, D was tossing in the pan and onto our plates.

Katie and I hadn't slept enough during the night, reliving the romance of our hike earlier that day. These days, I relished any romantic gestures Katie was willing to offer, especially if it prevented lectures about college and moving on with my life. On the warm, bumpy bus ride to Dilsberg, we nodded off over and over. We opened our eyes occasionally when D tugged on our sleeves to point out misty scenes of the Neckar River framing the white stucco walls of red-tiled houses. Gossamer haze softened the brick red to bleed into the pastels of other shops.

We snoozed until the bus lumbered up a difficult stretch of road. The groaning of the engine stopped to deposit us into the fairytale village of Dilsberg.

Cobbled streets, half-timbered houses, steeples, and an ancient city wall. Every feature of this minute hamlet enchanted me. I took Katie by the hand and told her I wanted to whisk her away to the top of the tower and kiss her high above this idyllic scene. Katie slipped her hand away. Her blank stare was less than idyllic.

D glanced from me to Katie and shrugged. Her look begged an explanation, but her one comment only related to food and drink.

We sat in the back room of the *Gasthaus* surrounded by wavy glass windows and rustic drop-leaf tavern tables. In the demi-light of the overcast day, I felt like we had traveled back in time three centuries.

While D and Katie ate and chatted about movies filmed here, I drank not one but two Schwarzbiers, losing myself and my worries over Katie in the inn's ambience, the wafting aromas of warm wine and cream, and the snapshot images of romantic village scenes peeking through the windows. I declared with great aplomb, "*Hier könnte ich leben und sterben.* I could live and die here."

"Now I know you are drunk, when you can say this in almost good German, too. But you would die of boredom if you had to live in this tiny village all the time! No money, no more work, no movies, no fun, just the church and the scenery. And the sadness. The people, they wait for something good to arrive. As if God will bring it or the fairytale castle. Come, let's walk." D pulled me up, shaking her head.

She continued her lecture a bit longer. "There would be no place for you, for you to love Katie. Not in the open, anyway."

I turned to look at D, to read her face and figure out why the dour talk. I was having some trouble following the conversation after my two beers. I hadn't meant to drink so much; it just seemed to go with the meal.

The air turned bracing and windy, whipping through arches and courtyards. Shutters on seventeenth-century cottages clacked shut, and pebbles grated softly against one another as they drifted downhill in rivulets of old stormwater.

The remains of the castle and its tower were playing peekaboo in the fog, but the old wall was still clearly visible. We would start here and make our way to the tower. We walked briskly against the wind in an attempt to reach the tower before the fog shrouded it—and before the crowd of recently arrived Sunday tourists clotted the stairs.

I wanted to lighten D's uncharacteristic mood. *And* I was still *blau*, her slang for "tipsy." I pointed to one couple as we passed. I made-believe I wore lederhosen and snapped imaginary suspenders over my breasts. Katie spoofed about the woman's old-fashioned dress-up clothes.

"*Ja*. I put on my go-to-meeting dress." Katie almost yodeled as she pretended to spread out her imaginary crinoline-filled taffeta skirt.

"*Ruhe*. Quiet." D waved Katie away, throwing me the stink eye. "You two are bad. They are a country couple, maybe even celebrating their engagement. This castle, you know, it's a big deal for them to come here. Big feast."

Yes! I had succeeded in distracting her. My parents had taught me about the poverty in Europe after the war. God knows, I had to eat all my veggies because foreign kids were starving, and they had been, my friends among them. But I was still somewhat plastered and enjoying a touristy escape from my beliefs and fears. Well, some of them.

After checking to see that the couple had disappeared into the thickening fog so I wouldn't offend them, I reached for Katie's hand. "Behind this pea-soupy veil, I search for your hand in marriage before this witness." I pawed the air in my imaginary hunt. "Where is your hand and where is our witness? Oh, where, oh, where have they gone?"

"Pina, cut it out." Katie sighed, brushing away my hand.

D clapped me upside the shoulder as we neared the end of our hike to the tower. "*Dummkopf*, here I am. Now you two must behave. This view takes your breath away. We Germans call it *mystisch*, mystical! And maybe that is why the people think the answers will come from here." D punctuated her words by blotting her eyes.

"Come, you two"—D grabbed us by the hands— "you must make a wish."

I sobered up. I was afraid to say mine. My wish was almost a prayer. That Katie and I would move in together. And that I would be free of Craney. I had almost forgotten about her.

Katie's response broke the spell. "Yes, for Pina to wear lederhosen!"

D lowered her gaze, mumbling, "I wished for peace and love for everyone, even you two silly geese!"

The crowd seemed to thin around us. The air was equally thin, making it harder to walk fast on the uphill, broken cobbles. The face-slapping wind rendered speech useless. We inched forward in silence.

We had arrived at the top, but the fog was still thick. I leaned over some of the broken bricks to see if Schloss Hohenzollern in Heidelberg was visible, then turned abruptly to get Katie's attention. I really wanted her close by my side, to bridge this gap between us. She stood way over on the other side, wedged between doe-eyed couples and families.

Through a sudden opening in the thick haze, I caught a glimpse of just how high up we were. My stomach turned, my knees gave way, and my back felt like a toppling stack of dominos. I faltered. Would I collapse? Up here? Close to the edge?

Panic. I knew this old sensation well. I swallowed hard. I bit my lip. I shook off all trace of alcohol to tell myself over and over I could do this; I could fight off the dizziness, my fear of heights. I would not faint. I closed my eyes. I counted. One, two, three… I stomped the uneven ground under my feet. I groped for a hand, any hand. "Katie, D," I called. Or was that in my mind? And then there was the sharp corner of brick I grasped. I could hold on to. I clutched.

I was safe. I could open my eyes and avoid looking down. I heaved a sigh, still clasping the wall, and turned a degree in what I thought was Katie's direction. And where was D? My vision blurred.

A bolt—a sharp blow—to my back broke my conscious world apart. I crumpled under the burning pain. I turned my head to face my attacker but saw only black. Another jab pitched me forward. I lost my hold. Lost my footing. The outer ledge of the tower seemed to rise up in waves, coming closer and closer. I knew I would die here. No, I knew nothing.

I was out. I heard and felt the rumbling vibration of the subway tunnels through every nerve ending in my body, and I felt the warm pee flow out of me and turn cold. I saw the white light and then nothing. I had fainted many times before, each time believing I had died.

Four monstrous hands came at me from out of nowhere. Four firm grips held my arms fast. Were they pulling me back or thrusting me forward? I emerged—

one degree of consciousness at a time, I woke from my stupor. I fainted, again.

Their touch was rude and strong. Their slaps bracing. Yet huge, hearty laughs rang out. The mouths seemed detached from the hands. Whose appendages were these? Was this hell? Someone had surely drugged me. I continued to hear guffaws. A man whispered, "Rescued!" He wore a black wool hood, his eyes beady underneath the cowl.

Rescued? If these were rescuers, they behaved strangely. I now stood. Dumbfounded. My feet were on solid ground. Alive, I turned from side to side. Was this real?

I suspected that I was not, in fact, safe. On either side of me stood the jouster and the maiden, re-enactors like the ones from the pub. They whacked me on the back in jest, laughing about the dramatic show I had just presented. They acted as if nothing had happened, that this was just a show for tourists. Had someone slipped me a mickey?

These were fever dreams, the kind people had when they were sick. Or maybe, just maybe, this *was* hell.

They continued to shake me awake, winking. "Nice show! You fooled us all." Sotto voce, they mouthed, "Just play along. You're safe."

Like hell I was safe. And where were Katie and D? I called for them amid the brouhaha and scurrying about on the tower. I struggled with the knight as I screamed, "Katie! D!"

Who the hell were these people, Craney's stooges? Yet they were holding my arms, keeping me away from the wall, whispering in Italian, "Craney *scappata*— escaped!"

I freed one arm and jabbed the damsel in the breast with my elbow, hard, thrusting her back, as Katie and D emerged from the ruckus.

"Get this bastard off me," I shouted.

Katie tugged at his hand; D bent his fingers back. Both blocked the damsel from approaching. I clawed at the knight's face and attempted a swift kick to his groin. Not a direct hit, but he put up his hands and stepped back. The damsel placed her hand on her beaded bodice, urging us to be calm. "Please, we explain. We go down, yes?"

"What the hell?"

D grabbed my wrist to stop me from lunging at the knight. She made me focus, holding my gaze for what seemed to go on and on. I heard her say, "Stop! We will hear this explanation. Down. Off the tower."

I trusted the warmth in D's eyes, her calming look. She was safe; I wasn't convinced I was, but I breathed slowly along with her.

"*Gut*," she said. "Good."

Katie seemed to surface from out of nowhere. "It's okay, Pina. We've got this."

Although I wasn't sure what "this" meant, I wanted so badly to believe Katie's saying, "We've got this." This event. Here. Today. Our relationship. Our future.

I felt D shake me alert. "Open your eyes. Pay attention. Please, Pina."

The knight told us they would go down first. They promised me we had nothing to fear. I still had my doubts, but I understood that someone had tried to shove me off the tower, not these re-enactors, but who were they anyway?

Still up top, Katie, D, and I exchanged questioning

glances. We heard sirens down below and assumed the police were there.

D nodded. "We will go down slowly."

"Hold on! We're not going off anywhere with them." I growled.

Both of them agreed.

Down on the ground, we saw the re-enactors speaking with the cops. When the clear blue lights of the police car flashed away, we heard the knight ask his damsel: "*Ha scappato lei?*" They were definitely speaking Italian when they asked if the culprit who had pushed me escaped. D recognized now that the would-be actors had been following me for days, first in the pub, then later at the dorm. That day, she had actually mentioned that she thought there would be a performance. I slowly started to imagine that these were the good guys.

I turned and managed to form the words "*Lui* or *lei*?" I had to know if it was a he or a she who had escaped. The woman pretended to congratulate me on playing along, whispering, "*Lei*"—she. Another knight signaled and discreetly pointed to the road, shrugged, and tapped his helmet to indicate he didn't know anything more.

The three of us remained silent and ashen. Eyes glazed, mouths slack, we stood there, shoulders slumped, arms akimbo. The knight and lady apologized again, saying in German that they must treat us to drinks. In Italian, the lady spoke to me, saying I was safe now. I still wasn't totally reassured, but I knew we'd be safe in the pub.

Installed in the bar, we drank some cognac at a table by ourselves. D leaned in very close to Katie and me, wide-eyed. Her jaw moved, her mouth opened.

Somehow, words came out. "*Ja.* It was Craney, definitely Craney."

"Did you see?" I formed the words, biting my lip.

"I saw her hands. Horrible. Monster hands…"

"Where'd she go? I mean, how'd she get away?" I threw up my hands.

Katie continued to chew her lip and do that thing with her hair.

D took a long sip. "The crowd just swallowed her up. You didn't see the confusion? Sorry, of course you didn't."

Katie said nothing. No rubbing my shoulder, no sigh for me, just the damn hair-twirling.

"Katie, stop!" I filled my lungs and blew out a quiet breath. "I wasn't just going to let them grab me…"

D patted my arm. "You did well. We did well. You know, I have a knife. We could have used it."

Katie held her head in her hands, shivering. "Think…" She burst into quaking sobs.

"Katie, breathe," said D, turning to me with a glance that at once melted my heart and made me want to sob. A warm glow filled me. I felt her love and protection. D would always be there. I needed that so much now, and Katie…I curled into D's side, not thinking, and immediately sat back up. I couldn't let myself go. Not here. Not now. "Okay, I'm okay. Think? We safe or not?" I blew out a roomful of air.

The knight leaned over to us pretending to wish me, "*Prost,*" and slipped me a note: "Leave tomorrow on the train at ten. Not to worry. We watch you now."

He clinked his glass again and in a loud voice ordered us another round of cognac before whispering he had a taxi waiting and "good people" at the dorm.

Chapter Twenty-four

Personal Secret Service

We huddled together in the taxi, too stunned to speak or move, virtually blinded by the set of headlights targeting us from behind—when we did risk turning our heads. Our driver seemed oblivious to them.

I watched the lights on the dashboard, losing myself in the warm yellow-orange turn signals in the black of night. Their clicking sound jarred me. I was still numb, frozen with the attempt on my life. What would I do? Would the car turn left or right, right or left? The car bore left. I ruminated: I could leave. Yes, leave. Go. Go home. Back with Katie. Yes. Then I leaned into D as we made a right turn. Click, click. Warm amber lights on the right side of the speedometer. I could stay. I would stay. Yes, I have to stay.

Left, right. Right, left. Yes and no. My mind raced as the car crept along the sixteen kilometers back to the dorm. Left signal, I had almost died. Right signal, I couldn't run from Craney. I had to stay and fight.

⚜ ⚜ ⚜

When we entered the dorm, a new student stood sentinel at the end of the floor. D remarked that he appeared too stiff and spooky to be a student. We agreed that he was one of the "good people."

We remained relatively mute, outside of grunts in the direction of the room Katie and I shared. The tacit understanding was that all three of us would lock ourselves in this room for the night.

D peeked outside and quickly pulled her head back in once she spotted the guard close to the door. "He is there." She nodded.

"So, we're safe." Katie hesitated.

I finally curled up in the bed, holding on to my knees for dear life. In between convulsive sobs, I muttered, "I could have…I almost…"

Katie finally embraced me. D sat on the bed on the other side of me.

"Shush, we are all here, all right. We will keep ourselves safe."

I swallowed hard and finally sat up. I had to believe we were safe. Had to believe that we could travel back to Paris. My jaw relaxed enough to mumble, "I think so, too."

There was a dry knock on the door. D checked through the spy hole. Someone saying, "*Telefon.*" D slithered out.

When she eased her way back in, she spoke in staccato bursts. "*Polizei*—Craney gone."

We squished together in the bed. D forayed out and back to grab some snacks and water. We tried to laugh, recalling scenes like this at Albert. Safe scenes, party scenes.

"I think I can sleep." I finally mustered a whole sentence.

Katie pulled me over and hugged me lightly. D kissed us both on the forehead and whispered, "*Gute Nacht.*"

We awoke itchy with crumbs in the bed and very sweaty armpits. It was early, before dawn. D was the first to lumber off the bed—to check on our night watchman. Still there.

As the dusky light brightened into a pale shade of butter yellow, Katie and I packed our bags and dressed. We paused only briefly to reach an arm out to each other and hug. We had so much to say and nothing to utter. Somehow, all three of us stood suspended in the same silent instant of love and trust. In our strange state, we couldn't risk a word.

The taxi ride to the station was equally silent. We moved through the last remnants of night as one and boarded the train, links of one unbroken chain.

D kissed us goodbye, but in spite of our reassurances, she wouldn't leave. A short stocky woman wearing a tight kerchief around her head and a crucifix dangling from her belt approached us selling food. Mère Paul? Incognito. Beyond belief.

She uttered a few words in German about a good breakfast and a safe trip, putting her finger to her lips to silence us. She refused to take D's money for the food.

Mère Paul lowered her head to whisper in my ear, "No, you are not crazy. This holy day weekend always, the French-German Résistance fighters reunite in Heidelberg. Père Sablé and I knew we'd be attending. So, it was okay that you were coming here. We did not say a word so you could be on your own."

I pulled D over to hug her again and whisper in her ear, "Mother Paul," and winked. D did the same to Katie, whose eyes had become gigantic blue orbs.

I heard Katie's "Really?" D flashed a huge grin and was starting to move out of the compartment when the conductor asked for tickets—in horrible German.

I stifled a guffaw when I saw Père Sablé in an ill-fitting German Bundesbahn Railroad uniform. I nodded to Katie and D and blew a final kiss to D, who put her hand to her heart. As she turned to disembark, I saw her swipe at the tear wending its way down her cheek.

The train grumbled to a start. Vibrations took hold of this steaming black colossus and moved us down the tracks toward Paris.

It was a while before we actually spoke. What twilight zone had we entered? Vapidly staring out at the bland suburbs and farmland while mindlessly chewing black bread took up the time. I reached my hand across to Katie's knee.

"Hi," I said.

She smiled. "Hi."

"Katie, we've got to talk." I couldn't believe I started this. Not here. Not now. But I was tired of this tension, all this tension.

"I know, but, Pina"—Katie softened her gaze, or was it just fatigue?—"now? We can't fix everything. Now? Craney? College? Especially now." Katie turned to look out the window.

I sighed, spent. For the moment, everything seemed empty—my mouth, my mind, my nerves. My heart was beating; my lungs pumped oxygen. I took it on faith that other parts of me were alive, too. Katie sat opposite me, a mirror image.

After our change of trains at Mannheim, accompanied by our discreet escort, Katie raised her chin at me. "Psst!"

I lifted my gaze to take her in: soft, pretty Katie. Katie who always soothed me—in the past. Katie. That was the extent of my mental and soulful mobility.

"Did that really happen?" Katie spoke slowly in

a hoarse voice.

"What part?"

"Sister—sorry—Mother Paul and Father Sablé?"

I craned my neck to see if they still patrolled the corridor.

"Yup."

"And they're really…I mean they…"

"They're part of a network." I must have put that irrational acceptance together from Mère Paul's explanation and tales of their Resistance work and political engagement.

"Huh? Maybe my imagination can't stretch right now…" Katie let her voice trail off and turned to look out the window, eyes blank, mouth agape.

"Not to worry." I started to chew on my finger.

I stared at the coat hooks above Katie's head and the netting for small personal belongings. Things like that were important. The nuts and bolts of life.

The trip would last another three or four hours, plenty of time to contemplate nuts and bolts or more pressing topics. For now, we both gave in to sleep or something resembling la-la land.

I woke to Katie's touch shaking my arm. "I think we're in France."

We caught a glimpse of the French flag hanging from small stations we passed and of Père Sablé dressed in his soutane, fingering the beads of his rosary in the corridor.

Mère Paul also walked by the door to our compartment looking like the nun she was, a vision in black and white. She poked her head through the door, announcing she would only join us as we approached Paris. She had a car waiting to bring us to the foyer. She smiled at Katie and took her hand to say,

"Mademoiselle, I am now officially Mère Paul. I am content to make your acquaintance."

Katie bowed her head and managed, "*Merci!*" A tear sat poised at the corner of her eye.

After Mère Paul left, Katie whispered, "Where will I stay tonight?"

"In my bed. Just to sleep."

"Huh?"

"My roommate, Cassia, is strange." I had almost forgotten about Cassia.

"Uh-oh, what else?" Katie groaned.

"She's lovesick over us. So, no public displays of affection in front of her."

"What? What the hell, Pina? What's been going on?"

"Nothing. I mean, Cassia's curious…" Oh, man, what did I mean? How was I going to explain?

"And public displays of affection? Are you and Cassia having a thing?"

"Jesus, no!" Shit. Were we? "Katie, look, Cassia… I think Cassia may be lonely. No, nothing has happened, but you know…" Shoot. Where was I going with this, and how red was my face?

"No. I better not know."

I tried to coax a smile out of Katie by making a bug-eyed face and saying, "I only have eyes for you." I joked some more, trying to keep any sign of worry—or guilt—from creasing my face. Man, I didn't want to deal with Cassia's stuff.

A half smile crossed Katie's face.

We quieted down and held hands under the protective cover of our German newspaper. Before long, we were pulling into the Gare de l'Est, and Mère Paul stood knocking at our door.

Chapter Twenty-five

The Catacombs

As promised, Mère Paul gave us a lift to the foyer in the very black tinted-windowed Citroën DS. During the ride, she informed me that Mademoiselle Lesage's mother was clearing out her apartment for Katie and me to move into Wednesday. Surveillance would be better there.

The driver took the scenic route, affording Katie great glimpses of the Halles, bustling with new deliveries—fragrant with the aroma of fruit, fowl, and seafood, freshly culled from land and sea—and a gray Notre-Dame, almost devoid of tourists and practicing Catholics alike in the aftermath of the holy days. Katie oohed and ahhed as she spotted all the cafés, bookstores, and cute Parisian girls on the Boul'Mich and laughed as we passed the sign for the catacombs in the Denfert-Rochereau area. She made me promise to take her there.

Mère Paul embraced us before shooing us up to my room, whispering, "*Pas de soucis!*" It really did feel like we wouldn't have any more to worry about. That is, if we could manage Cassia's enthusiasm.

As soon as Cassia's image danced across my mind, some live wire sparked in my chest. Hmm. I had warned Katie. *My* body had almost forgotten how electric Cassia was, to me, too.

Distracting myself from that idea, I helped Katie up the stairs with her bag and explained the light system. She could hardly listen, she was in such a rush to get to my room and meet Cassia.

"*Les voilà!*" Cassia threw open the door, crooning "*Bienvenues!*" and kissing each of us the requisite two times on each cheek. She almost floated a foot above the ground, hovering about us with such élan, and helping to remove our bags, our coats, almost anything that wasn't glued on. I felt her tiny touches—accidental?—all over my body.

Apparently, Katie felt them, too, judging from the unique shade of fuchsia tinting her face. She clasped the top placket of her button-down and smiled a honeyed grin at Cassia.

"Hi, I'm Katie."

"*Oui.* I know you already. I have your *belle* photo next to my bed." Cassia sighed.

Katie blushed. I coughed, beginning to feel like chopped meat.

"*Salut*, Cassia! Did you miss me, too?" I nudged her, a bit on edge. Shoot, why didn't I just give her the brush-off?

Cassia rambled in rapid French for a few minutes while Katie rooted around the room. She smiled at the fireplace she must have recognized from my letter and narrowed her gaze at the sexy picture of herself looking down from the wall onto Cassia's bed. She coughed so hard, I offered her some water.

"Yeah. I think I need something…"

I poured her some water while Cassia all but tripped over herself to offer Katie a chair. Cassia couldn't do enough, almost stooping to fan Katie when it was really Cassia who needed to cool down. Instead, she struggled to express in English just how gorgeous Katie was.

"Your eyes, yes! They are seas—like the Riviera, in big, big coves, coves for your blushes." She sighed, her chest heaving. "Your hair—long, so long, locks, lovely, with a glow—you light my heart." Cassia put her hand on her heart.

I rolled my eyes and thought I'd gag.

"*Oui, oui*, Cassia. That was so moving. Right, Katie?" I poked her with my elbow. "Aren't you just so moved?" My voice dripped with sarcasm.

Katie sat there speechless, but she turned a menacing look in my direction followed by cow eyes at Cassia. "*Merci*." She sighed.

Cassia suddenly placed her hand over her mouth. I thought she was trying to compose another "ode" on Katie's beauty.

"*Pardon! Excusez-moi*," she said, pointing to the door and the stairs. The last we heard as Cassia flew down the stairs was the word *WC*.

I glared at Katie. "I told you!"

"God, Pina, she's harmless and so sweet."

"Yeah. Like treacle."

"Damn, you're jealous." Katie guffawed.

"Am not." I started unpacking and throwing clothes on the bed.

Katie got up to stop my unpacking. "Look at me! You've got the hots for her." She stood an inch away from me, leering, reaching over to pinch or worse.

"Stop! Do not!" I rolled onto the bed; Katie followed. She held my writhing body down and pushed herself on top of me, kissing me fully and deeply. My moan came loud and unexpected. I was hungry for her and groped her rounded bottom as the door burst open.

Katie jumped off the bed. Cassia, mouth open and scarlet, stood in the doorway, covering her parts. Her hand could have been a fig leaf.

"Oh, I am—how you say?—in *de secret*?"

"No, Cassia," I said in a flat tone. "We have been indiscreet."

Katie excused herself to find the bathroom once Cassia relaxed and stepped aside out of the doorway.

"Cassia, listen. Katie and I have to stay here tonight. Tomorrow, we will go to my former instructor's apartment. It's necessary for security reasons." I spoke with a sudden sense of detachment to steel myself against any more of Cassia's theatrics.

Cassia seemed to sober up, saying, "Yes, my father received the news about Dilsberg. He said Craney is probably back in Italy or…" Her face started to puff up in sadness. "I am scared for you. You were right about Craney, and I did not believe you soon enough."

As she wiped away a lazy tear, Cassia tapped herself upside her head. "Ah, but we must celebrate before you leave. We go to the catacombs today, *oui*?"

"*Oui*, Katie will like that."

Katie smiled her typical smile when she returned and heard about the outing and acted politely normal with Cassia.

❧❧❧❧

On the Métro, Cassia spoke with enthusiasm about the catacombs and the Louvre, which Katie would visit the next day. All fell back to normal.

Typical, that is, until Cassia's face lit up.

"*Ah, oui*, the Louvre. You must see the Impressionists."

"Yes, I'm dying to see van Gogh and Monet,"

Katie said.

I started to lose myself, staring at billboards for wine and gym classes on the walls of passing stations, as well as at the long-haired lovely in tight blue jeans topped by a big bulky sweater and a painter's smock. But I briskly turned back to Katie and Cassia when I heard Cassia raving about Manet.

"Oh. You must see Manet, his *Le déjeuner sur l'herbe.* You know, the lady is in birthday suit at picnic—all the men with their parts hidden, but the sexy lady with hair there and breast... I make joke, I tell Pina—Pina and I go do that nude, and we prepare a picnic with you, all nude!" Cassia smiled, I think so proud of her English. I just wanted to silence her, pinch her loose lips together, locked.

Katie stared at me and turned back to Cassia. "You say, you and Pina already made a naked picnic?" Katie reduced her English to basics.

"All ready? Ah, Katie, you want to do it today?" Cassia asked.

Katie glanced at me and grabbed my hand a bit too firmly as we stood to exit at our station. "What the hell?" she whispered.

I whispered back, smiling the whole time, "No, she suggested it. We never did. I've never seen her naked—"

"Ha! You didn't say she hasn't seen you naked." Katie was still smiling. Her smile was far from heartfelt.

Cassia was aware of our smiles but had difficulty following the bits of English she heard through gritted teeth.

"Katie—later!" I said, pointing out the late-blooming asters and lilies for Katie to smell in the square Denfert-Rochereau. I softened my gaze, giving her my best melt-your-heart-and-your-parts smile. I had to do something to steer her away from my Cassia story.

"Now. Stop. Forget floral scents. Think pizza, cookies, anything but flowers. Stand here and smell this," I said.

"What is it?" Katie asked.

"Smell the butter and the wine and the garlic. How about the parsley?"

"Got it," said Katie. "It smells so sizzling, like the wine fumes are almost rising, wafting up my nose. And, and it's fish...or...Oh, wow! Snails."

Cassia jumped up and down. "*Oui, oui*, I know the just place."

I spun around on Cassia, grabbed her by the elbow, and whispered in French, "*Mais, pas de picnic nu.*"

She made a sheepish grin and agreed there would be no more talk of naked picnics.

We entered the steep stairway down to the entrance of the catacombs. While the smell was not as bad as in the sewers, it did reek of dust, dirt, and death. Not decomposition, but...deep, ancient excavations, the kind for quarries—which this had been at one time—the kind for burials, but these bones migrated here much later, exhumed from their original graves when their cemetery walls collapsed.

The first view of skulls almost amused me in a bizarre way. The skulls seemed like furnishings or some sick take on interior decorations. They were arranged in a tight pyramid. We passed stack after stack of yellowing, gray-white, chalky ulnas and tibias, some square piles, others rectangular. The air turned more sour, maybe from urine and mildew. A heaviness overcame me. We were all dust and rust.

I turned around to touch Katie. I wanted her

comfort. She was not there.

I hung back from the swarm of people moving forward and spotted Katie in an area with no overhead light. Cassia was working her arm up Katie's back and rubbing up close to her side. *Merde!* I coughed extra hard as I approached Katie.

"Stay with me," I said to Katie, who eased away from Cassia.

"Mmm," she responded. Paris seemed to have reignited our passion—or maybe our jealousy.

The undulating crowd enveloped Cassia, snaking its way along the serpentine tunnels, and the group was now almost out of sight behind the wall of skulls stacked like firewood in an end-pillar pattern. The dust and darkness magnified the fading echo of tourists' footsteps. The off-white skulls remained cold and rigid.

Katie and I hung back some more and tucked into a nook by ourselves. I took Katie's smooth face in my hands and stepped closer into her embrace. We heard footsteps and pulled away from each other. The slap-dap-splash of feet running in shallow pools of muddy water sounded close. I figured it was Cassia in hot pursuit and grabbed Katie by the hand. I pulled her farther into the blackened alcove. The echo of feet followed. From which tunnel? Pea gravel shifted, a few pebbles, then silence. Then slap-dap, then stones grating. Cassia was certainly persistent.

In the far reaches of the area we were in, I could barely make out a barrier in the darkness, some sort of sawhorse. Katie and I loosened a few slats to clamber over and filed through four more passageways. We stopped to catch our breath and listen. Silence. No more footsteps. No more Cassia. Just air staler than before, as if no living soul before us had ever breathed it.

Alone finally. I leaned my back against the naked, sweating wall. No skulls, no spiders. I reached out for Katie's sweet face. We both laughed. I eased her against the wall and rubbed my breasts against hers. She whispered, "Love you," against my lips, nipping at them, and pulling them apart slowly, teasing. Her tongue filled my mouth and danced with mine. My knees buckled. She throbbed into me with her whole body. I felt her wetness and her heat.

After a few minutes, I opened my eyes and gently stroked her cheek with my thumb.

"We've got to go," I whispered, but I desperately wanted to stay. Whatever love potion Katie had swallowed after Heidelberg, I would buy her a lifetime supply.

"Phew! If I can move."

"Katie, we've got to. Listen, steps. Heavy steps."

"Wait. Where are they coming from?"

"Uh. They stopped. What the—"

We heard distant pebbles scraping, slushing. Grating sounds echoed through the network of tunnels. The clatter, like a pile of stones chafing and tumbling, followed by a definite kerclunk, the vibration of some object landing closer to us, much too close.

We took off. We ran. We turned left, sure that was the direction of the main tunnel the crowd had continued down, but when we heard a deafening silence, we circled back. I inched forward to locate the next branch of the tunnel and turned back again.

I turned left and then back. I leaned my head forward to locate the next tunnel and turned back again. Everything was pitch-black in this area.

"What is it?" Katie asked.

"I don't know where we are."

After a half hour of turning left, right, and back again, I announced, "We're lost."

"Maybe not just lost, but in an enclosed area?"

"What do you mean?" I begged for answers from Katie, whose spatial skills were more acute than mine.

"It feels like we're sealed into a kind of maze. Like with no exit."

"That can't be. We got in."

Katie held me by the arm a sec. "Let's think…"

We had a small pocket flashlight and a whistle. I opted for the flashlight first. No exits that I could see. But we did crunch something. I was afraid to look. A rat? A finger?

I flashed the beam at my foot and gasped, holding on to Katie. She grabbed the light and bent down. She stood back up with my skull in her hands. "Pina" was scrawled indelibly across the skull's forehead.

I bent over, my stomach turning. Katie reached for me and pulled my hair back. Holding on to Katie, I was grounded. I breathed in her scent, her Canoe essence, her air of home. She exuded safety and intimacy again. I stood back up.

"Give me the whistle, quick!" She blew three sharp blasts. She stashed the skull in her shopping bag. Mumbling some soothing sounds, she rocked me and started another round of the three-blast emergency signal.

There weren't any other skulls or bones where we were. And a quick examination of the walls in the poor glow of the flashlight revealed recently quarried rock.

"Ideas?" I asked Katie.

"More lovemaking?"

She ran her hand down my hair, saying, "I love

how calm you've stayed."

"Do I have a choice?" I managed to laugh.

"Shush," Katie said, sniffing. "Exhaust fumes."

"Good Parisian diesel?"

"Yeah, and fresh air."

"Was it starting to rain when we smelled the flowers outside? I hear raindrops."

We started groping our way toward the odors when Katie shouted, "Escargots."

Katie stood relishing the heady bouquet of the snails, the ones from the café at the entrance to the catacombs. The raindrops seemed closer and closer overhead, and Katie said she believed she saw a flicker of light. We ran toward it and found an old, partially obstructed set of stairs to the far end of the catacombs. We managed to remove some rubble and poked our hands above ground enough to signal passers-by.

Footsteps. Good footsteps. Running footsteps. They raced in our direction.

"Eh oh!" People shouted to one another for help as they took our hands in theirs. Warm, safe hands.

Safe, we were safe. We heard scraping and felt heavy vibrations, blows breaking cement above our heads. A point of light leaked in. Gravel and dirt sprayed down and then an arm, two arms. More pounding, more light. A smiling, bearded face peered down.

"*Ça va?*"

Yes, we were okay.

"Patience!" Another voice.

After another shovelful or two of dirt and debris, we could see a crowd cheering and clapping. They hoisted us above ground, dusting us off and embracing us. Men doffed their caps and berets; women made the sign of the cross.

There were more French kisses and cheers when Cassia rounded the corner and ran to embrace us.

"You naughty girls! You fuck in the catacombs," Cassia whispered.

"We were trapped in the friggin' catacombs," Katie said in an uncharacteristically direct style.

I held up my hand to make it clear to Cassia that I didn't want to talk about this yet. Her grimace eased into a soft smile. "You're fine, Pina. Let's go get those snails."

The scent of fresh air with accents of sizzling snails smelled like true release after our imprisonment in the catacombs. We followed the intoxicating aroma of wine and butter-slathered snails to a minuscule café.

The trifold doors—advertising in very French handwriting "*Spécialités: Escargots, Soupe à l'oignon, Huîtres*"—opened onto the street. Once inside, we walked along the bar on the sawdusted white tile floor to a tiny back table tucked between the bar and the side exit. We immediately collapsed onto the bent wood chairs and served ourselves water from the carafe on the table.

Cassia studied Katie's and my weary faces for a split second and took charge. She signaled the waiter to order a triple serving of escargots for the table and three glasses of red wine. She turned back to us and double-checked my face.

"Can you talk now?" She reached across the table to lightly tap my hand.

I leaned my elbows on the table and rubbed the back of my neck. I blew out a bunch of air.

"We lost our way in a side tunnel where we tripped over…" I fished the skull out of Katie's cord shopping bag and, draping it with my jacket, flashed it at Cassia. "This."

I gave her the short version. No emotion, no exclamations. I had no idea where or what my emotions were, besides avoidance. My mind quickly traveled away from the table. I barely heard Cassia exclaim, *"Mon Dieu!"*

Katie threw me a look. "Cassia, we have to give Pina some time."

"Of course." She turned her full attention to Katie. "It was atrocious for you, no?"

"I'm okay. It's okay. Pina will work this out."

Cassia stifled a snort. "Did you two sneak off to kiss?"

"Well, kind of...but not really." I heard Katie's obvious lie.

After Katie gave Cassia a few more basic, censored details, I lost track of things, except the snails. I savored the slightly chewy morsels in my mouth. I breathed in the rising fumes of garlic butter and wine. A few bites of butter-soaked baguette washed down with red wine, and I really was fine.

I would go to see Père Sablé the next day. I pictured him munching on bread, smiling his leprechaun smile, telling me how he found, not Jesus, but love in the war-torn hills. I hadn't found Jesus in the snails, but a kind of peace. Père Sablé would help me identify this French relic, this skull. As for the owner of the footsteps? Just another hired thug.

I tuned back to reality when sunlight suddenly danced off the stainless-steel snail grabbers, blinding my eyes, already sticky with splattered garlic butter.

Cassia was demonstrating for Katie the fine art of eating snails. She leaned over close to Katie and manipulated Katie's hands to grab the shell with the metal clamp and extract the snail with the little fork.

Katie licked her fingers and smiled a buttery grin at Cassia. Both red-cheeked, they drank a few more sips before clasping another snail.

I coughed to announce my re-emergence from timeout. Katie smiled. I smiled back in silence. Katie even claimed it was the best thing she had ever eaten. Cassia wore a Sylvester grin but gloated tacitly over her snail lesson to Katie.

It was late, and Katie and I had to leave for school by eight the next morning. I signaled to Katie to meet me in the WC. I needed to eliminate any possibility of Cassia's funny business.

"Listen, tonight we sleep, that's it." I yawned, tired of Cassia, weary, just weary.

"Ah, yeah? You thought we'd do a show-and-tell for Cassia?" Katie shrugged at me.

"Man, Katie. She's sweet and all that, but you see how she is."

"Wow! You really think I'm dense?"

"No. Just a reminder. Please. I don't have anything left in me tonight."

"Got it." Katie placed a kiss on my cheek and took me by the arm to rejoin Cassia.

The three of us rode the Métro home with few words. The clicking of the hall lights and the soft shuffling of our steps were the only sounds accompanying us up to the room. I dove under the covers half-dressed after blowing kisses from a distance over to Cassia. Katie slid her longer, cooler legs alongside mine from the opposite end of the bed. A certain stillness filled the room.

Chapter Twenty-six

The Morning After

We had forgotten to lower the metal blinds, and now an eerie light leaked into the room. I slept in fits and starts, conscious at one point of Cassia creeping about in the half light. She mumbled something about water.

In another flash, a ghost-like Katie moved slowly across the room, clinking change together and rolling the towel bar. When direct sunlight painted the entire room golden, I saw that I was the only one still in bed.

Sweaty and dank, I still wore my shirt from the night before. I grabbed my towel, some change, and a clean shirt and underwear, then flew down the stairs to hit the shower. Both doors were closed.

As I leaned against the frame of the shower room, the door eased open. I blanched. I said nothing, just watched.

Cassia stood naked, clutching Katie. She held Katie's head and kissed her firmly on the lips. Slippery with soap, she moved her hips into Katie and separated Katie's lips with her fingers and her tongue. Katie stood stiff, arms at her sides until Cassia slid down Katie's body and took her breast in her mouth, over and over, sucking and pulling.

Katie came to life when Cassia grabbed her behind. She put up her hand, but her flushed look and arousal were obvious. Was her hand raised in submission or resistance? She caught sight of me at the door and ran naked out of the shower and up the stairs.

I slammed the shower door on Cassia and followed Katie up, locking the bedroom door behind me. Katie's sobbing choked her speech. She mumbled, "Sorry…I uh…She…Shit, Pina…"

"Get your clothes on," I said, ice in my veins.

Katie tried to hug me, stroking my head, groping for my hand. I stepped out of her embrace.

"We're late. Hurry. And get all your things. We're not coming back."

I put on some clothes hanging on my bedpost and took a swipe at my tangled hair with the brush. Then I just stared at the brush in my hand. I couldn't figure out where to put it. Pack it? Leave it? I hurled it across the room, threw my jacket over my arm, and unlocked the door, nearly knocking Cassia down the stairs.

Cassia attempted to say something to Katie, who brushed past her. I pushed Katie in front of me and turned to Cassia, gritting my teeth.

"Don't! Just don't." I snarled.

Outside the foyer, Katie struggled to keep up with me. She tried to explain. Her words rolled off my back.

"We'll go to the Institut. A guide will take you to the Louvre—a security person who will bring you back to school to meet with Père Sablé and me. Just don't say a word. I don't want to hear it!"

Katie stood nodding at me as if she were afraid to get yet another thing wrong. How could she?

I stewed all the way to school. What the hell was Cassia thinking? I knew the answer to that. Maybe the real question was: What was Katie thinking? A little Parisian spice? In the friggin' shower?

We arrived at school, and a tall, thin person in the French version of the compulsory spook crew cut opened the door of a black Citroën DS for Katie. She attempted to hug me. I spun away.

I sat on the deserted curb. The ever-present aroma of black coffee and chicory nauseated me, and the street noises boomed their deafening sounds. I kicked a large rock, which pinged off the hubcap of a parked Renault.

What the hell was I going to do? I couldn't think straight. I gave out a bitter laugh to myself. Katie and I had never had that discussion—the one that goes, "Oh, you're leaving for four months; you're not going to go with other girls, are you?" Shit, I just assumed. I mean…Damn! Even in that first telephone call when I was going kind of crazy, we took for granted that neither one of us was going to cheat. And with Cassia?

I kicked the ground. I made a fist and thumped it into my leg. If I could just…what? Shake the anger out? I squeezed my eyes shut. I was bleeding crimson rage. I slumped over. No, not anger. I hurt all over. How could she? A distant voice in my head whispered, "And you?"

I ran for the *toilettes*. Locked. Stifling a public cry, I knocked and then barged in as the person exited. I wailed, seated on the toilet. No words could say what this meant to Katie or me. Enough whimpering. Getting up, I blew my nose and tried to get the red out of my eyes with drops. Everything hurt less now, dried up.

How was I going to speak to Père Sablé about the skull? What was it he said to me about the tower? Yeah.

If I needed to hide. If I needed to get rid of my enemies. I had no idea what I was going to do with myself. How the hell could I know what to do with Craney? Cassia? Katie? Not throw them off the tower... Well, maybe Craney.

I began to think more clearly. I'd wait for Père Sablé at the tower door.

※ ※ ※ ※

Père Sablé peered over his glasses. After chiding me for cutting his earlier class, he threw his arm around my shoulders.

"Come, it's time for a break."

He leaned forward and looked me in the eyes. "I see you can use a big break, too. *Ça ne va pas, hein?*"

"Nothing is going right." I choked out as few words as possible.

As he opened the door to the tower, he handed me a man's large white handkerchief with an embroidered red cross in the corner. "A gift from Mère Paul to me," he said.

We climbed a few steps before sitting down to rest. He tore a piece from the baguette he carried and handed it to me.

"*Alors,*" he said, twisting a piece for himself. He pulled the soft white inside out and rolled it into a ball before popping it into his mouth. He tossed the crust on the next step.

"So?" I said, eyeing the crust.

"So, I tell you war stories. I think you've had a few lately. Mère Paul knows about the skull; she called me. But I see there are other battles. The war of the heart, yes?"

"*Oui,*" I mumbled, grabbing the crust from the other step.

Slapping my hand, Père Sablé passed me a fresh piece of bread, explaining, "My crusts are for the birds."

He scratched his forehead and seemed to look into himself.

"So, the war. You know Mère Paul and I hate war. I don't like even to hurt my enemies, but back then, there was this evil spreading like sickness, and there was this love growing." Père Sablé coughed. "Yes, I confess, Mère Paul and I were in love, and the only way to go away with her was to join the Résistance. Her parents had promised her to the church, an old tradition when their prayers for something were answered. Well, you know where love leads. We won the war—love triumphed over hatred—and Mère Paul and I promised eternal love to ourselves and to our people. But I could not forgive myself. I made her break her vow—you know, the physical one.

"But you know redemption. She forgave me. She loved me, but maybe Jesus more, and of course, she had to honor her parents' promise. We vowed to continue our love through what you call *social action*—and she would go to the convent and me to the priests. There, that is my story."

He handed me another chunk of bread and pulled the middle out of his own piece. He rolled it and chewed it slowly.

"And your story this morning?" he asked.

"Well...the skull?"

"That is not bringing tears to your eyes," he said.

"She...she was letting Cassia kiss her," I babbled, unable to hold it any longer.

"And? You hurt..."

"Yeah…"

"And? You don't know"—he turned to look at me—"if Katie loves her?"

"No. Of course Katie doesn't love her."

"Eh?"

"Well, I don't really know." I chewed on some more bread. "I didn't actually see Katie do anything."

"Ah? You think Katie is tempted? But she loves you? And she has done nothing wrong?"

"Well, not really," I grumbled, remembering Katie's stiff arms at her sides and her raised hand.

"So, no one made her break any vow? We conquer our enemies with love, eh? That is my story."

And my own vow? Had I broken it? Why didn't I ask him about that?

I passed Père Sablé the inside of my bread. He took it in silence and winked. "I think you are smart. You can learn the redemption game. You learn to kill with kindness. Come, we go to God's country."

We went to the roof and sat. Bells chimed at noon. They seemed to do a call and response sequence as so many nearby churches rang out for the noon prayer.

"Now show me the skull," he said.

I took it out of the bag.

"*Eh, bien.* It is a fake. No worries."

"I don't get it."

"Someone, anyone can buy these. It's not old. So, not Craney herself, but a stooge. She's not here." He raised his empty hands to demonstrate "nothing."

"But we were trapped."

"Eh? But I see you here." Père Sablé smiled that broad grin.

He looked at me like the good teacher he really was. His eyes urged me to think and pull together some hypotheses.

"Yes, you do. And we had actually wandered off."

"There is a time to worry and a time to *worry*. You know *Le petit prince*, another war story, *hein?* You remember the little prince even tames the rose with the big thorns. And how?"

"You want me to cut Craney's thorns?" I shook my head, but with a big grin.

"Maybe shrink them? She has no love. You, lucky girl, you do. Lots of people, they love you. Cassia has no love. No hope for her, either? Really?"

My head started to spin. Père Sablé was asking me to believe—not in any divinity—but in hope and love. He interrupted my thoughts, saying, "Trust!"

"Look," he shouted, "we have finished the bread. You must trust that people will take care of you just as you take care of yourself and other people. I bet you will always find things to eat."

With that, he jumped up and looked at the sky. "Ah! God's country? Maybe we also go to the land of the little prince's planet. But you have to wait until dark to see it smile and laugh. And by then, you will be smiling and laughing, too."

We went down the steps slowly, holding on to the cord. Père Sablé waved goodbye. "*Pas de soucis, eh!*" I waved back. Right, I thought. Yeah, right, not a care in the world. Boy, I had a lot to think about.

I lifted my head to check the hall for Katie. Not yet. What the heck did he mean about things to eat? Unless there was a famine or I ran out of money, I'd have things to eat.

And there he was again, at the end of the hall opening the door for Katie—who was carrying a bunch of little bags from the gourmet food shop around the corner.

As Katie stepped down into the hallway, a shaft of sunlight laid a golden carpet for her to walk on in my direction. Off to the side, Père Sablé turned and winked at me before disappearing.

I approached Katie and spun her around in the opposite direction. Holding her by the shoulder, I steered her out the door. Neither one of us spoke. I took her arm as we walked toward the Jardin du Luxembourg.

Katie didn't ask where we were going. She didn't say a word. As we neared the park, I nodded. She struggled to remove a throw from her shopping bag as we neared the park.

"Hold this, please." She handed the bag to me.

I looked at her over my glasses—I hadn't had time to put my lenses in that morning. Her eyes begged forgiveness as she chewed her lip. I smiled with every inch of my face, trying to reassure her.

We found a spot tucked away farther back from the boulevards and the busy noonday streets. I spread the throw and opened the goodies. Looking up at Katie, I extended my hand to her and whispered, "Please."

Katie took my hand and eased herself down. She held on to my hand and kissed it. Her eyes welled up.

"Shush," I said. "Let's eat first. Père Sablé told me I would have good things to eat."

"I don't understand. He didn't know," she said, savoring some olives.

"No, he was telling me to trust that life would take care of me."

"And you believed him?"

"I had to. You were standing there with the most wonderful treats possible."

I spread some *pâté de campagne* on bread and lifted it to Katie's lips.

"Mmm. God, this is good." Katie chewed slowly, then stopped. She did that thing with her hair, kind of twirling it. "I…uh…want to explain."

I loaded a clump of bread with a very runny, really stinky Camembert cheese. I licked every drip oozing from my lips and finally looked up at Katie. I breathed deeply. "Okay, if you're ready."

Katie stared at me, eyebrows raised. "Aren't you…?" Her voice trailed off.

I chewed on that thought for a sec. How much was I ready for? What if there had been more than what I saw between Katie and Cassia? And what about Père Sablé's message?

Smiling a smile I wasn't sure of, I nodded. "Yes, I am."

Katie pushed the bread and the salami aside and touched my hand. Her look asked for permission.

"Okay. I went down to take a shower. You know that, sorry. Partway through, I couldn't load the coins for hot water, and I thought I heard someone. So, I cracked the door just enough to ask for tokens. And you know the rest."

"No, Katie, I don't." I almost pulled my hand away, but I realized Katie had no idea what I had seen and what it looked like.

"Well, Cassia pushed herself in, babbling about the right coins and then…then pushed me back against the wall and kissed me so hard before I even got what was happening."

"You liked it." I tilted my head in her direction.

"I…uh—"

"Was very aroused," I finished her sentence.

Katie blushed and started to cry. "I've never been kissed like that by anyone."

"Anyone?"

"Anyone but you, and that's after heavy-duty making out for a while. But you're right. I was totally excited, and that's why I uh, I was completely in shock."

"That didn't look like shock to me."

"I know it's crazy. But my body just went wild, and my mind went dead, like my body was telling it to shut up and go away. My arms and legs just froze, like they were anesthetized. Pina, that sounds really weird. I'm sick to think that if she had kept on driving into me and putting her fingers all over my butt, my whole body would have…I mean…I didn't want to, well… I'm so sick over this."

"Shush." I sighed, and looking at her long and hard, I could see she was in a lot of pain—the last thing I wanted.

"Stop," I whispered, leaning over to pull Katie against me. "I'm sorry I was cruel to you earlier." I stroked Katie's face and rubbed her tears dry. "I want to say I forgive you, sweetie, but then, it's like I think you're guilty. And I don't." My own tears bathed my face and Katie's as I kissed her eyes and stroked her soft, curly hair.

"You don't?" Katie pulled back and stared at me. "Are you okay? I mean, you seem so calm."

A knot of guilt started low in my stomach. I had to undo it. "Shush," I said. "Just let me look at you and kiss you."

I brushed her lips with mine and put my finger to them when she tried to say something. "Ah, so you don't want to kiss me," I joked.

Katie laughed, quietly mouthing, "Thank you,"

and finally, "Yes, I do, but not here and definitely not like this!"

"Good 'cause I'm bringing you to our new apartment—all *ours* for now and near Montmartre."

Hugging me, Katie giggled. "I like your makeup present. What am I going to give you?"

I didn't dare say what I wanted. I was afraid I'd jinx this Parisian spell that Katie was under.

We packed up the remains of our treats and headed for the Métro to Rue du Faubourg Poissonnière. Katie repeated at least a thousand times how sorry she was. I repeated how much I loved her *and* Père Sablé. Katie winked and agreed he must be very lovable.

Chapter Twenty-seven

Love Trumps Hate

On our way to the apartment, Katie asked about the skull, studying my face for signs of a grimace or anxious tics. I explained that Père Sablé said the skull was fake. I laughed at the leaves dancing down in front of us, tossed about by the breeze blowing at our backs. There was a new lightness in the air as we almost sashayed down the boulevard.

"And the news about Craney—she's almost certainly not in Paris. So, finding my name on a skull is not the same as almost toppling from a tower."

"Wow! Père Sablé must have given you a real pep talk."

We both guffawed as we skipped down the steps to the Métro, where a concert awaited us. Accordion music drifted our way, a song about Paris skies. Katie clapped her hands, shouting, "Man, this is neat!"

"Wait till you hear the rest," I said as we rounded another tunnel. The accordion seemed to duel with a violin almost singing a Bach cantata. The whole station throbbed with life.

I took Katie's arm and fell in love all over again when I saw her dab at her eyes.

"I can't help it. It's so beautiful, and you're so gorgeous, and I almost screwed everything up."

"No, Katie. It's Paris, and everything here is

magical. Well…almost." I stood, grinning at her as the train pulled in.

❧❧❧❧

As we exited from the Métro, I named the monuments and neighborhoods in all the different directions to orient Katie. She made me promise to take her to nearby Montmartre, Pigalle, and the flea market.

After two more blocks, I pointed to the number 169 above the old coach door and teased that I should carry Katie over the threshold. I greeted the concierge, who eyed us from our American loafers up to our American hairdos. She smiled an unconvincing smile as she wiped her hands on her apron. "*Attention au bruit*," she barked.

I nodded and explained to Katie that even though the apartment was on the third floor, concierges always complained about noise.

"You think we're that loud when we do it?" Katie grinned.

"Shush!"

Although Mère Paul had already described the apartment to me, when I threw open the heavy oak door, it took my breath away. Katie dropped her suitcase and just stood there, mouth open.

"Ours? All alone?" she asked.

"Yup."

I brought in the bags, took Katie by the hand, and quickly shut the door behind us. I bowed to Katie and wished her "*bienvenue*" before kissing her passionately against the closed door.

She lifted her head. "This, too, leaves me

breathless!"

I covered Katie's eyes, dangling keys. "What's first? The tour or, you know, some hot stuff?"

She pulled my hands away and gave me a quick kiss. "Show me around so I can choose which bed to warm up."

We entered a huge sunbathed room. Floor-to-ceiling windows, opening to the courtyard and partially veiled in gauzy, undulating curtains, reflected our image—our perfect couple—and funneled in the essence of beef *bourguignon* and pastry, perhaps a marzipan cake. The tall walls were covered in a tan linen fabric accented by hunter green chair rails. A huge metal-framed bed occupied the corner beside the fireplace.

Katie flew to the second and third doors in the hall, a deep closet with things acquired over the youth and student days of five Lesage kids and a second bedroom also boasting a fireplace.

Now we knew the layout, but Katie continued to run her hand over eighteenth and nineteenth-century furniture. "Oh, Pina, the wood is so smooth. And look at the drop-front desk!"

Another sofa bed and a richly oiled drop-leaf table completed the furnishings. Katie flopped down on the sofa and held her hand out to me. I pulled back.

"What's up?" Katie squinted at me.

Oh, man! What got into me that I had to spoil the perfect moment, the perfect setting? Something bizarre happened when I saw Katie's eyes go crazy looking at the beds and running her tongue all around her mouth. For a split second, I flashed on Cassia. In the blink of an eye, I imagined Cassia chasing Katie all around the bed and licking her all over. And then

Cassia was moving against me, and I felt those tingles, that throbbing just imagining Cassia.

"*Merde!*"

"Pina, damn it, what is it?"

"I'm sorry. I've got to talk about Cassia."

Katie drew out the word *okay* until it had about ten syllables.

"I've got to understand." I ran my hand through my hair. "I saw her touching you in the catacombs, right? Didn't she?"

"You know, I was so out of it with all those bones and people crying, I don't really know. I had this idea that everyone kind of huddled together among the living—like we were one breathing, moving being—*alive*, not dead like the bones."

"Hmm. And what about before that, or I know, during the night, last night, Cassia was creeping around in the middle of the night. Did she get into bed with you?"

"Sweetie, we—you and I—were in bed together." Katie looked at me like I was obsessed. Maybe I was.

"I know, but…You noticed your picture on Cassia's wall, right? When she saw your photo in my things, God, she was almost drooling. She was really strange—as if your picture aroused her. Seriously, she looked at your photo every night and kissed it." I started shaking my head and banging my foot on the oak floor.

"Shush. The concierge." Katie leaned back against the wall, scratching her head. "That is really bizarre. Did she ever—I mean, has she touched you?"

"Jesus, Katie, no. I'd smack her down!"

"Well, I'm not the only sexy one around here."

"Oh, shoot. She did sleep in my bed once—

sleep…I think," I mumbled, mealymouthed.

"Oh, ho!"

"Nothing happened." I coughed and looked away. I couldn't let myself wonder about that now.

Katie stifled a guffaw. "I trust you, but…" Katie doubled over with laughter.

"You're laughing, but I'm serious. How far would she have gone with you in the shower? She was building up a full head of steam! Man, I should have—" I stopped cold. My conscience was tugging at me.

"What, Pina? What should you have done?"

"Never mind!" I turned my head away from Katie.

"Listen, you've got to get this out and let it go."

I huffed, and I puffed. "Père Sablé," I muttered. I looked toward the wash of sunlight bathing the floor and squinted, trying to remember what Père Sablé had said about Cassia not having any love.

I ran my tongue around my teeth. Another conversation about love came back to me.

"Katie, she said she never knew love."

"Who? I thought you said Père Sablé."

"Don't you see? Père Sablé asked if I thought there was no hope for Cassia. He didn't mean hope of seducing you or me. He meant…"

"Yeah?"

"Well, Cassia said her parents provided for her, but she never felt loved. Her folks even sound like they don't like each other very much."

"So, Dr. Mazzini?" Katie laughed. She loved it when I tried to analyze relationships.

"Cassia was so moved when I talked about why I loved you and how you cared for me. You know, from your letters and phone calls."

"So, you want to share me?" Katie rolled her eyes and hugged me. "I'm teasing, but you're saying she learned about love through your eyes and our voices."

"Yeah! She fell in love with love."

"Uh-huh," said Katie. "So, what do you want to do? Invite her over here? Now?"

"Maybe forgive her." Shoot. This was really about forgiving myself. I just had to tell Katie, but my mouth was wide open, and my foot was going deeper and deeper into it.

"Really? What happened? You were ready to rip her head off a few minutes ago."

"I don't have to. She needs kindness."

"And?"

"And…I have an idea."

"Oh, Pina." Katie threw me that look.

"We'll find her someone to love."

"Yeah, Pin. 'Wanted: One lucky person for Cassia to adore. Must love showers.'"

"C'mon, you doofus." I poked Katie.

"Sweetie, I'm just ragging on you."

I snapped my fingers. "Got it! I'm going to take us all to Chez Moune."

"Who?"

"A lesbian cabaret, my dear. We'll get a date for Cassia yet."

"Good Lord!" Katie roared with glee. "*What* exactly did Père Sablé say to you?"

We continued to sit for a while, quiet.

"Now about that invitation." Katie broke the silence. She fluttered her eyes, consuming me from head to toe.

"You want me to call Cassia right now?" I said, playing dumb.

"Actually, I want to ask you over to my big bed in the corner."

Katie took my hand and led me to the bed. As we lay down, we stopped our snappy talk and just held each other. Katie brushed the hair from my face and gazed into my eyes so softly for a long, long moment.

"We've got all the time in the world here in this lovely place. It really feels like our home," she said.

"No, your eyes are my home." I kissed Katie's eyes and breathed in her scent—fresh air, citrus, and lavender. She smelled of the earth, of our roaming free and safe. "With you here," I continued, "it does feel like home."

As I started to kiss her lips, I had a split-second flashback to waking next to Cassia that morning after the sewers and the cognac. Did Cassia and I actually do it? I didn't think so. And I really didn't want to think about that now, now that all I wanted was Katie—*and* she wanted me. I struggled to turn off my head and focus on Katie's full, luscious mouth, the mouth that said she trusted me.

Katie kissed me first, a deep, inviting kiss as she slid her hand under my shirt.

"Take it off," she said. "Take it all off."

I kept my lips locked on hers as I wriggled out of my pants with her help. I pushed into her mouth with my tongue, and slipping my hand under her skirt, I eased down her pantyhose. Only then would I let her loose to pull off my shirt. My other thoughts had disappeared.

Chapter Twenty-eight

My Gladiator Fight in the Arena

In the early morning, I opened my eyes onto a crisp half-light accenting different aspects of the apartment I had begun to claim as my own the previous night. Katie's dark shiny hair curled softly about her shoulders still cloaked in the comfy flannel sheet blanket.

The air was still, a kind of vacuum locking us away from the concerns of daytime and life in the streets, which would start to pulsate in a few hours.

Sleep lingered in the air, as well as subtle hints of the onion soup we dined on before its soothing richness put us to sleep.

I looked over to Katie above the peaks of the comforter that had migrated to my side. We needed to see the sunrise together. Not here, but I knew just the place.

Brushing my lips across Katie's forehead, I whispered, "I love you."

Katie blinked several times and smiled. She stretched and mouthed, "Me too."

"We're going to do time travel today," I said, nuzzling her face.

"Oh. What time is that?"

"It's five now, but I mean Roman time." I teased Katie awake with a feather I found on the nightstand.

Katie shook her head and opened her eyes wide. "Roman baths, what?"

"C'mon, we've got to get there for the sun's show."

❧❧❧❧

We were still groggy when we stood at number 49 Rue Monge in an old Rive Gauche neighborhood. Katie threw me a dirty look, asking whom we were visiting at this ungodly hour. "I thought you said sunrise."

"Open the door. Go on," I urged.

Katie slowly twisted the large brass doorknob. She jumped back, rubbing her eyes.

"Where am I?" Katie's eyes opened wide with fear—or wonderment or panic. I couldn't tell.

We stood before a first-century Roman arena, Les Arènes de Lutèce, which in the gray pre-dawn set an eerie stage more fitting for a tragedy than for a sunrise ceremony.

"Really, where are we?" Katie shook herself. "Am I dreaming?"

I put my arm around her shoulders as I reassured her and led her into the arena.

"No, sweetie, you're really seeing these ruins. We're here to catch the sunrise."

Katie tucked her head into my embrace. When she lifted her head, eyes open, she wore that look of love, which melted every cell in my body.

"God, it's beautiful—and so are you."

We walked along rows of stone bleachers and sat facing the east. Gardens framing the outside rim of the arena soon wore a golden hue. We sat snuggled together as the pinkish-yellow glow bathed the frosty sky, the opening act for the sudden burst of orange. We applauded the sun's performance.

Katie kissed me softly, murmuring, "You bring me the sun every day, every minute."

I rubbed her head, so happy that we could witness this show in these ruins. I didn't want to do a history lesson, but I found myself blabbing about how this used to be an evil place, where the powerful witnessed gladiator fights and Greek tragedies while slaves and prisoners awaited their fate. I pointed out the cages beneath the bleachers.

"I could lock you up and lose the key," I said with a cunning smile.

"Is that what you really want for me?" Katie chewed her lip. "Sorry, that was mean."

"Creep," I cried before chasing her around the center of the arena. We fell over laughing.

"I'm sorry, Pin, you were beginning to drone on. And all I wanted was to pledge undying, eternal, faithful love to you, up there, on that stage area."

I laughed, running to the stage with Katie, but my conscience was echoing her word *faithful*. Shoot! I still had my doubts about what Cassia and I had done.

Katie and I hugged on the stage and renewed our old vows from our blood sister days in Maine.

"I am yours," Katie said.

"I am yours, and you are mine," I answered.

I told Katie I really needed a few minutes by myself to chew on everything Père Sablé had said to me. Katie's lingering look of affection as she wandered off to explore the arena sent a deep shiver of love—and guilt—through me.

I went off to sit on a bleacher all alone, no one in sight. Yet I had this sense of exposing myself in front of the ancient crowd of fifteen thousand spectators.

Undying, eternal, faithful: the words stuck in my throat. Was I a liar? I couldn't answer that question. I didn't really know what Cassia and I did. Nothing, I hoped. I mean, I wouldn't have...but I sort of wanted...I did.

Hmm. I did think she was cute and exciting. I really did have to tell Katie. I was not a cheat. That word made me gag. Did *fraud* fit me better?

Man. I had to decipher Père Sablé's whole long speech about forgiveness and redemption, about taming people with love. If you did, you were kind of responsible for them. Like him and Mère Paul.

Well, that was what Katie and I did for each other. I had to trust that Katie could forgive me if...I got up and started to pace.

I couldn't think. He was daring me to go deeper. Like, could I believe in hope? Hope that people could redeem themselves, do the right thing?

This was crazy. Too much for this early.

I flopped down on the bleacher again. God, I was dense. All these people, Mère Paul, Père Sablé, Katie, Dorotea, even Cassia had given me the message that I deserved their love. I started to get it. If I couldn't trust myself to be lovable, then I couldn't trust other people.

All those people, there for me. Of course Craney hated me. Not one person rooting for her.

I was not Craney. That sounded friggin' crazy. But I wasn't crazy. I didn't take what I didn't deserve. And I was certainly not a cheat.

I knew what I had to do. Where was Katie now? I needed coffee, and I wanted it now.

I had been sitting on the bleachers so long, the crisp November air numbed my legs. I ran around the arena to warm up. My craving for hot coffee—satisfied! I saw Katie ease her way through the doors from Rue Monge, carrying two steaming cups of coffee and a bakery bag.

"You read my mind." I took a cup from her. "Let's go sit on the stage."

We leaned against the wall, snuggled side by side. Katie handed me the bag of croissants and sipped her café au lait.

"You all thought out?" she asked.

I swallowed hard, almost burning myself. I set my cup down and fanned my mouth to cool it off. Fanning my anxiety, too, since the words that needed to come out of my mouth were scorching the tip of my tongue.

"Katie." I sighed deeply. "I want to make another vow to you."

Katie turned to study my face. Her eyes darkened as she squinted first, then smiled. "Which one?"

Her gaze held me. I hoped I read forgiveness there, absolution without a confession.

I paced a few seconds and sat again. Katie wrinkled her forehead and reached over to me. "Pina, c'mon, now you're scaring me."

I squeezed her hand and whispered, "You know I love you."

"Yeah…"

I held up my hand. "Let me. I don't know if something happened with Cassia."

"Huh? I told you—"

"No, with me. We had a lot to drink, and uh…I found her in my bed late at night. I don't remember a thing."

Katie looked as if she were trying to identify Cassia. She squinted and started twisting her hair.

"Ah, is that what you meant when you said, 'Nothing happened, I *think*'?"

"Yes, when you laughed and said you trusted me."

I chewed on my lip when Katie turned her head away. Was she reviewing in her mind each word of *that* conversation?

"I laughed?"

"Yes, you were teasing me about worrying. I am not a liar. I should have told you everything that day. I wanted to, but—"

"You were scared I'd give you the silent treatment you gave me? When I didn't know if you'd ever believe me? If you'd forgive me or send me back to the States?"

"God, Katie, I am so sorry. For this and for scaring you like that. I should have believed you right away."

Katie dropped my hand and took a sip of coffee. I tried to pull apart the look she turned on me. Was she reminiscing about our past, all nine years of it? Was she writing the final chapter?

Katie took me by both shoulders and pulled me to her. She caressed my head and covered my face with soft kisses.

"How can I forgive what I don't know? And how can you punish yourself for something you can't remember?"

"Oh, Katie..."

Katie's eyes twinkled with that shit-eating grin. She smacked her lips, saying, "Must have been so scintillating, you couldn't remember it!"

I slapped Katie. "Stop! Please, please, just say the words—"

"I forgive you?" Katie dropped her clown mask

and took all of me in that look she gets. "Pina, I do forgive you."

We held each other for a long time, until magic white crystals kissed our noses. The surrounding trees already wore a light coat of winter white. I giggled, my body sensing every first snow I had experienced this way, with Katie, outdoors, totally open to receive it and everything coming our way.

Chapter Twenty-nine

Communication

On our way out of the arena, we noticed its historical plaque. It explained how the arena belonged to the past but also to the present and the future. Our present existed in the momentary life-stopping silence of snow.

After our breakfast of ham and cheese crêpes and crêpes oozing *marrons glacés* and whipped cream, we took the Métro back to the apartment.

Now that I had raised the sword of guilt far above our heads, so far that it reached the clouds—and maybe that was why it snowed—Katie and I felt freer. Freer to tease about being turned on by certain Frenchies on the Métro, by their tight dungarees and their clinging cashmeres. Freer to joke about which one of us would flirt with which one of them.

I loved this slightly bawdy side of Katie. Of course she would never play it out. Not really. I think. But I wasn't ready to play Truth or Consequences with this emerging lusty Katie.

When we arrived at the apartment, the concierge pointed to us, waving a letter.

"*Souvenez-vous! Pas de bruit!*" she reminded us.

I thanked her for the mail and agreed we'd walk on little pussy toes. Katie chuckled at my explanation and then beamed when she saw that the letter was from her father and Joe.

We settled on the daybed, where Katie started to read the letter out loud. She winked at me, saying, "No secrets!"

Dear Katie and Pina,

We hope you're enjoying Paris. We feel more comfortable knowing you're in the protective hands of Mère Paul and Père Sablé. At the recent Albert board of directors meeting, Mademoiselle Lesage told me so much about them and their connection with her father during the Resistance. Joe has also alerted his contacts in security services.

Speaking of connections and Fifi and his buddies, we can't divulge exact whereabouts, but your disappearing pal, A, with whom you used to share Vin Santo, will soon make an appearance. Go have fun.

We are so glad you two did the expedited academic program in two and a half years. Amazing! So that brings up the topic of future college plans. Katie's squared away, but, Pina—I may be pressuring you—I can get you where you need to go. Please don't drop your dreams to follow Katie's.

"Damn it, Katie, have you told him about our talks?"

"Not really, but he knows. He's always asking what college you're going to."

"Yeah, he's right. He is putting the screws to me."

"Can I finish reading?"

"Go on. Read."

Fifi is so looking forward to celebrating your successful sleuthing two years ago in Maine, as well as your early graduation from Albert. He wants us all to meet for Christmas in Pina's grandmother's village Giuliana, in Sicily. Her parents are set, as are Joe and myself. Of course the disappearing friend and Dorotea are welcome, as well as Mère Paul and Père Sablé.

We're also giving you an early gift. We will be sending you to a cooking school in Sicily for Thanksgiving. Invite friends from past Thanksgivings, if you like. We know it's short notice, only two weeks away. The info is on its way.

We love you, Katie, and you, Pina!

Love, Dad and Joe

Katie tossed the letter aside and yawned. "Do you have a clue?"

"About which part? The 'disappearing friend' is obviously Alda."

"Well, what about the cooking school?" Yawning again, Katie scratched her head.

"Sounds good to me—and mysterious."

Katie eased her way down on the daybed to a napping position. I wanted to talk with her about one more important thing before she conked out.

"Hey, sweetie," I said, wiggling my shoulders. "I'll make you a coffee, okay?" I hoped to arouse enough interest in either me or coffee that she would postpone her nap until I went out to talk to Cassia. "I need to tell you something else about Cassia."

She managed to pry one eyelid open.

Chapter Thirty

Fear Talking

Sipping our coffee as the midafternoon sun bathed the apartment with its fall haze, I saw Katie's face flicker between loving concern and anticipation.

"What else, Pina? What more is there to explain about Cassia?" Katie's tone sharpened. The tension in the air thickened.

"This isn't about you," I said. "Or me."

"Phew."

"Well, it is about me in a way. I have to forgive Cassia."

I also breathed out a sigh of relief when Katie reached over to take my hand. "Hey. How about I make a fire? Can it hold for a sec?"

As Katie lit some kindling and a small log, I watched the red-orange sparks and first flames lick the dry slivers. Katie's face took on a golden hue. My face softened, but my eyes burned big and tight. Something else was working its way to my surface.

When Katie sat back down at my side, we stayed quietly mesmerized by the crackling, shooting flames for a few minutes.

"Cassia…" I started, trying to stay focused on *that* topic. "I have to forgive her. Before you came, she told me how alone she felt, not just lonely. That aloneness, Katie, I've felt it. It's like when you're not with me."

Katie breathed deeply. I read impatience on her face and worried that she would interrupt me, initiating *that* conversation about my needing to be more independent. I hurried to finish my sentence, and as I did, my anger over Doc's letter almost bubbled over.

I stopped my explanation and started to stand to go see Cassia. Katie glanced up at me and quickly turned back to the fire.

"Sit!" she said, her voice tightening. She looked back up at me and offered me her hand.

The snap and pop of the sappy wood was the only sound breaking the thick silence. I sat.

"Go on," Katie said. "It's going to come out either now or in some explosion over a minor 'accident.'"

The cold tension rising up and progressively claiming every cell in my body eased as Katie touched my arm. I wasn't sure what I wanted to say or where I dared to begin.

"Is it because I told my father and Joe about our college conversation?" Katie almost gritted her teeth.

"Yeah. I think so. Maybe more."

"Go on." Katie leaned over to poke the fire.

"Gee, you get so pissed when I talk about wanting to protect us. I want us to continue as a couple; I thought you did, too."

"I do—"

"But?" I cut Katie off, piqued by a burst of simmering anger.

"Sweetie, you can't be my bodyguard at college. You've got to be your own!"

"Huh?"

"Don't you see?" Katie took my hand. "I love you, but I love you as you, not hovering over me, afraid I'll abandon you or someone will steal me away."

"Well, look at Cassia." I wiped a tear.

"Life happens, Pina, and life that doesn't happen dies."

Katie got up without warning and left the room. I feared the worst as the red shame of begging crept up my neck and cheeks. I closed my eyes and started breathing deeply. Katie came back in, smiling. She had some papers in her hand. Aw, shit, college applications? She eased herself down by my side and brushed her lips across my cheek.

She took my head in her arms, whispering, "Pina, honey, I am *not* breaking up with you. Stop it! All I'm saying is you have to grow. Otherwise—"

"I would stay stunted and die and kill our relationship."

This was the first time in a long time that we'd had a conversation like this. My esophagus seized up. Sour juices flooded my throat. My heart beat with a strange percussive rhythm. What I most feared was myself. I was so unlovable—of course Katie would abandon me. And here I was trying to hold on to her, and I was squeezing the life out of us.

Katie kept on petting my head and comforting me with her soft blue eyes.

"And then I would lose my sweet Pina, the Pina I fell in love with and love still..." Katie's voice trailed off as she shuffled through her papers.

"*This* Pina!" Katie held up one of the pages. "I wrote this in my diary ages ago. Please, stop crying."

I sniffled, I snorted, I swallowed hard. I wiped my nose on a shirt I thought was mine. Katie laughed at her snotty sleeve and mussed up my hair.

"I can listen now." I sat up.

"From my diary, December 26, 1959: 'Pina? What's to say? She's just Pina, like the sister I never had: a mirror of me—well, a part of me, the brave part, the part that stays in the shadows. Pina says what she thinks and dares to do the hard stuff. But then she can get all freaky and scared if she thinks I'm mad at her. Oh, and wow is she competitive, smart, good at what she does, whatever she does. And then there's the part that treats me the way I wish my mother had: caring, warm, safe, taking me in her coddling, strong arms, those huge hazel eyes beaming down on me, saying I'm perfect the way I am.' That's my Pina!"

I was a basket case again. Katie grabbed a box of tissues for me. "Do you need your mom's hankies?" We both laughed about my mother's stock of hankies, usually stashed in her bra or up her sleeve.

"Pina, that's who I want. My brave Pina who succeeds, even when—ahem *if*—she fails. You've always been a risk taker. C'mon. You can risk four years of college—"

"*Not* the college talk. No, this is enough."

"Okay, but—"

"Katie." I bit my lip and turned to look her full in the face. "Now you'll really want to leave me."

Katie sucked her teeth.

"I'm so afraid I'm just like Craney, a lecherous, evil thing!" I pounded the floor and just wailed.

"Jeez! No."

"I mean, I wanted you physically."

"Oh, Pina..."

"Well, are you totally cool with this lesbian thing?"

"Stop! Yes, I am. I've been reading a lot and"—Katie shook her head—"it's other people, our flipping, phony society telling us we're not *normal.* Look, here in Paris, everything is much more open, right?"

I stopped sobbing. "You're right." I started to picture girls I'd seen in the Métro. I thought about Mère Paul, too, hiding her affections. Well, I didn't want to be a nun.

"Hey." Katie slapped me upside the shoulder. "Remember that club you were talking about? Chez Moo-Moo or something."

"Chez Moune."

"Yeah, yeah. Well, we're going to go. You invite Cassia, and we'll make a date. You'll see who's not evil. But I-I am going to be a devil!"

Katie pushed me over and tickled me for a few seconds before tenderly holding my face and kissing me deeply.

Our lovemaking was brief but passionate. It felt free and mutual, far from the desperate and cloying way I had been feeling.

As I got ready to see Cassia, I became more and more curious about Chez Moune. I couldn't wait to see more local lesbian color.

Katie helped me with my jacket, cackling, "You sure you don't need a Craney cloak? Ha! Ha! Ha!"

I grabbed her by the waist and bit her somewhat gingerly on the throat. I croaked back, "All the better to eat you, my dear!"

As I turned the doorknob, Katie stroked my head. "Forgive yourself, Pin."

Chapter Thirty-one

Relief

As I approached the Métro, I tried to process one thought at a time. Flashes of black academic gowns superimposed themselves on images of Cassia as Cupid.

I focused on the delicious smells wafting through the vents in the bakery door. Almond paste melting with butter through paper-thin layers of flake pastry. I could almost savor the custard of the Gâtinois cake on the presentation platter displayed in the slightly fogged-up window.

In the Métro, I'd caught a fleeting glimpse of a youngish Muslim girl in a black *abaya* robe. My mind immediately flew to Craney, imagining her at my age. Had she always been out for sex? I pinched myself. I had to concentrate on the person—any person—who looked the least like a naked cupid or an arthritic, evil monk. I was neither Cassia nor Craney; I needed no reminders of whom I had to deal with. *But* I had to forgive Cassia.

At the foyer, I took the stairs slowly and quietly. I knocked lightly on Cassia's door and entered.

Cassia, who had been propped up on the bed reading *Les liaisons dangereuses*, sat up, eyes wide, hand to her mouth. She lowered her head into the crook of her arm. After a deafening silence, she mumbled, "I hide my head in shame."

I took a few steps into the room, stuck. I didn't want to touch her, and I hadn't prepared anything to say.

"Look up," I whispered, smiling more with my eyes than with my lips. I shook my head. "Shame is no good." I wrinkled my nose. "It stinks!"

"But…" Cassia lifted her head. Her eyes begged forgiveness.

I sat on the edge of my bed, facing Cassia. "I should have told you that we wouldn't be staying here. Sooner. That was unkind of me." I leaned over to hand her tissues.

A flood of garbled French started to pour forth from her mouth. I put up my hand.

Cassia stopped for a moment and managed to squeeze out, "But I was wrong, and I am truly sorry."

She got up, removed Katie's picture from the wall, and handed it to me. "I didn't deserve your trust."

"Cassia, shush. You deserve good, trusting friends. You've got to reach out and ask for love. But first—believe with your whole heart you deserve it. That takes guts. I know about that…" I let my voice trail off. My conversation with Katie was fresh on my mind.

"So, you are not hating me?"

"No. Katie and I both like you and forgive you. I remember everything you said—about your family. You do deserve good things."

"Really?"

"Yes, my dear." I leaned over to pat her hand. "And Katie and I are going to take you out. Do you know where?"

"To confession?"

I rolled my eyes and whispered, "Chez Moune!"

"*Hein?*"

"We are going to take you to a club, a *lesbian* club, if you like."

Cassia was jumping up and down, grinning like a fool. She ran to her closet, pulling out outfits and flashing them in front of me.

"I take it you like this idea?" I laughed.

"*Ah, oui!* And maybe—"

"Yes, just maybe you will meet a charming person who will see how charming you are!"

"Oh. I love you! Oh, no, I mean, *je t'aime bien!*"

"Thank you for clearing that up. Don't want your new potential girlfriend to be jealous."

"But I do love your friendship. Thank you, Pina."

I finally hugged Cassia. She cried on my shoulder. I told her we would call her soon. As I started to turn the doorknob, Mère Paul peeked in.

"*Ah, bien!* Come walk with me," she said.

Outside in the garden, Mère Paul took my arm. She looked deeply into my eyes, assessing. "You are not sleeping well, eh?"

I started to fudge, but she shook her finger at me, touching the side of her nose. "I can tell. I know the look."

I sighed and nodded.

"I have herbs. Come." She pulled us along into the main building and up the stairs.

Mère Paul took me to her barren cell. A cot-like bed covered in a rough, off-white woolen blanket, flanked by two plain wooden tables took up most of the room. A small crucifix hung on the wall above the bed. A short tower of books almost concealed—or protected—an old photo of Père Sablé in rough clothes out in the hills and another photo of a woman with very short hair and old men's clothing. Both photos were vintage 1940s.

Mère Paul pointed to the pictures. "I learned love there in the Résistance, and I carry the marks, all the marks of love and of the Résistance with me forever. The love helps. I know about dreams and pain, not just the physical kind, and the fear that creeps in at night. Ha! I still hear those shells going off around us—and sometimes into us."

I nodded, afraid that if I opened my mouth to say anything, I would cry. She somehow knew about my nights, my fears, and my angry outbursts. Maybe Cassia…

"You need these *millepertuis* herbs." She handed me a bag of dried green and yellow leaves. "And you must do a prayer—not a Jesus prayer, if you don't like, but a kind of mind prayer. You know?"

"*Merci mille fois.*"

She patted me on the shoulder. "Shush. You don't have to thank me. The tea from this will help calm you so you will be able to see your path."

I smiled. I could risk speaking now. "You and Père Sablé, you are showing me a path." I put my hand on my heart and bowed my head in a quick nod.

"Oh," she said with a twinkle in her eye, "you now have a vocation?" She guffawed and slapped me on the back. She put her finger to her lips, saying, "No more words. Go. We are watching out for you."

I almost flew home. My pockets were full of these herbs to help me sleep and to calm down. Mère Paul had shared beautiful things with me about love. *And* I began to feel safe. Thanksgiving was still almost two weeks away, but I had a lot to be thankful for in the here and now.

Chapter Thirty-two

Alda

I tiptoed into the apartment, afraid that Katie was still sleeping. An orange cast with occasional cream yellow flickers enveloped the main room. These shades were alive with fragrance as aromas of melting Gruyère and sweating caramelized onions drifted on the waves of heat from the fireplace. Katie appeared from the kitchen, bathed in the glow flooding the room and carrying two bowls of steaming onion soup.

I yelled, "Success!"

Katie nodded at the bowls and responded, "Success!"

She set the bowls in front of the blazing fire lighting up the room as some stars made their presence known in the darkening sky outside our windows. I hugged Katie, marveling at her newfound culinary skills.

She patted my bulging pockets. "What is that?"

"I'll show you, but let's eat first. I'm drooling." I patted her hand.

We blew on the soup and pulled apart threads of the crispy, bubbling cheese. This was wonderful. I dared to look at Katie. "We're playing house."

"I know, just what you've always wanted." Katie quickly laughed, probably so I wouldn't start up about moving in together when she left for college.

I let it pass. I just wanted this tranquil scene to continue and to share my good news. I sipped some of the broth before removing one of the bags of herbs from my pocket.

"This might be the answer to all my problems." I shook the loose herbs in the bag.

Katie pulled a phony pout, saying, "And I thought I was."

I pushed her gently. "Go on, keep it up. You'll see." I put on my most serious face, announcing, "Overnight, this bag will make me the only thing you desire."

Katie wrinkled her brow.

"Seriously, these herbs may calm me down, so I can sleep, so I don't have to panic every time someone looks in my direction. And you know, my weird dreams—not the grandma ones, but the flashbacks—well, they might go away."

"You're serious, right?" Katie put her bowl down and sighed. "Oh, man, that would be such a relief. Tell me more."

I talked about Mère Paul and how these herbs helped her, explaining the symptoms I thought Mère Paul was describing as *fatigue de combat* from the Résistance.

"Battle fatigue?"

"Right. Mère Paul was talking about the creepy stuff, the dreams, the weird attacks of anger over nothing...all tied to some event that really shocked all of a person's senses."

"Like a mugging or...Craney?"

"Yeah. I'm going to make some of this right now."

Katie leaned over to stroke my cheek. "I hope it

works. I really do."

I got up to boil water. As Katie cleared the bowls, she slapped her forehead. "Jeez! I almost forgot. Look, Pina."

I quickly turned away from the two-burner gas stovetop and almost crashed into Katie. She was waving a note at me.

I took a sip of my tea and exaggerated calmness. I slurred, "Wha izit?"

"Let's go sit down and find out," she said, breaking the seal. "Someone slipped it under the door, and when I looked out, no one was there."

As we went to sit back down by the fire, Katie squealed, "My God, it's from Alda."

I propped us up with pillows as we both deciphered Alda's loopy, fancy penmanship.

My dears,

I am nearby in a Sicilian monastery as a witness. No, not a Jehovah, and no, I haven't found my calling, just a safe haven, so the other big boss, not God, can't reach me. You will learn the details when you arrive.

Katie's dad asked me (through my indirect channels!) to research this Sicilian cooking school called Gangivecchio, and they reserved the Casa D'Annunziata for you.

Doc has arranged transportation to this safe *dolce vita* refuge. It will be the location of your Thanksgiving 1961.

I love you two,
Alda

"Wow!" I shouted. "It's going to happen. We'll see her there, I'm sure."

"Maybe. Same old Alda. *And* she's telling us it's safe, *and* she's been there for a while."

In my mind, I was already planning my trip, but I felt somewhat calmer. I didn't have to get up and pack right away, *and* I wasn't worried about Craney, even though she was supposed to be in Italy. Besides, Sicily wasn't really in Italy, according to mainland Italians.

Katie interrupted my thoughts. She leaned over and kissed my eyelids, which were almost at half-mast.

"Sweetie, you're almost asleep. Your tea's working." Katie helped me get up off the floor. "Off to la-la land with you."

Katie kissed me and started to shut off the light. When she saw my one eyebrow raised, she added, "Yes, we'll plan the Chez Moune club excursion tomorrow morning."

I managed to say, "All's well with Cassia," before a gentle snore sneaked up on me and escaped from my mouth.

Chapter Thirty-three

Chez Moune

School had become almost an afterthought. I went most of the time, but my real focus was on Katie, my friends, and upcoming trips and excursions. I was totally wired about going to Chez Moune and cut out of school early to get ready for the evening's fun. A part of me was also a bit tense: I had never been to a real lesbian bar, even in the States.

Cassia met us at the apartment since it was close to the club in Pigalle. She oohed and ahhed over the fireplace and the antique furnishings. While I was busy putting the finishing touches on my outfit—I would dress in *nouveau beat*: a paint-spattered denim smock, dungarees, and a silk neckerchief—I overheard Cassia speaking to Katie in English.

"Oh, Katie, I must apologize, please."

I heard Katie try to brush it off as nothing.

"I insist," said Cassia, "that you listen. I was in the wrong. I confess I did not know how to appreciate you from afar. I am, as you say, new to this."

Cassia was sobbing as Katie finally made some soothing sounds and apparently offered her some tissues. After several seconds while Cassia blew her nose, Katie said, "It's okay. Believe me—it's really okay. No harm done."

When I walked back into the room, I saw Katie

place an innocent hand on Cassia's shoulder and Cassia touch Katie's hand. "I see why Pina loves you so much. You are too good." She beamed.

I guffawed, "Aha! No, she is the devil incarnate. Watch!"

I tickled Katie, who said, "Yes, I promised I would be diabolical tonight and curse the person who didn't fall for you at the club, Cassia."

Cassia laughed hysterically. "You really think you can scare up a lady for me?"

I smirked. "Well, maybe not a lady—maybe a sweet chickie."

❧ ❧ ❧ ❧

It was dark and cold outside. We walked briskly. Katie wore an old tux and a worn skin coat, both of which we found at the Marché aux Puces. Cassia was the height of femininity in a flared organza dress with a wide white collar. She looked too pixieish in the high-fashion dress than we imagined for a lesbian bar. As we neared Place Pigalle, we found a secondhand shop where Cassia exchanged her clothes for a type of sailor suit with a low-cut midi blouse. She also wore a French sailor's cap placed jauntily at a slant.

The music, old accordion tunes pouring forth from some doorways and old jazz licks from others, told us we were approaching Pigalle. A few streetwalkers darted from tiny alleyways, and neon bulbs began to decorate entranceways to sleazy-looking bars. Barkers winked at us but pulled at guys' arms, hawking dancers with naked breasts, pasties, and fig leaves.

We all started walking closer to one another, a strange trio: a beat, a tux, and a sailor girl. The looks we exchanged reeked of doubt when we all but stumbled into a large bouncer-type man/woman/being—we didn't quite know. The voice said years of smoking Gauloises mixed with early morning cognac. The breasts said woman. The muscle said, "Don't mess with me!"

She eyed us over and nodded. "*Dix-huit ans?*" She asked whether we were legal.

I nodded and slipped her a ten-franc bill. Winking, she said to Katie and me, "*Amusez-vous bien,*" and to Cassia, obviously single, "*Bonne chance!*"

The room was decorated in early cathouse. Red velour drapes with gold filigree-encrusted tassels framed the stage. Red isinglass-paneled lanterns sat on tables in the midst of molded black-and-red-satin booths arranged in tight clusters. Off to the back, a cave-like alcove offered a private area. We only guessed it was occupied from the intermittent flickers of candlelight on writhing forms.

A buxom waitress escorted us to a table, sliding her hand down along my back past my waist. She lowered her lashes at me, saying, "For you, I have a tight table." I wasn't sure I had translated correctly, but I immediately pulled Cassia and Katie down beside me.

Waves of circus-like music came from backstage, where they were rehearsing the show. Patrons milled about—older, younger, some in austere, tight men's suits with carnation boutonnieres and red satin ascots. Others wore dramatic Chanel-type lady's suits, while still others sporting extreme crew cuts wore worker-blue overalls.

A sweet youngish girl in a clingy turtleneck and an artichoke haircut nursed a Vichy water while cruising our table.

As the lights dimmed and the curtain rose, I nudged Cassia, saying, "A chickie for you." Even in the semi-darkness, I saw the crimson rise to her cheeks.

A vaudeville number with full-breasted women and women dressed as male pimps premiered. Debonair younger women dressed as men rescued the damsels, seemingly in distress from the exploiting lechers. The emcee, dressed in an impeccably tailored tux, thanked everyone and introduced the next act, an Édith Piaf look-alike. Cat whistles welcomed her, and shouts of "*Je t'aime*" echoed throughout the room.

I noticed the sounds of shifting about in our booth and caught a glimpse of the sweet chickie easing into the narrow space next to Cassia. I didn't hear any protest.

As the last notes of the song *Non, je ne regrette rien* faded away, several women sobbed quietly as their dates handed them their handkerchiefs. Katie and I gawked at some of the guests, as we had only read about the early lesbian scenes in the States.

During the intermission, Cassia's friend introduced herself as Sophie. She appeared a bit shy and admitted her reluctance to stay.

"I do not know my way here. I am a student, and these are much older people," she said, sneaking sidelong glances at Cassia.

I started to ask about discrimination when Katie kicked me under the table. So, I just nodded, saying, "Oh, Cassia, like you!"

Cassia almost hid under the table, but Sophie gently placed her hand on Cassia's similarly cut hair and said, "Yes, a student just like you."

Cassia seemed speechless. I shot her a look,

begging her with my eyes to say *something*.

Katie said, "Yeah, Cassia, you two have the same haircut, maybe from the same salon."

Finally, Cassia opened her mouth. "*Oui*, I have a haircut…"

We all giggled, and sweet Sophie cooed, "And I love it."

Cassia sighed. "Oh, yours is so much more *chouette*."

Ah, there was that word again. At least the two of them were cool with each other's hairdo. I glanced over to see them laughing at Cassia's outfit while Sophie pulled another turtleneck from her bag. The two of them disappeared, apparently for Cassia to change her top.

The show resumed for a short time, and then a slow song was announced. The emcee reminded us that only one dance was allowed, and if the *flics* came, the music would change, and we would have to pretend we were learning the minuet.

The slow song was an old forties tune by the Ink Spots. People partnered up, and as *If I Didn't Care* began, the butches—I was just learning the terminology—started pressing their large-buckled belts into their skirt-wearing femmes for a slow grind. A few dancers paused up against the wall, and murmurs of "*embrasse-moi*" and "*encore*" almost drowned out the music.

Katie commented that they could have updated to Connie Francis's version to really get in the groove. I almost spit out my Schweppes when she suggested we do a tango. I was somewhat intimidated by these women who had the courage to risk police raids night after night. Where was mine?

There were those prickly sensations—the ones that often tingled right before I asked myself *those* questions about my cowardice and my queerness. And my badness. I started thinking I'd have to drink a lot more of those herbs when I heard Katie ask where Cassia was.

We couldn't see her. After we combed the place almost until it shuttered, we went outside. Neither Cassia nor Sophie was anywhere in sight.

As we ventured into the back alley, through a few squirming couples, Katie turned to check me out. "Are you worried that something—"

"No," I answered immediately. "I think Sophie's safe."

Katie gritted her teeth. "I mean, you have that look on your face. Could someone like Craney be messing with you?"

I stared hard at Katie. She did take my Craney phobia seriously, but I was feeling quite calm about Craney now. It was just the other stuff.

"I really don't think Craney has anything to do with this."

Katie still wore a worried look until one of the huddled couples slowly inched apart and, bleary-eyed, started checking their watches. There were Sophie and Cassia, fine—a bit disheveled but fine.

"Oh, sorry," Katie said, seeing their blushing and startled faces. "You missed the dance."

"We lost track," said Sophie.

"*Pas de problème.*" I reassured them everything was cool.

Cassia pulled me aside. She cleared her throat and whispered, "How to say this…"

"Go ahead. I have a good idea what's on your

mind."

"Do you think we could stay in your extra bedroom tonight?"

I stifled a laugh. "Sure, *mais pas de bruit*." I reminded her of the concierge's warning about noise.

We took a taxi home, with Katie and me sitting up front. We thought we heard some smooching coming from the backseat and kept up a scintillating conversation with the driver about late-night traffic.

Katie and I showed Cassia and Sophie to their room and, grinning widely, repeated, *"Pas de bruit."* We wished them a good night and shut the door.

❧❧❧❧

I sat up terrified in the totally darkened room. It was three in the morning. Craney had worked her way back into my dream. Shit. What did I have to do to be free of her? This was a new version of her, dressed in long black pants with a stripe down the leg and a high-notch-collared, starched white shirt closed with a black satin bowtie. Her cutaway jacket was skintight and only parted at the waist to reveal a huge silver belt buckle with a stylized Nazi eagle embossed on it. She pulled me onto the dance floor as eerie xylophone-like music played. I felt the imprint of her eagle in my groin as she thrust me into this deadly tango with her bony hips. In my sleep, I went berserk, desperate to scratch Craney's eyes out. I almost succeeded—unfortunately, it was Katie I almost mauled.

Katie startled but caught my flailing arms in time. She held me, rocking me, whispering I was in her arms and safe. "You're good, Pina. We are good. No worries." She said it over and over as if it was a mantra—maybe what Mère Paul called a mind prayer. She made me whisper those words with her. When I started to say Craney's name, Katie put a finger to my lips, saying, "No. Not tonight. Not here."

⁂

For breakfast, Katie and I served sparkling cider with the brioches and croissants Katie had run out to get. Cassia and Sophie emerged from the room looking as if they had already been drinking. Their moods were equally bubbly and their cheeks totally flushed.

Cassia gushed her thanks to Katie and me while Sophie recited Jacques Prévert's poem *Déjeuner du matin* and apologized that it was not a happy poem but the only poem she knew about breakfast. We toasted to friendship and love. Finally, a bleary-eyed Cassia shouted, "Yes, love triumphs hate!" and collapsed, crying tears of joy and exhaustion.

We all applauded and ate our fill until the happy couple returned to the room to, as they said, "straighten up." They re-emerged after an hour, claiming it was sufficiently clean now, thanked us, and left, floating on air.

⁂

As the sun continued to pour into the apartment after Cassia and Sophie left, we continued munching. The late night and early morning events finally caught up with us, and I fell asleep on the daybed, only to feel Katie join me a short while later. I woke up to Katie fanning me with a thin package.

"Maybe the instructions to the kingdom of Sicily."

Katie wiggled the envelope and did a little dance.

I yawned. "Can we wait until I'm really awake to open that? I need some water."

Katie brought me a glass of water, giggling about our success with Cassia.

"We really did work magic, didn't we?"

"I wasn't sure we would survive our walk through Pigalle. That was far from magical!" Katie groaned.

I yawned again. "Just locally colorful. But what a hoot, huh, that club?" I wiggled my torso in front of Katie.

"Uh, c'mon, Pina, tell me what you really think about Chez Moune."

"Well, I didn't know it was a cabaret."

"Oh, and I know how you just love musicals. But c'mon, I saw that look on your face during the dance."

"Oh, that one…" I flicked crumbs off the daybed.

"Damn, you're stubborn." Katie scratched her head hard. "You think I don't see, and then you go and have that ugly dream. All that fear and ugliness bottled up inside ferment and from that damned underworld, pop your friggin' cork. And you bawl that you're bad."

"I, uh…" I had a knot in my stomach. That was what I knew, and I knew that Katie was right. "Katie, every time I go to say this to you, I get scared that that's how you'll see me."

"Well, shoot! If you really see yourself that way—the little you said about the dream was obvious." Then Katie took my hand. "I'm not mad at you. Please don't start to cry. I just hate your beating yourself up. You ask me to take care of you while you tell me you're not worth it. Pina, look at me!"

Katie shook me until I put words to my fears. "I know what the dream says. It's pretty clear: I'm as dirty and as ugly as Craney—"

"And you're destroying yourself as you try to destroy Craney." Katie finished my sentence as she drew me to her.

I lay my head in Katie's lap, convulsed in tears.

"You'll never be old and ugly. You're good and wholesome, but, sweetie, *you* have to believe you're not bad. Love is not bad."

"I know, I know," I mumbled. "I've got to go back to that club and dance. I know that sounds crazy, but when we come back from Sicily…"

"We will, we really will. And no, that's not crazy at all."

I sat up and dried my tears. "Besides, Craney has bad taste in clothes."

"Huh?"

After I described in minute detail every article of clothing and accessory that Craney wore in my dream, we laughed. Maybe it was a good dose of comic relief, but the image of Dracula crossed with a Nazi scientist brought good tears to our eyes.

"C'mon," Katie said, "let's look at my father's package."

"Boy, am I ready for that!"

We sat on the floor in front of the fireplace and tore open the package. Tickets, photos, maps, vouchers, all fanned out across the floor. It was all there: the three-page plane tickets from Le Bourget, Paris to Rome; Rome to Catania, Sicily; the hired car to pick us up; and the best news—we'd be leaving in two days.

Katie flashed me an old black and white photo of the cooking school at the monastery and the stone house, Casa D'Annunziata at Gangivecchio. Blotting a single tear, Katie read Doc's words. "*Baci, baci, baci* from all of us. We've seen to it that you'll be safe, and we regret that we can't be there to celebrate Thanksgiving with you. But at Christmas…"

I put my arm around Katie's shoulder, laughing. "God, they're great."

Katie waved the letter. She sniffled. "I'll go write a thank-you. We'll clean up later."

I looked up at Katie, my eyes dancing with glee and gratitude.

I leaned my head back against the wall, smiling at the dimming rays of the sun still bathing the apartment. I was upbeat and grateful—now. And the upcoming Thanksgiving trip and reunion with Dorotea and Alda excited me and promised to be reasonably safe.

Chapter Thirty-four

Pre-Thanksgiving

Katie and I had been planning and packing for Sicily most of the morning. Tomorrow was the big day. We had an early departure in the morning, so we went to bed shortly after dark. We were so excited that we slept fitfully and briefly. We hoped we could cuddle and nap a bit on the plane before arriving in Rome.

After the short drive to Le Bourget, we cleared through all the formalities in the small airport and stood admiring the Alitalia propjet that we would soon board. We joked about our first plane ride together two years before and the physical exhilaration of the acceleration and thrust we experienced *up front* and personally.

"Do you think…?"

"Exactly what I was planning." I fluttered my eyelashes coyly at Katie.

Katie slapped me gently as we lined up to board. We took the two seats in the last row and immediately covered ourselves with the forest green Alitalia blanket. We held hands and undressed each other with lingering glances. Although it was early, I was already excited.

Katie laughed, reminiscing, "Poor us. Back then, we thought we'd be going directly to our own dorm room upon arrival after all that precoital buildup."

"That was before Dorotea and Alda."

"Talk about sexual frustration!" Katie quipped.

"What did you know, oh, virginal one?"

"Speak for yourself, toots." Katie combed my body with her seductive look.

"Shush. I think we're about to do countdown. Ready for takeoff?"

Katie passed her hand gently over my torso. I took a deep breath as the plane accelerated faster and faster, its thrust pushing us back against the seat while it propelled our insides forward and held them there, suspended. Suspended until it was no longer possible to go faster, higher, tighter, and then, the final burst. Katie and I looked at each other, mouths open, speechless. It happened again just like the first time two years ago, and all our parts were smiling!

Our deep breathing became more regular and smooth. Our soft, open gaze became even softer as our eyes slowly blinked closed. Whatever was left of our energy dissipated, leaving us asleep before any stewardess could inquire about our needs. We had already done a good job seeing to our own needs.

I drifted off to dreamland. I was away at college, or rather I was away with Katie, who attended college. I attended to Katie's needs. She had the best outfits, crisp and clean, and she indulged in gourmet meals lovingly prepared by none other than me. Awaiting her arrival after class, I prepared something cold for her to drink and a few canapés served on the best Limoges and Waterford. And I delivered all this with a beatific smile on my face, a smile destined for only Katie. After dinner, Katie entertained me with the latest scientific theories and the most astute political arguments. Our life was ideal.

In my dream, I did appear somewhat shorter and visibly younger. I experienced difficulty following some of Katie's discussions and developed a nervous tic. In an attempt not to push Katie away, I struggled to hide my emerging imperfections. I worried, though, that I was regressing and signed up for spousal counseling. They prescribed a bottle of individuation pills and the film *I Want to Live!* with Susan Hayward. They said my disorder wasn't necessarily fatal, but…

I woke up in a sweat. I glanced over at Katie, who appeared lost in thought. I tugged on her sleeve. "You awake?"

"Yeah. Heard you talking. Mumbling about 'my heart's desire for dinner.'"

"Right. I was dreaming about college."

"Oh, Pin, that's great. Man, you're finally willing to talk about it. Whoa! Where?"

"Where what? At your place."

"But I haven't decided whether I want to go to Berkeley, Stanford, or Vassar. It's kind of late, but my father could help you."

"Damn it! I don't want your father's help. I just want yours."

"Okay, cool it. I don't want other people to hear. What do you want me to do about your college?"

"*My* college? No, this is about you."

"All right. You have totally lost me. What the hell is going on, and please keep it low."

"I just want us to move in together. That's what my dream was about."

"Oh…And they lived happily ever after?" Katie's cheeks flushed a brighter shade of crimson. She closed her eyes and sighed loudly.

"You don't have to be so sarcastic. I know you

don't want that."

Katie breathed deeply. "I want you to be a star. I want you to grow, too. I want to be able to love you when we're seventy-five because we're both full of life and smart and dynamic, not die-namic! Can't you see that?"

"Damn it! Yeah. In my friggin' dream, they sent me to a shrink because I was going backwards. They gave me individuation pills. I think I've heard that term in my Human Behavior class. And I'm supposed to watch an old movie called *I Want to Live!* There, are you happy?"

"Oh, sweetie, it sounds like a nightmare. I'm not abandoning you, but I certainly don't want a maidservant or a mascot. I want an equal. You, my dear, have all the qualifications *if* you'll get off your derrière and move on with your life. Oh, shoot, Pina, please don't cry."

I took several deep breaths and wiped the tear beginning to form. I choked back a few silent sobs, blubbering, "I have to work on this, I know. It's really hard. Like I don't deserve to—"

"Say it, Pina. *Live!* Yes, but it's got to be for you, not for me."

"Okay, okay. That's all I can hear right now." I bit my lip.

Katie took my hand and caressed me with her gaze—for about five minutes—and then grinned like a fool, pulling me over to her, calling me her beloved doofus.

We were quiet, just craning our necks to catch glimpses of Roman monuments as we circled Fiumicino Airport. As the plane veered tightly to the right, Katie leaned into me and sneaked a kiss on my neck, pretending to get a better peek through the window. We thought we spotted the Forum and the Colosseum, and then, almost without warning, we were on the ground with a lackluster landing.

We didn't have much time before boarding the small plane for Catania, just time enough to be and wowed by the luscious women with wavy dark hair, all somewhat resembling our Alda. Most men wore their suit jackets draped over their shoulders; some walked arm in arm with their friends; some even held hands. Most likely none was homosexual.

We looked forward to the next flight in an even smaller plane and boarded as soon as the agents announced the plane was ready. The flight was brief, our altitude fairly low. We could actually appreciate the boot and toe of Italy. And then the triangular Sicilian island appeared swimming in aquamarine waters. Etna spoke for herself in smoke and plumes in one of her frequent eruptions.

Once on the ground, we located our driver, who wasted no time loading us and our belongings before speeding off. Etna lit up the sky in an orange haze, thick with particles of ash. Other mountaintops still possessed their mostly intact castles, and shepherds still herded their sheep on the sides of roads. We were under Sicily's spell.

Beautiful and magical, this view, and finally I was here for real, here where my ancestors had lived. How far we Mazzinis had come on our journey as immigrants, and here I was, free to travel back and forth, with (Doc's) money and education backing me. Somehow, those two words, *journey* and *education*, set off an itching in my mind. What was it Craney had said about journeys? Right, she had called me a kindred spirit, a crane person from Chinese mythology, a person who could magically transform into a crane and fly away on journeys. Shoot! She even called me her fledgling, who she wanted to take under her wing. She could have protected me; she could have. Whatever happened to that lofty vision she'd had of herself? When did it shatter into a broken, eerie jigsaw puzzle of pure lust and power?

Shaking my head to sweep away the image of a broken mirror, I focused on the almost crimson rays of the setting sun and forced myself to peer over the edge of narrow, precipitous shoulders. Craney was gone; I remained.

I had a hard time staying awake through all the hairpin turns and narrow passes. Occasionally, a sign broke through the fog with names of towns we'd heard Fifi visited in the past to locate a *strega*. I joked that maybe a *strega* could give me some herbs to help with my individuation illness. Katie rolled her eyes at me. "Yeah. Maybe Alda is our local *strega*—a good witch."

As we entered the brick-walled estate of Gangivecchio, flanked with Italian pines and poplars, we became aware of the ancient red stone and stucco monastery off to the right. Pine and rosemary wafted on the gentle breeze as bells from the chapel tolled vespers.

The driver opened the door for us, and the chill of the early evening enveloped us. A dim light cast shadows from the upper windows of the monastery when a nearby lantern lit up our path. There at the end of the slate walk to an old stone cottage stood Alda, very much alive, larger than life itself, arms outspread, face glowing with the warmest, most loving smile imaginable. "*Ciao, care.* Hello, my dears."

Chapter Thirty-five

Catching Up at Gangivecchio

We hugged, we kissed, we jumped up and down. We hadn't seen each other since Thanksgiving two years ago, when Alda mysteriously had disappeared from Albert Academy. I patted Alda all over, as if testing to see that she was real.

"Yes, I am." she said with a stronger, sexier Italian accent than the one I recalled.

Katie smiled softly. She seemed to have no qualms about gently stroking Alda's cheek, unlike the Katie I knew a couple of years ago.

Alda clasped Katie's hand. "You're lovely as ever," she cooed. "But we must give our Pina an Italian haircut."

Katie roared out loud. While pulling disobedient strands from my ragged ponytail, Alda said, "This is passé!" Alda winked, adding that the witness protection thing had taught her a lot about changing styles and disguises. "But that is for another conversation! Come! I will show you Annunziata's cottage."

As we opened the cottage's small wooden door, we came upon a tiny kitchen twinkling with candles on the windowsills and on the table. An old ewer filled with asters decorated the rectangular farm table worn to a lustrous patina from several generations of Sicilians rolling pasta dough.

Alda showed us to our room. A canopy bed, topped with a tatted lace veil and covered with a cadet-blue satin duvet, stood against a stucco wall decorated with an oil of a Madonna and a cherub. The far corner boasted a beehive fireplace with its rounded hood and oval opening. All was stone, brick, and stucco. Gauzy curtains danced in a slight mountain breeze whispering through the small-paned window.

Alda helped us drop our bags and rushed us back to the kitchen. Handing each one of us a covered plate and a glass, she escorted us back to the canopy bed and made us close our eyes. We heard the pop of a cork and the sizzle and snap of paper and kindling catching the spark from a match.

"*Ecco!*" Alda cried out with a clap of her hands. "Open your eyes. Here it is."

She had prepared a blazing fire, plates of cannoli and struffoli, and Vin Santo.

"Now," she said. "I will tell you the story of my life, but first a toast." We clinked our glasses. "To Pina and Katie, who taught me friendship!"

We drank to that. I continued, "To Alda, may you forgive me for doubting you!"

Katie added, "For teaching me grace under fire."

We turned a quizzical look at Katie, who responded, "What? We really did accuse you of almost everything we couldn't explain."

We drank again.

Alda's tanned cheeks actually reddened as she broke into a subtle grin. "I never knew I was so powerful."

This new Alda—softer, quieter—still warmed our hearts with her deep-reaching, caring love, warmth, and acceptance. Her hair, now blond and straight, may have changed to conceal her dark Mediterranean loveliness, but her heart remained beating with her inner fullness and beauty.

"Come, let's eat," Alda invited us to the feast.

The cannoli were freshly made, the ricotta cream silken and sweetened just enough, the shells thin and crisp. No words could describe the smoothness and the mellow aging of the Vin Santo.

"Yes," Alda said without preface. "I have moved around—rather I have been moved around. Wolfie, my father, is hidden elsewhere. The family here, Giulia, Gina, and Lorenzo, have cared for me on and off since I was a child. Giulia is my good witch, you know, my *strega*. Gina and Lorenzo enchant me. I am in love, but I don't know with which one and in what way."

Katie's eyes shot open. "You don't mean you're… with both of them?"

"Oh, *cara*, even I am not that talented. No, it is as you say, precoital."

I almost choked on my cannoli shell. "Sounds like they're almost brother and sister to you," I said, winking at Katie, who had described me as the sister she never had.

"*Proprio!* And that is the question. Which one is the brotherly/sisterly love and which is romantic?"

"*Santo cielo!*" Katie remembered one of Alda's favorite expressions, a variation on "holy smokes!"

"But you? Pina? Katie?"

We kissed a virginal kiss to save words. I sighed then and rubbed my chin. "Well, you know, Craney and my anxiety are back. My herb tea helps me handle most of the regular anxiety, but Craney—"

"For now, Craney seems to be in northern Italy," Katie said.

"So I've heard. Sounds like the authorities are on

to her." Alda held out her hands in an Italian gesture that showed disdain for the Italian police. "But the Corsicans and the Americans—"

"*Grazie a Dio!*" I said.

We agreed to postpone any more serious talk until the next day when Dorotea would arrive. I lifted an eyebrow at Alda when she mentioned Dorotea's name.

"*Va bene?*"

"Yes, it's really okay between us. We've both grown up." Alda shrugged with a sheepish grin on her face.

"A lot." Katie and I both yelled out, feeling the Vin Santo flow through our veins.

We all fell asleep on the bed, bellies full, hearts warmed, and safe in our kinship. This was family. This was home.

❧ ❧ ❧ ❧

Early the next morning, warblers outside our window sang morning songs accompanied by the tolling of the old abbey bells. There was a vague dry crackling sound, which I imagined were acorns dropping on the tile roof. Vapors of pistachio crescent rolls and heated cream blended with the aroma of freshly ground coffee.

I opened my eyes when I heard a distinctly different bell tone ring out. A nearby bell tinkled, and I sensed filtered coffee wafting almost under my nose. Dorotea stood there, finger to her lips, extending a steaming cup of coffee to me. She silently motioned me outside to the kitchen.

A fire crackled in the kitchen hearth, and the table was set with both Sicilian and German breakfast treats. Dorotea hugged me hard. I took a sip of my coffee and took Dorotea by the arm to the outside patio.

"Here? So early?" I asked.

"Yes, I couldn't wait to see everyone, especially Alda."

I tried to read Dorotea, who had not been on the best of terms with Alda. "Have you had a chance to talk much?"

"Not really. But it is all good."

We walked through the grounds, the site of an archaeological dig dating back to the third century BC. Dorotea and I fondled some shards. She looked at me with softened eyes as she took my hand.

"You are okay?"

"Yes and no. I take herbs for the anxiety, St. John's wort."

"I like that you are so honest with me. You do seem better. And the *no*?"

"The nightmares of Craney are back. The angry outbursts are back."

"*Oh, schade!*" Dorotea said, stroking my cheek.

"Yes, it is a shame, but I have to learn to pray— well, not *pray* pray, but like meditation."

"Oh, yes, I know this. In Heidelberg Medical Faculty, they study different ways of healing. We will ask Alda for the library and read about this, *ja?*"

"I am so glad we're all here." I hugged Dorotea and wiped the tear that was threatening to fall from her eye.

"*Ja*, but *schnell*, we must make coffee for the others. Come."

As we turned to go back inside, Katie joined us, already holding a cup of coffee. She threw her arms around Dorotea and then kissed me quickly on the lips. We sat quietly on the patio watching the fog creep across the surrounding hills. A medieval tower pierced through the soup.

Dorotea spoke about the sentinel towers of hill villages in Europe. She said the villagers from the town with the tallest tower would build the fire to signal safety to all the friendly villages, to connect them in a web of kinship.

She winked. "Who builds our sentinel fire? Who is our tower? Hmm?"

Katie laughed. "Sorry, guys, I have no fire this morning. Ask me after my second cup of coffee."

I took Katie by the arm, whispering, "Let's send Alda out. Maybe she'll be the friendly fire starter."

"Ha!" Katie responded. "That would be in character—ah, I mean, the flamboyant part."

"Hey, D, we'll get more coffee going. Go commune with the ancient spirits."

Katie and I tiptoed back into the cottage and got into the bed on either side of Alda. We tickled her nose and fanned steaming coffee vapors toward her. She opened her eyes, smiling.

Katie put her fingers to her lips and handed Alda a cup of coffee. "Go claim your surprise outside. No questions asked."

Alda yawned and dragged herself out of bed and onto the patio through the bedroom's French doors. Pretending to go prepare more coffee, Katie and I hid behind the curtains to make sure things were all good between Alda and Dorotea.

We did see Alda immediately put her coffee down and run to hug Dorotea, who tolerated the hug, arms to her side. We didn't expect to see Alda's tears, subdued but flowing.

"Dorotea, I am so ashamed." Alda rubbed her watering eyes. Her voice lacked the old flamboyance and bravado. She took Dorotea's hand, insisting, "I was a bully, a thug. Like my father. And now there are consequences. Please..." She wiped wildly at her eyes.

Dorotea stroked Alda's new blond hair. "But what is this yellow? No more Italian tootsy look?" Dorotea chuckled. "Come, we were stupid then. I was so naïve and—how you say?—righteous-self?"

Alda looked up and chortled. "You? Self-righteous, ready to turn on Pina and me?"

Katie and I worried the tone might turn sour again. And then we heard Alda and Dorotea burst out laughing and squish each other in a bear hug.

"Come, we eat!" Dorotea commanded.

Food seemed to be the order of the day. Alda announced we would celebrate Thanksgiving later. Giulia, who was starting a cooking school here, would prepare the dinner with Gina and Lorenzo.

Alda toasted us with freshly squeezed blood orange juice, saying, "We will have a lot to be thankful for. Giulia makes magic with food and herbs. She makes love with her cooking; cooking is her prayer, her grace!"

Katie leaned over. "Pina, that's what you need."

Alda, Dorotea, and I shouted, "What?"

Alda got that old twinkle in her eye. "She needs to make love?"

Dorotea smirked. "*Nein, nein*, she needs magic."

We all groaned, but she continued, "Hush, hush, I mean, prayer magic—good magic."

Katie rolled her eyes. "You guys, she needs to cook."

"Uh-oh, you didn't like my dream about keeping

house for you." I guffawed, but Katie seemed to grit her teeth while Dorotea whispered, "Oops!"

Alda sat back, chewing some biscotti, and looked from right to left, checking us all out, one by one. "Eh? Why can't we do things Sicilian style? *Domani*, you know, tomorrow! There's plenty of time to talk tomorrow." She snapped her fingers and, in the Alda style of her former life, made a sweeping gesture and said, "I will fix everything *domani*."

We all laughed. Alda patted me on the shoulder, quietly saying, "Giulia will help you find the right herbs for you to cook up your solutions."

Katie smiled a warm, open smile at Alda, but her eyes gave away a hint of sadness.

Dorotea became serious, utterly serious for a few minutes, to remind us that tomorrow often brought separation and crisis. She recalled how the Berlin Wall had appeared overnight earlier this year. Alda dropped her gaze and nodded. Pulling on a strand of her hair, she said, "Who knows? I may have to change my blond hair to a new shade of red tomorrow and go hide as a witness in Timbuktu." She recovered immediately, flashing a broad grin. "No! *Domani* we go to Sperlinga, a nearby town settled by troglodytes."

"Troglodytes?" Katie and I asked, making goofy faces at Alda.

Dorotea yelled, "Cave dwellers."

"Oh, Pina." Katie's tone softened. "Is that okay? I mean, would it be too freaky to go to a cave after our catacombs scare?"

"No, I'm really feeling good about this. I sense Craney's not here. We are." I raised my orange juice triumphantly.

"*Grazie a Dio!*" exclaimed Alda.

Chapter Thirty-six

Giulla's Thanksgiving

As I started to clear the table, Alda placed her hand on my shoulder. "Stop, *cara*! You have important things to see Giulia about. The rest of us will do this." She held my chin in her hands. "My sweet, we all have to grow up."

I couldn't be angry. Her gaze held me tight. I knew she was right. She pointed with her chin in the direction of the abbey.

Walking through the fourteenth-century arch, I sensed a different atmosphere in the outer and inner courtyards. I imagined monastic life; everything here was poised to await a procession of men with tonsured heads and cloaked in sack cloth. Small cells lined the sides of the quad. A larger opening that emitted the smell of lilies and incense seemed to be the old chapel. I located the almost-bare kitchen at the far end of the courtyard opposite the loggia.

A somewhat round, full-cheeked woman raised her sparkling blue gaze as I entered, my heels striking the granite floor announcing me. She tossed her reddish-brown frizzy hair over her shoulder and wiped her tomato-stained hand on the white apron around her waist.

"*Ave! Buon giorno! Pina, si? Che piacere!*"

"*Sì.* The pleasure is mine," I answered in my

rusty Italian.

"Taste it," she said, handing me a spoon.

The red sauce was divine, made extra thick and rich from tomatoes dried over five days outside in the sun.

"*Squisito!*" I struggled to say the perfect thing about the food.

"*Pian piano!* Slow down. You don't have to be perfect. Just put *love* in your cooking and in nature—the rest is just the rest. You add your favorite people. This is how you make the glue. Eh? We must all be connected. You grow like you grow your garden. You add good stuff, you tend it, and…you pray."

My face must have wrinkled with that word again.

"No, no. Not the monk's prayer, but blessings to the earth. Here, taste heaven."

Giulia smeared my mouth with some grains of rice, sticky and herbed with rosemary, saffron, fennel, and mint. My mouth watered for more as my chest and stomach dilated, overcome with a calm I hadn't experienced in a long time.

"That is love—and the ancient earth. Trust yourself. Put your love and your hope in your dishes. And *magic.*"

I leaned against the huge black cast-iron stove. Rubbing my forehead, I closed my eyes, a bit dizzy. For a split second, I thought I saw an opalescent flash.

Giulia shook me gently. "I see you can feel my cooking. Here, take this." Giulia handed me a sack of dried, pungent herbs. "They will open your heart and your mouth so you have the words you need to guide yourself."

I sniffed the sack. The bouquet was a bit vile.

"Shush. Carry them with you. You will know when you need to take more. You keep them till that moment. They are very strong. I just gave you a tiny, tiny dose. Now shush. Go with your friends, your kin. We feast later. I call it agape—love feast."

No longer dizzy, I thanked her and left. I sat in the courtyard, imagining a Gregorian chant—maybe more like a lullaby. I drifted asleep. When I stood, I was afloat on a wave of love and checked to see if there was fire in the tower on the hill.

⚜ ⚜ ⚜ ⚜

Dinner, or "love feast" as Giulia called it, followed a short while after my cooking lesson. We sat in the upstairs refectory, a long austere hall with a fresco on the far wall, a Catholic religious scene peppered with pagan elements: cupids and mythological symbols of wheat and pomegranate for Ceres and Demeter. Fitting for this room whose light peeked in small doses through tiny windows high up near the cornice.

Giulia made us all hold hands and give a double kiss to everyone. We sat as Lorenzo and Gina, who were seated next to Dorotea and Alda, respectively, left to bring in the dishes.

I had sampled some dishes with Giulia, but now I drifted through the meal in an altered state, transformed by a lasagna "out of this world," a wild turkey and root vegetables braised in wine, and local vegetables sweated with local fruits, olives, and chestnuts.

Katie took my hand several times as her eyes glazed over with the intoxicating richness. I flashed on Thanksgiving with my folks, who always mixed Italian and American specialties on this holiday.

I noticed Lorenzo teasing Dorotea as they played a kind of guessing game, her eyes shut, his fingers offering new flavors. "*Cara,*" I heard him whisper, "tell me the flavor of love."

"Red," she slurred. "And hot…and chili!" She was radiant, ripe, ready to burst.

She opened her eyes, staring into his, smitten. He took her hand and, looking around to see if anyone would notice, he placed a Baci chocolate kiss in it and closed his fingers over hers.

I poked Katie when I heard Dorotea struggle to catch her breath. Katie stared off in her direction a second and, leaning into me, took my own breath away with a deep, passionate, pasta-flavored kiss.

Alda caught my eye once and winked, but her attention soon froze on Gina, who was raising a glass of vintage Nero d'Avola to Alda's nose. I heard Gina just above a whisper. "Breathe. *Sì. Respira.* Deep." Alda would lose herself in the heady blood red wine. The next time I glanced over, Alda was smearing some truffle paste on Gina's lips.

Giulia sat proudly at the head of the table. She appeared at ease, queen of her realm, pleased with her work.

Chapter Thirty-seven

Cave Dwellers

Early morning light danced off the ceiling while the lacy veil of morning dew crystalized on the drying asters out in the patio garden. Inside, a lazy moth clung to the curtain shimmying in the draft.

I lay awake fitting picture-puzzle pieces together. What had happened the night before? The meal was scrumptious. I thoroughly enjoyed the family, and they enjoyed us. Apparently, the siblings enjoyed Alda and Dorotea in particular.

As I thought about Lorenzo and Gina, images of Cupid and Eros flashed in my mind. Was it the memory of the painting on the wall, or had the chef dished up a good serving of flirtation? I recalled that Katie and I had left early, feeling quite amorous. Looking at the bedclothes, that wasn't just a feeling.

The grins on Dorotea's and Alda's faces when they suddenly appeared at our door also suggested Cupid had been busy over at the abbey.

They brought bread, cheese, and pastries and brewed lots of coffee for us. They crawled into bed with me, even over a dozing Katie. Breakfast in bed with Alda and Dorotea, giggling and spewing crumbs all over as they competed, raving about how enamored they were with Gina and Lorenzo, respectively.

Katie yawned and brushed off the pieces of

semolina bread and flake pastry. "Why so early, you guys?" Her eyes were slits.

"We're going to Sperlinga, remember?" Alda mumbled between bites.

"And," chimed in Dorotea, "we woke up really early after a good night's sleep."

"Sleep?" teased Alda.

"Whoa!" I said. "No show-and-tell, but I am so glad that love triumphs."

Katie scratched her head, trying to keep up with us, her voice thick with sleep. "Must have been the love feast for us, too." She turned a shade of fuchsia—her body working faster than her mind.

❦❦❦❦

We piled into Dorotea's Fiat 600 with a picnic basket packed with prosciutto, salami, mozzarella, bread, and wine. A short drive later, the old town of Sperlinga appeared almost out of nowhere. The rock face of the hills served as a pedestal bearing the medieval castle sculpted into it. After a quick visit to the remains of the castle, we scouted for an empty cave hollowed out of the rock face. Most were still inhabited by locals.

Removing a flimsy board, we crawled into a fairly spacious cave with two distinct rooms. One with a carved-out, domed ceiling had been outfitted as a kitchen. We chose the larger hollow area whose blackened ceiling revealed centuries of use in both summer and winter.

I built a small fire while Katie, Alda, and Dorotea spread the blanket on the beaten dirt floor and chatted about Dorotea's intro classes at Heidelberg

University's Medical Faculty. Alda hemmed and hawed, finally admitting that she might not be able to pursue her art studies at the University of Palermo. Her future depended on the ongoing safety of her current relocation. I really wanted to tell Alda I knew that out-of-control feeling, but I sensed the direction the conversation was heading.

Katie coughed when Alda and Dorotea turned to ask her about college. I understood her discomfort and crawled out of the cave to gather more wood. When I sneaked back in unseen, I heard her saying she was dying to go to Berkeley near San Francisco.

My heart sank. Although I knew about this, Katie's enthusiasm when she spoke about advances in science and Berkeley's expert faculty and lecturers socked me in the gut. Dorotea quietly asked, "And Pina?"

"What?" Katie sounded miffed.

"What will she…" Dorotea's voice trailed off.

I saw Alda become quite still. She whispered, "She'll die, all alone—"

"Shoot, Alda! Pina's got to grow up—"

"Or just grow. Give her time," Dorotea said.

"Alda, I can't babysit Pina. She's got to get on the stick!" Katie banged the loaf of bread on the hard ground, breaking it in two.

Alda picked it up and started to hum. Quiet set in for a while until Alda looked around, saying, "*Dio mio*, where is our Pina?"

I pretended innocence, walking into that room with a few chunks of wood. "What?" I said as if surprised by their concern.

Alda followed me with her gaze. I swear they were signaling me that I was safe. "*E tu?*" she asked.

Katie rolled her eyes. "Don't ask!"

I threw two chunks of wood on the fire and turned back to the group. "I'm going to college now with all that I'm learning."

Katie let out a harrumph.

Dorotea held her hand up to tell Katie to back off. "What are you learning, Pina?" Dorotea asked softly.

"I'm learning about forgiveness." I held my arms out to include the three of them. I had to wipe my eyes before I could say any more. "All of you are teaching me to forgive, just like you forgave each other yesterday. And about understanding—how to understand Fifi or D's father, or Wolfie, your father, Alda, to see how they struggled to redeem themselves after the mob and the war. So, there's hope."

"*Ja*, but just how much to forgive and forget?" Dorotea said.

I laughed. "Yeah, like I forgave Alda even when I believed her dad would hurt Craney—on account of me."

Alda slapped me upside the back. "Aha! That's only because that would have solved the Craney problem."

Dorotea became very serious. "You forgave me for telling Craney you were a lesbian."

Katie, who had been icy quiet, threw us a tense look. "But she can't forgive herself!"

"Wait, Katie," I said. "*You* just can't forgive me because I don't want what you want." I chucked a piece of wood into the flames and turned to face Katie.

"Oh, you smartass. You don't want to learn, to discover things? Why? Because you don't deserve it? Damn it!" Katie put her head in her hands and cried in loud, convulsive sobs.

I tried to reach for her hand. Nothing. Empty air.

"Hold on, you two. That's really personal," said Alda while Dorotea patted Katie's back.

"I'd have to forgive Craney to forgive myself," I said, breathing hard.

"Huh. Could you ever?" said Alda and Dorotea.

"Uh…well, I'm learning to understand love. If somebody never experiences the love of even one person, how can they help but be jealous…or hate themselves and…They've got to think they're evil or just plain *nothing*."

Dorotea whispered, "I was jealous of you."

Alda quietly added, "I never had any friends. Thought I lost your friendship. Lost everything when I had to leave Albert. *Minchia!* I even lost my identity."

"Could you ever forgive Craney?" Katie asked, sober-faced.

"Well, I think Craney hasn't known love. I mean, like, ever. I don't think she really meant to destroy Emily Whitfield, but—"

"Or *you*?" Alda interrupted.

I continued, "When Emily—"

"Or *you!*" Dorotea repeated.

"—abandoned her. It had to feel like pure hatred and evil itself to Craney," I said.

Katie looked up again. "Pina, we're talking about you. Could you ever forgive her?"

"Well, not if she's drowning me. I could understand why she would want to, but…"

"Hey, how much of those herbs did Giulia give you?" Alda smirked.

"Oh. I'm supposed to wait until I really need them."

Dorotea and Alda laughed. "Yeah, but we need

some wine now. C'mon, Katie."

"Wait, Pina, could you ever—because I think that's what you really need to do to forgive yourself." Katie burst out crying. "I love you, but you've got to live!"

We all held Katie *and* drank some wine. I fixed the fire again as Alda and Dorotea slowly inched over and hugged me. No more words were necessary as we sat soaking in the messages of the cave people.

Chapter Thirty-eight

Back To Paris

The moonlight disappeared and reappeared, playing hide and seek as the storm system rolled in from the Mediterranean. Our drive back to the cottage was slow and quiet.

I started to nod off, my head against the cool window. Lines of old songs about moonlight becoming you and dancing by the light of the moon drifted lazily through my head when I felt myself go tense. The poem, the one by Byron that Craney had recited to me, the one about no longer going roving by the light of the moon, that one socked me midchest.

Early on, Craney had been inspired by beauty and love. Maybe she had fallen in love, not lust for Emily Whitfield. Emily was—no, *is*—gorgeous, and smart, so smart. All of us students loved her. Maybe Craney would have loved me that way when she was my age. God, it must have killed her to see all of us, so young, so free, so sexy. When did she become so bitter, so entitled that she had to take us by force or destroy us?

"Who's gorgeous?" Katie shook me, thinking I was asleep and dreaming.

I must have slipped and mumbled some thoughts out loud. I opened my eyes wide and shook myself alert into the crisp nighttime air of the car.

"You are, my sweet." I brushed Katie's thigh with my hand.

When we arrived, we decided to hang out for a while and turn in early since Katie and I had to fly back to Paris the next day. Walking to the cottage from the car, we marveled at the occasional planet turning on its sparkle in the otherwise pitch-black sky. Dorotea exclaimed, "The sentinel, look!"

Alda laughed, a bewitched sound. "Fire on the mountain."

All four of us stopped and huddled together, crying tears of joy. I had never cared for anyone as much as I loved these three.

"You four are the glue," said Giulia, opening the cottage door for us. She pointed to a gigantic bowl of pasta and a bottle of wine. "Go, make a fire in the cottage and *mangiate*." She kissed me and Katie goodbye. "Remember the love feast."

We made a fire in the beehive oven and ate spaghetti from the communal bowl. Alda rocked in a rocking chair, the three of us at her feet. She sang old Italian folk songs, filling the room with distant voices of long-lost friends and kin. There was magic in the night air. Words were superfluous. Occasional sniffles, the snap-crackle of the sappy wood, and the squeaking of the rocker accompanied the songs.

Dorotea stood first without disturbing us. She kissed the crowns of our heads and left. Alda blew kisses next, promising to ring the bells for us in the morning.

❧❧❧❧

In the morning, Katie and I got up and dressed

quickly to stay warm in the mountain air. We could hear the hired car idling outside as the bells tolled our departure. Two windows in the abbey brightened as Lorenzo and Gina waved candles for us.

Like fairies, Alda and Dorotea flew to our sides out of the darkness that cloaked the fourteenth-century arch. They hugged us closely, smothering us with kisses.

"Until Christmas and the big reunion then," I yelled out the window of the car.

Alda responded, "*Si, ci rivediamo, care!*"

The bells tolled as Dorotea put her hand on her heart and sobbed, "I love you two!"

❧❧❧❧

Katie held me in her arms as I slept all the way to the airport. And again for most of the flight to Rome, even through takeoff. On the last leg back to Paris, I managed to stay awake, and for the first time since Sperlinga, we talked openly with each other during the rest of the flight.

"I have a lot to think about between now and Christmas. I mean, when the whole family celebrates in Giuliana, back in Sicily."

"You're right. You do." Katie took my hand. "I will try to be supportive, whatever you choose to do."

"Thanks." I sighed. "And me keeping house for you seems to be off the table."

"Yes." Katie's yes sounded indifferent. Twirling her damn hair, she quickly added, "Oh, any decisions about forgiving yourself?"

"Yeah. No matter what, I have to return to Albert to graduate. Maybe right after Christmas." I looked out the window, trying to avoid a head-on confrontation again.

"Shoot. Graduation's almost an afterthought. We've basically done everything we have to do before graduation."

"But you still have to make your final decision about your college pick." I wanted to probe her feelings behind her choice, but her response left me flat.

"I know what it is."

"Yup. Berkeley." I started to fidget with the control for the reading light.

Katie touched my hand briefly. We were quiet a bit.

"I need to have some long talks with Mère Paul and Père Sablé about meditation and psychology. Dorotea and I never did get to the library."

"Psychology?" Katie seemed as puzzled as I felt.

"Yeah. I don't know where that word came from, but it just floated out of my mouth."

"Do you still want to go to Chez Moune tomorrow?" Katie's face closed in on itself as if she was afraid I'd say no.

"Yes. Sure." Was Katie giving up on me?

I couldn't think anymore. I just wanted to sleep. Did I have the guts to make those decisions about college for myself? Would the herb or meditation or counseling or *forgiveness* help? I could go to the club and dance. I definitely was sleeping better. But truly believe in myself? And if Katie dumped me?

I remembered one more thing Alda had said to me while the two of us were watching the sentinel fire. She reminded me that at Albert, I had stood *against* Craney, which was good for that time in my life, and now I had to stand *up* for myself. I could only do that if

I believed I deserved to live—Katie or no Katie.

❧ ❧ ❧ ❧

Back in Paris, we invited Cassia and Sophie to our apartment. We decided to visit the church at Sacré-Coeur de Montmartre on our way to Pigalle. Walking was difficult because of the icy breeze, but we wanted to pass by some of the salons and clubs known for artists like Cézanne and Toulouse-Lautrec. Katie and I chatted up Cassia and Sophie, who were doing quite well together. I didn't really know about Katie and me.

The wind picked up, and Cassia and Sophie decided to take the funicular instead of the millions of steep steps up the hill to the church and the best Parisian viewpoint after the Tour Eiffel. We agreed to meet in a café up top.

As Katie and I walked in a semicomfortable silence, she took my arm. "I still love you, you know." What the heck prompted her to say that, and what did it really mean? Then, neither her words nor their meaning mattered at all.

A screech tore the sky apart. A spark three feet long shot out from the funicular with a crackle and a crash. The car hung suspended. Rail ripped up, and people in the street screamed as debris fell, wounding pedestrians.

"Oh, shit. Cassia and Sophie!" I covered my mouth. The horror of what was happening flooded me instantaneously.

I looked at Katie, petrified. It was my fault. It had to be. Craney was back because of me. I-I was supposed to be on that car. My friends would die instead of me.

Something let loose in me, washing away all

traces of the relative calm I had been practicing. I was wild. I ripped at my hair. I hit the ground with my fist, shouting at Katie, "Don't you see? Can't you see? I didn't deserve to have all these good things and people in my life. I had to pay."

Katie grabbed me firmly and shook me. "Stop! You, Pina, had nothing to do with this. It's not your fault. No matter what, it's not your doing. Horrific, yes, but you can't do anything about our friends. Look at me! Where are those herbs? Take them, damn it!"

I could just about focus. Katie strong-armed me into a café and got me some boiling water. I sipped slowly and fought hard to ignore the sirens and ambulances in the street.

The herbs were working. Katie made me repeat, "Fuck Craney. It's not Craney. It's not me." I closed my eyes, mumbling, and found myself instead saying, "The light, the opal, the fire on the mountain, gold and yellow." I could feel the golden light—cosmic light— penetrate the crown of my head and descend into my chest to spiral around my heart. My heart expanded, and I felt radiant heat and light and a different lightness.

I turned to Katie. "I think it's gone. Everything bad is gone." I shook my head, trying to empty out the stupor.

We overheard firemen saying that the wounded had just a few cuts and bruises and that everyone was safe. Some clunky debris had fallen on the rails, causing the car to jump the rail.

Katie's look contained mixed messages. Did she doubt either part of my story? The panic that had come on suddenly? And the golden light, which I knew was the cure?

She smiled a full smile and took my hand. "Let's

go find our friends."

We were having no luck finding them among the injured when we heard them call our names from the esplanade. We looked up, all along the railing.

"Here! Over here!" Cassia waved. "We're not hurt. We're good."

We ran over to them and hugged them hard, each of us checking to see the others were fully intact.

"Thank God!" Katie said.

I kept on smiling at them and stroking their heads. I had started to say, "I'm sorry," but instead just continued to shake my head. I had nothing to do with this. I had no other words left. I whispered to Katie, "I'm okay. I got it. It's not me." She squeezed my hand.

They explained that they had ridden up on the previous car. We hugged them again and stayed together on the esplanade for quite a while, admiring the cityscape. The golden glow enveloped the whole city. Paris was truly the City of Lights. The Eiffel Tower flickered on and off with red and green lights for Christmas. Spotlights beamed down on the Arc de Triomphe, illuminating its starlike avenues, scintillating rays from the arch and center flame for the Unknown Soldier. I said a prayer to the golden light.

We arrived at Chez Moune late but in time to hear the emcee announce two dances instead of one. She said since so many cops were stuck at the funicular, they probably wouldn't raid the place tonight. I took Katie by the waist and pressed her firmly to me as we danced. She nuzzled her head into my neck and sang along with Connie Francis's *If I Didn't Care*. I felt her move against me, and I was excited to show her (and me) off.

Then I felt a hand on my shoulder as two other

dancers took Katie and me for their dance partners. My new partner seemed quite butch, leading me firmly with her hand at the back of my waist. She whispered a question, "Kiki?" I understood she wanted to know if I was both butch and femme. I was having a ball and feeling somewhat excited—and not uncomfortable at that thought. When she tried to French kiss me, I pulled back, pointed to Katie, and told her I was a taken woman. She smiled a suggestive smile but nodded in Katie's direction, calling her the lucky one.

Katie seemed equally delighted with her partner, to whom she pointed me out. We switched again and shared another dance with Cassia and Sophie.

Cassia giggled. "Finally, I get to hold both of you," she quipped. She was laughing so hard, she could hardly hold on to me.

I flashed her a huge smile.

"And now, thanks to you, I have Sophie to hold, a lot!"

"Oh, Cassia," I said, "that's all your doing."

Katie and Sophie danced close by and overheard my comment. They both shouted to Cassia, "You deserve it."

Sophie pushed us together into a four-person dance. "I think we all deserve this, eh?"

We left the club, so grateful for the second dance. We took a taxi home, all of us in high spirits, and stayed up for a while eating cookies and cider in front of the fire. We invited Cassia and Sophie to stay, but they had an early event the next day.

At the door, Cassia hugged Katie and me two times in addition to the four kisses apiece. "You two have shown me friendship. You have shared your love with me, and I live more fully. I do deserve Sophie. *Je vous aime!*"

We all cried. I really began to appreciate parting words. They showed me that goodbyes also held the seeds for hellos and welcome-backs.

❧ ❧ ❧ ❧

Katie and I crawled into bed shortly after Cassia and Sophie left. Our arms brushed each other, and our hips touched. But something felt disconnected and distant.

"I'm glad we went to the club," I said, hoping to breach the emotional wall between us.

"Uh-huh." Katie flicked her cuticles.

"Yeah. I was so proud of you." I smiled at Katie and took her hand.

"Why? Don't you mean you were proud of you?"

"Well, yeah, but…"

"Pina, it's about you!"

"Yeah." I wasn't sure about Katie's tone. She sounded exasperated with me or just plain cold. "Well, is that bad?"

"Jeez! Figure that out for yourself. I mean, the herbs are helping, but this shit has got to stop."

"Whoa. You sound angry."

"You said you had to go back to the club, right?"

"Uh-huh, because I was uncomfortable with the dancing."

"Yes, just like you were uncomfortable with being a lesbian—"

"Right! That's why I really was glad to dance with you."

"Right. And the rest of the day?" Katie yawned.

The air seemed to grow even cooler. I thought

Katie was going to shut out the light and turn over.

"Man. I was glad Cassia and Sophie were okay, weren't you?"

"You lost it! You were so friggin' convinced Craney was after you. And everything was your fault. Damn it! It's all the same thing."

"Listen! The light, the golden light, I know it's real, and it's doing something to my image, my self-image. Like it's getting rid of the *bad*."

"We, all of us, have told you you're not *bad*." Katie threw up her hands.

"Yes, but I have to tell myself and believe it. That light was kind of like a prayer." I groped for Katie's hand. "God, Katie, you've got to trust me. I am working on this."

Katie breathed a deep sigh. Her face softened as she turned to look at me and brush my bangs aside. "I want to trust you." She leaned over to brush my lips with a kiss. Her snit fizzled out for the moment. "Now," she said, breathing another deep sigh, "tomorrow we'll get you a cool French hairdo to celebrate the new Pina, and then I'll drop you off at school to introduce Père Sablé to his new student."

"And how about some high-heeled sneakers so I can really grow?"

She shoved me gently. I finally breathed a sigh of relief, feeling the tension go poof and disappear, at least for the moment.

We kissed good night and cuddled. I shut the light and then my eyes, afraid to risk more and maybe hear the other shoe drop.

Chapter Thirty-nine

Family Therapy

True to her word, Katie marched us off to the beauty parlor first thing in the morning. I was fed up with my poor-waif look.

"*Quel style de coupe?*" asked the beautician, a Jackie Kennedy look-alike.

"Tell her, something really cool." Katie flipped back my bangs.

Jackie shrugged, looked at Katie and back at me, and started slicing and dicing my long, straggly hair to create a cut midway between Cassia's artichoke and a beat vampire with wispy, pointed bangs. Katie and Jackie shouted, "Voilà! The French cut!"

"Now walk out with a cocky attitude. Everyone will recognize the new Pina."

"Fine." I walked with an air of "Watch out! Don't mess with me!" Katie clapped.

As we approached the Institut, Père Sablé rode up on his moped, exclaiming, "*Mon Dieu! Qui c'est cette vedette?*"

I rolled my eyes and translated, "Who is this star?" for Katie, who spoofed back, "Bob Dylan."

Katie quietly split, leaving me to be fussed over by Père Sablé. He winked at me, slipping his arm through mine, and escorted me, la nouvelle Pina-Dylan, into the Institut.

"We will go to the roof. There is a surprise for us up there," he said.

Père Sablé and I climbed the stairs to find Mère Paul on the roof holding a tray of madeleine cookies. We all hugged.

Père Sablé sat down a ways off to read his newspaper.

I chewed the cookie slowly, savoring each buttery bite and running my tongue along the narrow grooves of this shell-shaped treat.

"I have heard from Cassia about the accident. And you, how goes it?"

"Mère, I think you probably know I kind of blew it."

"Blew it? For yourself? With Katie?"

"Yeah."

"And the tea I gave you?" Mère Paul scratched her cheek, doing that French pout thing.

"Your tea and finally Giulia's herbs from Sicily."

"Ah? And hers are better than mine?" Mère Paul slit her eyes at me.

"*Attention!*" shouted Père Sablé from his spot five feet away. "Don't get her jealous."

"Both are good, but the light, the golden light—"

"You saw it?" Mère Paul stared hard at me. "This only happens rarely, only when a person meditates."

"Yes, it was exactly like you said: a mind prayer." I had so many questions for her, but she put her finger to her lips to shush me.

"You know, in the Résistance, we saw so much evil. So we, that one over there"—she pointed to Père Sablé—"we decided to take all that evil, all that blood, all those bodies, all those guns and panzers, and make an image in our heads along with all the fear and ugliness they created in our guts. We coached each other and created the biggest, strongest image of a tank—in our heads—a tank nothing could get out of, only in. And then we put all the evil in that tank and sealed it for good."

"And then came the golden light," added Père Sablé. "It came, who knows, from God, from the minds and souls of all good people. It came through the crowns of our heads and kept on coming, down to our hearts—"

"And spun and rotated and filled our hearts with the healing light. And the evil that we had started to fear was in us disappeared. Everything in us was coated with a golden, healing light. And that is what we have shown to so many people who have been hurt by evil and hatred." Mère Paul sighed and finally caught her breath. She put her hand on her heart and glanced over to Père Sablé, who had closed his eyes and touched his heart.

I sobbed. I felt in my chest, in my gut, in every part of me what Mère Paul was describing. Mère Paul placed her hand on my back. "*Mon enfant,*" she said. "I study this now. And doctors, too, use this in emergency crises."

"You know, Pina," said Père Sablé. "I worked with the American Army at the end of the war. They, too, want me to train specialists. I don't know. Maybe someday. They say at this special school, Stanford, I could help the psychology department. Do you know about this school?"

"Yes and no." Katie had mentioned it. "It sounds really special if you can teach that."

"Ah!" Père Sablé stroked his chin and pushed out his lips. "Maybe you can help me. You could scout out this school for me."

"Oh, so you want to know if Stanford's worth it?" I laughed as he thrust his long Gallic nose up in the air.

"*Ah, oui.* I'm not just any *résisteur*!" He guffawed.

"Ha," said Mère Paul. "He can say that again! So, Pina, you've got to put on your thinking cap and take out your magnifying glass. Inspect it and send back a full report!"

"I'm not sure I can."

"Eh? And the new Pina-Dylan?" joked Père Sablé.

"Shush!" said Mère Paul. "We must listen to the bells."

As bells tolled from Notre-Dame, the Sainte-Chapelle, Saint-Sulpice, Saint-Séverin, and all the churches of Paris, red and white lights flickered on from La Tour Eiffel. The three of us huddled together. I swear we all felt the golden light.

"This will be a good Christmas," said Mère Paul.

Père Sablé made believe he was striking a match. "We give you the gift of light. Use it!" And with a twinkle in his eye, he said, "Let us be careful going down the stairs. Always look for the cord to hold on. There's always a cord in life."

❧ ❧ ❧ ❧

I had a lot to think about as I traveled back to the apartment. I stopped off at the neighborhood library and asked them to do some research for me on this Stanford place. I would ask Katie about it, too. Like why—if it was cool enough to teach that kind of weird, supernatural stuff—why wouldn't she go there?

I had so much on my mind that I closed my eyes a lot, walking the last few blocks to our place. I could only keep them closed a few seconds, but I saw lights, all kinds of light, all colors and hues and strengths.

Even some pretty intense gold sneaked in there for one split second.

❧❧❧❧

Before bursting into the apartment, I decided to make my life with Katie easier. I would keep that in mind when I talked about Stanford.

"Hey, hey, Katie!" I called out, doing a little dance. "I saw the light," I said and sang the old gospel tune. "Mère Paul showed me the light. Just the way I described the special light to you last night."

"You're not kidding, huh?"

"No. It's a real thing. I guess it's a kind of meditation, but it works, and they use it with soldiers and people who have had serious accidents."

"So, you mean you can learn to use it to stop the crazies?"

"Yup."

"And Craney?"

"What, Craney?"

"Even when she's not there, you see her everywhere."

"No. We lost her in Germany. And I'm not losing my mind over her anymore."

"That's great if... Come here and let me give you a big kiss."

"You're going to make me see different lights and stars?"

"Later, sweetie."

"Yeah. I've gotta ask you something else."

"Ha. Did Mère and Père do family therapy with you?"

"You know, they kind of did. So, how come you don't want to go to Stanford?"

"Huh?"

"Well, they said Stanford teaches all these cool supernatural-like things. Stanford even wants to hire Poppa Sablé to teach this meditation light business and something called image work in French. So, why wouldn't you want to go there?"

"Pin, it sounds like *you* want to go there."

"Well, I might. I mean…" I hurried to clear my throat. Shoot. What did I mean? "I mean, Père Sablé wants me to check it out for him."

"Oh?" Katie's eyes lit up, her smile broadened, and then she turned away from me, coughing. "Anyway, I want to study science first at Berkeley, and who knows, maybe do graduate work in psychology or psychiatry at Stanford."

"Oh." Now it was my turn to choke on the "what?" I almost blurted out. Katie'd never mentioned this before. So, she *was* interested in the psyche. Hmm! I wondered if she'd been studying me and my dreams and uh…I changed the subject so I wouldn't stumble into dangerous territory. "Hey, want to go to the cinema?"

"What?" Katie pulled a face, throwing up her hands. "Oh, okay, but what about Stanford?"

"Oh, yeah. Well, we've got to hurry to make the next show down the block. They're doing *Black Orpheus*."

"Right," she said, throwing me a sidelong glance.

ॐ ॐ ॐ ॐ

Walking back from the cinema, I lost myself in the afterglow of the film. My eyes still feasted on the carnival characters, my ears throbbed with the jangle and beat of the bossa nova music, and my memory zoomed me back to the Greek myth of Eurydice and

Orpheus.

I questioned if my relationship with Katie was also doomed. Just like Orpheus, the more I turned around to check on Katie's presence, the more she disappeared, and the more I stumbled. Where were my feet going? Was I going backward? Was I losing my gifts?

I walked quietly by Katie's side. My mood shifted. I reached for her hand and immediately dropped it as if it were a live wire. My brain sizzled as I recalled the preview for *The Children's Hour*, the same story that Craney had planted in its play version outside my room at Albert. Would Katie and I face the same scandal, a town turning against us because we were lesbians? Would I end up destroying myself?

Katie pulled on my arm, startling me. I shook myself from the image I'd retained from the play, of the main character swinging from a noose, and turned my face away from the blinding light coming our way. A locomotive at the station crossing brought me back to my senses.

Light? I did have the light, Mère Paul's golden light.

Katie took my hand. "It's okay."

I started to speak and stopped. Katie was sending messages, too. She looked at me as if she had heard all the noise clanging around in my head and spoke just above a whisper. "Pin, *The Children's Hour*, it must have reminded you of Craney."

I let that sit between us for a second or two. "I've got the herbs and the light stuff, and who knows, maybe even my grandmother's dreams."

She stopped to look at me, her eyes soft and penetrating. "And forgiveness?"

"I'm working on that."

Chapter Forty

Loose Ends

We snuggled our way back to the apartment in silence. The night was clear and crisp, and the quiet twinkle of the stars softened the lingering garish visions of *Black Orpheus*. At the apartment, we collapsed on the daybed, where I held Katie tucked in my arm and twirled some strands of her hair, so she wouldn't. Katie was too busy reading me and, if her flashing eyes were any clue, analyzing my mood.

"You don't have to be so fatalistic!"

"What?"

"Pin, the movies, life doesn't have to be that way."

"What way? The movies seemed to say, 'So little time, so many catastrophes!'"

"Look at me! Where's your damn *light*?"

"I'm just saying—"

"Myths, Pina—myths are just that! Big flashy stories to explain things ancient people couldn't understand. Native Americans have creation myths. Do you really think good and evil come from your right and left armpits like the Iroquois myth?"

"Huh?"

"Damn it, why don't you just focus on Orpheus's message, that old saying, 'Don't look back'? If you're so set on the past, try remembering your cocky, feisty self, the one that came out to your parents and drove

Craney away, crazy and powerless." Katie ran her hands over her head and just stared at me. "I am really tired. Let's go to bed."

"Yeah, guess you're right. *I* make my own bed, not the fates."

Katie's eyes twinkled as she yawned. "You can make it a bed of roses."

We both groaned and hurried to slip under the covers of our bed before either of us said another word.

꙰ ꙰ ꙰ ꙰

I smoothed my hand down the length of my iridescent green raw silk gown. Somewhat unaccustomed to the high, tight, gold-braided bodice, I pushed my breasts up and almost out, exposing them to the breeze flowing off the River Styx. The wind at my back propelled me away from the river in pursuit of the lovely long-haired goddess, at times just outside my grasp in front of me. We danced, floating on tiptoes to competing, throbbing notes of dueling lyres, until I stumbled, falling, stepping into a swirling mass of asps.

I heard an eerie sound, my goddess crying out in pain for me, as my spirit began to evanesce into the ethers. Lyre music swirled and floated in evaporating waves, disappearing and transforming into rhythmic beats and a chant as yet unknown to my people.

Men and women and heavenly in-between people wearing ibis feathers and paint on their faces danced with rattles and beads. They smoked long reeds from which huge curls of heady vapors escaped. Their loins were bound in leather and dangling beads, which they used to stroke the heads of the asps. As the incense rose, so did the snakes' heads along with their long graceful bodies, slithering in sync with the human dancers.

My legs caressed the snakes, now free to dance with them and the people called the Hopi. I petted the asps and urged them higher and higher.

As my love goddess appeared on the horizon, the asps waved in unison. A heartfelt adieu and Godspeed to me and my beloved. Feathers flew up to the heavens, the winds calmed, and the river dried. My goddess opened her arms wide, inviting me to take the space in the adjacent dune as we peered across the knolls and walked on in step with each other.

⁂

"Holy crow," I yelled, sitting up and laughing my fool head off in the dark of the night.

"Aw, come on, Pina! What now?" Katie was not amused.

"Katie, Katie, listen."

"Oh, jeez. A dream?" Katie's eyes flashed annoyance.

"You were right. Myths are myths. And I just put together the best one!" I snapped my fingers, breaking the silence in the room.

"Go on," she said as some distant church bells tolled 3:00 a.m.

"Well, I sort of dreamed about the real Greek myth of Orpheus, where Eurydice steps on the snakes—that's Craney—and goes to Hades."

"Charming. And you're happy about this?" Katie was sitting up, just staring at me, mouth agape.

"But I don't go to hell. I become a Hopi Indian and charm the hell out of the snakes. And my love and I live in a spacious and idyllic place."

"Sounds great, but you think you can forgive Craney before she poisons you more?" Katie started to puff up her pillow. She was done with this conversation.

"Don't you see? I could charm her and take away her venom. You know, tame her."

"You just had to throw in *The Little Prince*!" Katie yawned. "That 'spacious' place, huh? How about some space for sleep now and talk in the morning? Please?" Katie hugged me and fell back to sleep as soon as her head touched the pillow.

❧❧❧❧

Katie all but pushed me out of bed in the morning, complaining that I owed her breakfast in bed. I complied with my goddess's wishes. She asked if I understood the goddess's additional desires. I chose actions instead of words.

Our lovemaking was sweet and slow, kind of lazy like the pale butter yellow fall sun peeking through the windowpanes. Our days here in Paris had dwindled to very few before we would leave to spend Christmas break in Sicily, the graduation present and the reunion with friends and family. This Sicilian trip to my ancestral village would be another dream come true. We wrote a formal invitation reminder to urge our old friends and newfound Parisian friends to join with us in celebrating the old and the new together.

We propped ourselves up in bed, surrounded by a stock of Petit Beurre cookies and plenty of coffee. Both of us held ballpoints but only one legal pad.

Dear Friends,
We hope you will come to Giuliana, Sicily, and

join in the festivities on December 24, 1961, to celebrate with Pina and Katie:

•the New Year 1962 and new beginnings

•their old success in proving the innocence of Doctor McGuilvry and Fifi Gallo in the murder at Camp Minnetonka

•their upcoming graduation from Albert Academy

•the holidays in a land held holy by the Mazzini family and their ancestors

"Hey, Katie, we've got to say this trip is a gift from Joe's dad, Fifi."

"Yeah, you're right. Just add 'and to celebrate Fifi's generosity.'"

We finished the invitation and signed it from the two of us, adding that the big celebration would take place at the castle of Giuliana on Christmas Eve.

❧❧❧❧

On my way to the post office to mail the invitations, I stopped at the library. The librarian had collected an enormous tower of Stanford brochures, applications, maps, and program descriptions for me. I loved the university motto: *"Die Luft der Freiheit weht,"* the wind of freedom blows, and the redwood tree on the logo. Buildings looked kind of Spanish-style with red tile roofs, and the church had huge frescoes on its façade. This school was really cool.

As I combed through the papers looking for the psychology course descriptions, maps fell out onto the table. San Francisco and Berkeley jumped right off the blue, green, and white page, and there, just south of them, a red star indicated Stanford in Palo Alto. I just stared, speechless, and proceeded to search for the map's legend. Aha! An inch measured twenty-five miles. Roughly calculated, Stanford and Berkeley stood forty-five miles apart. Forty-five dinky miles. Hmm!

I quickly checked my watch, bundled the free pamphlets, and set off for the post office after folding the matchbook-sized map and the list of freshman psych classes. I managed to flatten the bulge they created in my skirt to an inconspicuous evenness.

At the post office, I mailed all the invitations, as well as the brochures for Père Sablé, with the exception of a short application form. I caught a fleeting glance of one requirement, an essay about the bearing of a historical event or period on one's current life's purpose. I saw one word in my mind's eye—*resistance*.

Fate socked me in the chest. My ribs, my diaphragm, my squared shoulders held me up. Standing power—*that* I had. I tapped my foot, debating whether to tear up the application. An essay…the essay. Hmm. I could write the friggin' essay. I could.

The walk back to the apartment with the small application form tucked in my underpants, hidden away from Katie's eyes, dragged on, long—the evening, as well. Katie fixed hamburgers for dinner and buried her head in a tour book of Sicily. I searched the apartment's bookshelves for anything on Sartre, Freud, or William James, an American psychologist who said as long as there was life, there would be possibility.

⚜ ⚜ ⚜ ⚜

Katie and I spent the next two days shopping for little presents, baking some cookies, and packing.

We were pretty quiet around each other, and I found several excuses to stay out in the park or at the Institut and read or scribble some thoughts on scrap paper. Katie also took several walks by herself. I often found her staring at me as if I just happened to be in her line of vision. At night, we snuggled; by day, we went about the silent business of preparation. For Sicily, yes, but for something else, which remained unspoken.

Père Sablé's note arrived on the third day. I sat by Katie's side on the daybed to read it out loud while she continued to flip through *Paris Match* magazine. He said he would come to Sicily, accompanied by Mère Paul. His letter was brief and direct with the exception of some cryptic remarks.

Pina, you will undergo your final tests there, some of which I will administer and send passing grades back to Albert. I will quiz you on realism, tragedy, and comedy. I do not know to what degree my teaching outside the classroom has affected you. If you've set up certain tests for yourself, as I hope you have, I wish you "*Merde!*" You know we French do not say "*Bonne Chance!*" It's how you say, "Break a leg!"

It was the last sentence that almost threw me. "*Merci pour the brochures.*"

Katie suddenly showed a burning interest in Père Sablé's letter. "What brochures?"

"Uh…I picked some stuff up for him at the library."

"Oh." Katie sighed and grew even pissier. "What's the big secret? You seem uptight."

"Huh? I was just wondering the same thing. You've been kind of incognito." I paused, and the words just poured out. "Will Sicily be our final test?" I looked away.

"What?" Katie froze. "We have three more months, February, March, and April before graduation." Katie twirled her hair as she spoke her weary words.

"And the summer?"

"Uh…I might start an early workshop at Berkeley. We've got time to talk." Katie's chest rose and fell as she sighed loudly.

"And the final test?" My voice rose. I worried steam might be coming from my nose and ears.

Katie shrugged. "I guess you give that to yourself."

I had no words. Sitting there stunned, I watched as Katie put on her coat, saying she was going for a walk. The door opened, she disappeared, the door closed.

⁂

As responses started to arrive, Katie's fog began to lift. My haziness dissipated, too.

My parents' card with my mother's scrawled "See you soon, honey" was a given, as was Doc and Joe's positive response. Katie and I laughed when her father wrote that Joe's father, Fifi, and Alda's father, Wolfie, would not be joining us. Joe thought each had been relocated again and were penitents at Lourdes.

Alda's card created the biggest surprise and joy for us. She and Dorotea would be driving with Giulia, Gina, and Lorenzo from Gangivecchio. Alda had not been relocated with her father and continued to live blissfully with Gina in the Casa D'Annunziata and Giulia and Lorenzo in the abbey. According to Alda, Dorotea jumped at the opportunity to see Lorenzo again and said she needed to brush up on her Italian. We didn't know if Dorotea meant her spoken Italian or her Italian boyfriend.

The last card arrived from Cassia and Sophie the day before we had to leave. Cassia wished us the best and hoped they could make it. If not, she said, they would ring bells for us, and if there were stars in the night sky, it would be them giggling and smiling down on us. Cassia thanked Katie and me again for teaching her about love.

❧❧❧❧

Katie and I lit a fire and sipped a toast of wine to each other and Paris on our last afternoon. I was also thinking about returning to the States sooner than expected since Père Sablé said I had already mastered the material covered. We walked to Sacré-Coeur and said our goodbyes to the City of Lights from the white-domed church. Our favorite monuments seemed to wink at us, and the breeze in the trees waved goodbye. The Eiffel Tower stood as a kind of urban sentinel, promising safety and the continuing light to see our paths. Katie kissed me, snuggling her face into the hood of my jacket.

"Tomorrow, Sicily," she murmured.

"Tomorrow, life," I whispered back.

"And today?"

"Life and love."

"Hmm…" was Katie's only response.

Chapter Forty-one

Sicily

Today turned into tomorrow, and the fog brought doubts about clear thinking and paths toward the future. We hoped the flight path to Sicily would be clear enough.

Katie and I struggled with the early morning departure, grumbling without our usual two cups of coffee. This deprivation compounded my grumpiness and set the stage for my emotional tango of hope and resignation. Would Katie and I make it?

After the taxi ride to Le Bourget Airport, my mood lifted, along with the fog, as the hope of a stirring, orgasmic takeoff flooded my mind and body. The Air France Caravelle loomed long and sleek on the runway. It lacked a certain propulsion of the propjet.

Maybe the so-so start of the journey served as an indicator of the calm to come. I could use some of that. No crisis with Katie. None of my mother's tantrums about not applying to college. And not one mention of Craney. I had my herbs and the light. I wished they could help me with Katie.

I looked over to Katie sleeping. Her soft breathing raised and lowered her chin, parting her lips a mere, luscious fraction. I wanted so badly to kiss her lips to make everything better. Afraid to wake her in a cranky mood, I turned back to the window and caught a glimpse of Mount Pellegrino, a kind of welcome-to-Palermo sign.

Our taxi ride from the airport to Giuliana brought us along Mediterranean coastal cliffs and through curvaceous hilltop towns. We gawked at the lushness of citrus orchards, wine grapes, and olive groves and snickered quietly at names of towns we recognized from gangster movies.

As we arrived at Giuliana, I took Katie's hand to help her out of the car and welcome her to my ancestral village. She smiled softly, slowly turning her head to take in the narrow stone confines of this tiny hamlet dominated by the Castello di Federico II, the thirteenth-century castle, rising out of the rock cliffs.

❧ ❧ ❧

"This is it?" Katie's face wrinkled as we entered a small, plain room inside the beautifully chiseled stone front of our *pensione*.

"Pretty simple, huh?" I knew Sicilians dressed up their façades while leaving the inside modest for only the family to see. "You don't need luxury, do you?" I bit back the rest of my thought, afraid Katie would think I was calling her a snob.

"Nah." She slumped on the narrow, squeaky bed.

"You okay?" I was sorry I asked almost as soon as the words were out of my mouth.

Katie looked at me and seemed to force a smile. "Just tired." She lay back on the bed still dressed in her coat, threw me a weary look, and quickly fell asleep.

I had to do something to stay out of my head and my worries over Katie. I got busy unpacking and occasionally peeked out the window to catch a few rays of the sun beginning to set on the white stone castle, a golden radiance resembling a fire dancing up its tower.

I had almost finished unpacking when I glanced over at Katie. My mind started racing ahead. What would the last three months at Albert bring? Would Katie and I be this distant? Was she preparing for the long distance, the end of the line?

Snatching my herbs, I bolted for the kitchen to boil some water before the crazies took over. Leaning against the stucco wall, I tried to sharpen my hearing for Sicilian sounds, anything to block out Katie's snoring and the trash clanging around in my head.

Someone sang *Bella ciao* in the distance. Its refrain echoed through the narrow back alleys we had seen on the drive in. The rolling glub-glub of boiling water almost drowned out a woman's voice singing out, "*A tavola*," calling her family to dinner.

I sipped some tea and lost myself in the music of this tiny village. A cat meowed, a canary sang. Its Italian notes sounded different from our domestic canaries. Multilingual chatter and giggles rolled in from a nearby room. I was focused on making out German, Italian, and English when the sound of a familiar curse—"*Minchia!*"—brought me back to the present. Alda and Dorotea had arrived.

I threw open the door and spread my arms to embrace Alda and Dorotea. Giulia, Gina, and Lorenzo, exhausted from the long drive, immediately escaped into their room. Alda and Dorotea and I danced about and ran to get Katie.

Katie lit up and insisted we open the wine Alda had brought to toast our reunion.

Alda wiggled with a look of impatience on her face.

"I've got a secret." She blushed.

Dorotea giggled, covering her mouth.

"I'll bite," said Katie.

"You and Gina?" I pulled Alda over and gave her a huge, noisy double-cheeked smooch. "She's great, Alda!"

"It's sort of new, but we have to be discreet here."

"Why? I switch rooms; I go to sleep with the old couple, Pina and Katie." Dorotea smiled her best cupid smile.

"Of course you can crash with us." Katie was twirling her damn hair. I merely raised an eyebrow.

"And Lorenzo? C'mon, Dorotea, what's going on with the two of you?" I asked.

She shrugged, turning absolutely crimson. "Maybe…he hasn't asked anything serious yet, and Sicily is far from Heidelberg." She sighed and started to say, "Like Berkeley and—"

"Hey!" interrupted Katie. "Let's go quickly up the hill to catch the last of the sunset or the moonrise."

Alda's gaze fell on me. She rubbed my shoulder, whispering, "It will work out. *Non ti preoccupare!*"

The four of us scampered up the hill in back of the *pensione*. We were bent over huffing when we heard footsteps. Lorenzo and Gina joined us carrying cheese and biscotti. We sat, all of us holding hands, passing the rest of the wine and snacks. Lorenzo produced another bottle from his jacket, which we willingly guzzled.

As the moon rose and the wine lightened our spirits more and more, we lay across one another with our heads on the next person's stomach. The first in line, Alda, let out a "ha," followed by Gina, who chuckled "ha-ha," and so on down the line. After three turns, we all convulsed in contagious laughter, unable to stop or to utter a word that made sense.

Most of us were still sober enough to cry with joy at the reunion. Alda stood and gave the last drop of wine to the earth and the gods for "*felicità.*"

"To happiness and love," we all shouted.

Dorotea, the only one who seemed drunk, tried to stand and sat back down. She cleared her throat as if to say something monumental and declared, "The gang's all here; the only one missing is Craney!" With that, she passed out, and we shrieked a collective "No!"

❧ ❧ ❧ ❧

The next morning as Katie and I navigated the springs and hollows of the mattress, we heard a lot of banging about in the hallway—and many exclamations of "Jesus, Mary, and Joseph." Our parents had arrived.

We managed to spot the clock despite our screaming hangovers. What an ungodly hour! It was 4:00 a.m. The flight from Rome to Palermo must have been delayed.

I went back to sleep. I had no clue what Katie did. When I resurrected myself at nine, I tiptoed to my folks' room. I smelled smoke, which meant my father was awake. He opened the door, maybe as psychic as I had felt at different moments of my life.

"Hey, toots!"

"Hey, Dad!" I threw my arms around his neck, which released a wave of his Bay Rum aftershave.

"Honey!" said my mom, rushing over to kiss me, still chewing on a chocolate she must have gotten duty-free. "Oh, mmm, you've got to taste this. Here, it's good for you!"

"Mom, I've got a headache. I need coffee."

"Your father will make you some. Barney, where's the heat coil you got?"

"Right here. One instant cappuccino coming up!"

I put my head in my hands. God, they were sweet, and shit, my head was pounding. "Got any aspirin?"

"Toots, drink this!"

"Thanks, Dad." I winced. It was coffee, but bad. "Uh…have you guys eaten?"

"Yes, with Doc and Joe. Katie wasn't feeling well, either. Did you girls eat something bad?"

I took a deep breath. "Yeah, something like that."

"They're probably still at breakfast. Why don't we go and get you one of the yummy cream crescents and say hello to Doc? After all, he does pay your way. It's the least you can do."

I thought I'd scream, but that would've just made my eyes cross more. "Right, Mom."

We entered the breakfast room. Katie raised her bloodshot eyes to me. She looked as bad as I felt. She smiled knowingly at me. Doc and Joe were on their feet—quietly. Katie must have told them about toasting the moon and everything else under the sun.

"I love you guys," I mumbled.

My mother poked me. "What kind of talk is that?"

I sighed. "A figure of speech, Mom. Let it be."

"Doc." I fell into his bear hug and mussed his mane of long white hair. "It's so good to see you!"

"You okay, Pina?" he asked quietly with a look indicating he meant okay with Katie, okay with life, okay with Craney.

"Yeah, except for this headache."

"Ahem!" Doc coughed so my parents wouldn't hear.

Joe flew to my side. "Hey, Pina, you're good. Don't worry. Katie told us you guys had fun last night."

I just smiled. I needed another liter of coffee. The four parents chuckled and laughed about the flight they had shared from Rome. Katie rolled her eyes at me, whispering, "You feel as shitty as I do?"

This was the first remotely intimate thing she had spoken to me for a while. I never thought alcohol drew people together. "Why don't we let them yackety-yack and visit with them in a bit?"

Katie was coordinating a walk with Doc and Joe, so I told my parents I would show them around at the same time. We hurried back to the room and collapsed in bed, shades drawn, Alka-Seltzer foaming in our glasses.

"Sorry," Katie mumbled.

"What for?"

"Don't know. Just sorry."

※ ※ ※ ※

I awoke to see Katie gone. I checked my watch—time to go walk with my parents. We set out for the castle. Completely sober now, I enjoyed seeing my parents smile over everything they were viewing. Here, in our ancestral mountain village, the earth felt like it was stepping its way up to the sky.

My mother sat on a bench, intimidated by the mounting steps in front of us. My father took my hand.

"You okay, Dad?" I noticed him breathing heavily.

"These sons of a guns are steep, probably even worse in the days of your grandfather Pietro and grandmother Francesca." My father was grinning from ear to ear as he sifted the grit from the steps through his fingers.

My father called my attention to the castles on the hilltops. "They used to build fires up there to signal friendly villages if enemies were coming."

"Yes. I think Père Sablé is actually going to do a Christmas blessing up there."

My father beamed and slowly put his arm around my shoulders, looking off to the hills in the distance. I saw a tear glistening on his cheek.

We stood peering down onto a narrow alley. My mother sat in one of the doorways, showing women how to do a tricky sewing stitch.

❧❧❧❧

On our way back, we bumped into Katie, Doc, and Joe. My parents walked arm in arm, and I mimicked them by taking Katie's arm. She rolled her eyes at her folks acting like lovebirds. I wasn't going to argue with her.

Her father sounded as if he were reading poetry. His normal doctor's voice was gone. He walked differently. He almost hummed.

"I feel the touch of these uneven cobbles on my feet, I brush the stone walls, and they give up their spirit, the spirit of so many generations. Oh, it's almost painful—such grace."

Katie made a gesture to me. "God, they're mushy." We overheard them wax eloquent.

"It's well...like we're all connected here. *Dolce vita.*"

I looked at my parents, oblivious to everything but each other. My father stopped to buy my mother more chocolate. She cleaned a speck off his cheek. Joe and Doc were almost prostrate before each other in the street. I looked at Katie, somewhat green, somewhat exasperated. Everyone swooned over this beautiful backdrop—everyone but Katie and me.

I threw Katie my best cow-eyed look of love. She walked straight ahead, sighing. She did grab for my hand when she almost tripped on a raised paving stone.

Our folks got real busy, for which we were enormously grateful. We attempted to find our friends, who like us were in pain. Dorotea had slept until three and could barely talk now at seven. All of us resembled paintings of absinthe drinkers: vapid and low on the IQ scale. We sat with the adults for pasta and excused ourselves to go stretch out on the hillside—without wine. As the stars began to twinkle, we got to our feet zombie-like and ambled off to try harder the next day.

Before crawling under the covers, Katie once again mumbled, "Sorry."

I yawned, blinked, and burped—the extent of my ability to focus.

❧ ❧ ❧ ❧

During the night, I lay awake, deciphering the word *sorry*. Had Katie already decided to end things? Everybody else was falling or growing in love. Katie was out of it. I tried to solve the riddle of the *final test*, Père Sablé's version and Katie's. I had more luck—or piss and vinegar—writing my essay on resistance in my head. She-it! Maybe that was the final test. And? Was I ready? Did I already know?

Light leaked into our room, washing across

Katie's wrinkled face, prompting one eyelid to ease open. She grumbled, "Morning," and shifted about in the bed. I turned toward her and gingerly placed my hand on her shoulder. "Katie, what is it?"

With a slight tremor of her lip, she mumbled, "Just blank. I don't have a clue." She buried her head in the pillow and reached for my hand. "I don't know. I don't know."

I didn't want to ask if this was about us. I breathed deeply before whispering, "Whatever we find out, it's okay."

When she smiled, I figured I had answered the right question, whatever it was. Maybe I was starting to believe that whatever happened to our relationship, it would be okay. Katie squeezed my hand. She yawned and formed what seemed to be a heartfelt smile. "Our friends said to meet them at breakfast. Beat you to the shower."

❧❧❧❧

Alda, Gina, Dorotea, and Lorenzo all wore the look of smitten cherubs. They chatted in half syllables as they stared into each other's eyes. After two cups of coffee and some pistachio crescent rolls, Katie and I livened up to the point where Katie actually kissed me on the cheek.

Dorotea chewed on her upper lip. "I must say sorry. I was truly drunk."

"Nah!" All of us laughed.

"*Ja*, you know, Pina, I was stupid to talk about Craney."

Alda shook her head at Dorotea. "Yup. You really blew it! Then your comment about distances and

Berkeley—"

Lorenzo apparently kicked Alda under the table while Gina started humming *Santa Lucia*.

"*Oh, merda*. I meant like in Sperlinga when we asked whether you could forgive Craney." Alda couldn't keep her foot out of her mouth.

Gina smiled a lazy love-addicted smile. "*Cara*, you still drunk?"

"No. It's just so important for Pina, no?"

"Hey, hey, you guys," I finally found the oomph to join in and put everyone at ease. "You didn't piss me off." I sighed, figuring out how to continue. "Craney-schmaney. I really think I could handle her now."

"And if she has a gun or a knife?" Dorotea said in a tiny voice.

"Well, I have friends watching. Besides, I would talk her out of it. She needs understanding."

"What?" Alda started to protest but burst into tears. "*Oh, minchia!* I love you all, and Pina's right. She knew when I needed understanding."

Gina leaned over to hug Alda. Both of them pulled me over to smother me with their affection. I called over to Katie. "You too, my sweet, I think I can do this now. Really."

"This? What is this?" Dorotea squinted with a diabolical grin.

Alda roared with laughter, slapping Dorotea on the back. Katie grinned broadly at me.

"Life, you turkeys, life."

After our breakfast, which ended in a short prosecco toast to life, Alda, Gina, Dorotea, and Lorenzo had to help prepare German and Sicilian specialties for the evening's festivities while Katie chose to be alone in church. I must have seemed totally floored by Katie's sudden religious conversion because Katie took my head in her hands, laughing.

"Pin, it's okay. Everything is okay. I just want some quiet."

"Should I come with you?"

"Damn it, Pina! I'm fine, and so are you. Go wait for Mère Paul and Père Sablé. Besides, I'm supposed to go shopping for seafood for tonight with your folks and mine."

I perched on a low hill overlooking the rural road and watched the chilly fog roll down the rocky hillside. Katie wandered off, slowly weaving her way over uneven cobbles to the smaller parish church. Maybe Katie was praying for me not to lose my mind, but I really did believe what I had said about Craney—that I could handle her.

Then I heard the gunshot and dove for the bushes. I shook myself off. I appeared intact. Looking around, I found every stone and boulder in its place; nearby café chairs and tables sat upright, inviting patrons; wires and lights still hung, strung taut for perching birds. Only one thing stood out—a huge Harley-Davidson lay on its side at the intersection.

No gunshot, no crisis, mere backfire.

Mère Paul called out to me, "*Salut*," while Père Sablé cursed the gravel on the road. They were unscathed, only their egos bruised.

I ran down to greet them, gawking at Père Sablé in full leathers and Mère Paul in a bomber jacket and a World War II helmet. We set the bike upright and seated ourselves in the corner café.

Two coffees later, Mère Paul asked if I needed more herbs now. I declined.

"And light?" Mère Paul's eyes twinkled.

"Who knows? Maybe tonight," I said. "They say there is a special star that comes out tonight. Isn't there a Bethlehem in Sicily?"

Mère Paul gave me a playful shove.

Père Sablé had gotten up to tinker with the rented Harley. He craned his neck up at us. "We, that one"—he pointed to Mère Paul—"and I, will say a blessing, but I think your ancestors are already protecting you—"

"And us," Mère Paul finished his sentence. "We could have been hurt, what with Monsieur le Père's driving. His wild days are not over yet!"

"To life!" I raised my water glass to him. "But it's true, I am feeling stronger. Maybe I don't need more protection."

"Eh? If that is so, then you have already passed your final exam."

"Tell Katie that."

"What? *Problèmes?*" Mère Paul wrinkled her brow. "Let me think about that."

"No. No more protection; I think I just need to see into people's minds and hearts, including my own."

Père Sablé rubbed his stubbly chin. "*Très bien.* You could be good at Stanford. You do know that school is close to Berkeley?"

"Eh oh. I believe Pina is saying love and empathy conquer all."

"*Amor vincit omnia.*" Père Sablé whistled.

"Ha. Just like a man to quote Latin when we talk love."

I laughed and laughed and hugged my two angels when Giulia's beat-up Fiat 500 roared to a stop at our feet. Père Sablé jumped up to give a piece of his mind to the thoughtless driver. Giulia started to give the evil eye to this Hells Angels look-alike, when Mère Paul and I doubled over with laughter.

"*Madre*," Giulia shouted through the open car window. "You fear I compete with your herbs, eh?"

Still chortling, Mère Paul yelled back, "Oh, no. I am afraid yours are better."

Giulia got out of the car, pumped Père Sablé's hand, and quipped, "Snazzy outfit, *Padre*!"

Père Sablé took in Giulia's long black dress and her black shawl. He winked. "Pretty appropriate, yours too."

Mère Paul got up and labored over to Giulia. "A pleasure to meet you. *La petite* has told us many good things about you." With a lowering of her coiffed head, Mère Paul added, "And you, too, know the light. Brava."

Giulia smiled her best Anna Magnani smile, earthy, sexy, and diabolically spiritual all at once. "Come," she said in her heavily accented Italian French. "I want to introduce you to some fellow Résistance pals." Giulia gestured to the back of the bar.

Old war heroes sat in a group at the far end of the café bar, lifting huge glasses of red wine to toast the Italo-French connection.

I started back up the incline as the sun began to set. Katie joined me at the next fork in the road. Without speaking, she slipped her arm through mine and leaned her head on my shoulder as we walked back to the *pensione*.

❧ ❧ ❧ ❧

Katie decided she needed a nap before the feast, which wouldn't start until nine. I stretched out by her side but continued to gawk wide-eyed at the image of the castle on the wall.

I thought about tonight and tomorrow and our final meals together. I was ready…ready to leave, ready for home. I could…

Père Sablé had given me my grades. I had already been fluent in French upon my arrival, and he said I'd seen enough realism and drama. I was more than conversant with French tragedy and comedy. Passed with flying colors.

And my final test with Katie? She and I still hadn't had *that* conversation, but I was ready. Ready to go on with or without her. We would always grow as friends; I believed that. I could live on my own. Without her as my lover? I would survive. I had come to trust I was lovable. I deserved good things. I wanted them; I wanted growth.

Craney? What if she reappeared in the States? I shifted my weight in the bed and flung off my covers. And? She could…but I couldn't hide. The FBI was certain to track her down.

I sat up scratching my head. The fear of Craney—the external Craney—was gone. Something had switched places with it. I got up and grabbed a jacket and crept outside. I paused and stooped to pluck some late wrinkled grapes and sat looking at the golden twinkles in the blackening sky.

A meeting. I would want a face-to-face with Craney. That's what I needed. Crazy. A meeting of my "internal" Craney with the real thing.

I was not Craney. I was loved. I understood that now and totally got what Craney had desired—to be loved—and when she learned she couldn't get that from me, she tried to destroy my potential for it. Not just sex, but the love she had never known, never been shown—the love I was receiving from Katie, all these friends and family.

I would tell Craney that she had helped me. I shook my head. It was clear to me now: she really had. Because of her, I could believe in myself and in the others. Shit, she helped me grow. I chewed on some more late-season, sugary grapes. Could I help her? Ha!

A chilly wind picked up. I shivered more at the idea of someday confronting Craney. My fear had disappeared. I was free. The breeze turned warm again as I returned to my room, and to Katie's side, and a profound but short sleep.

Chapter Forty-two

Christmas Eve on the Tower

The aroma of sun-ripened tomatoes stewed for hours with wine and olives, complemented by the succulent brine of oyster juices, wafted down the slopes from the castle. Various dishes decorated the tables for the feast on the castle's terrace. Lobster claws and muscles surrounded mounds of spaghetti while oval platters bore roulettes of prosciutto, melon, and dates. Cannoli arranged in columns surrounded by pyramids of chocolate-slathered profiteroles kept company with cream-topped chocolate panettone. Nero d'Avola, white grillo, and inzolia wines awaited blessings and toasts.

Père Sablé silently blessed the food as Mère Paul lit candles and torches. Adults and kids filed into rows of white folding chairs with parents claiming space for their broods. Each of us carried a small votive, which we lit as Père Sablé called out in Latin, "*Lux*," and light bathed our whole community.

He explained that the eve of feasts allows our hopes to live, to take the spark and unite us in one passionate moment of love. "I bless you," he said, "with the gift of light. Love one another and live your hope. This is the message of creation in all cultures. To life!"

We all embraced one another, and Giulia, Gina, and Lorenzo poured wine for each of us. We all sang out, "To life!" and toasted one another and the network of stars beginning to illuminate the sky.

"*Mangiate tutti!*" Giulia cried out.

My mother already sucked her fingers after brushing off the powdered sugar spraying off the cannoli that had drifted onto her black nubby wool coat. My father held out a lobster claw for me, afraid I hadn't seen them. Doc and Joe were winding massive spaghetti twirls in their spoons under the approving gaze of Giulia, who had cooked most of the meal.

My friends and I drank, hugged, and fed one another while dancing around from table to table. Gina and Lorenzo led us in *Astro del cielo*, the Italian version of *Silent Night*, while Dorotea's soprano moved us to tears with *Stille nacht* in German.

Wine flowed; tears flowed. Mère Paul and Père Sablé smiled and nodded in what seemed like meditative prayer.

Stopping for a moment to study them, I too bowed my head and closed my eyes. They had taught me so much. I absolutely had to climb the castle tower to feel one with the night sky and with this communal meditation.

I stole away from the group and began to mount the stairs and meditate on my time in Paris and my growth. As I focused on different stages of alternating glee and panic, the tower's steps grew steeper and more difficult. I had almost reached the top step. These would be some of my last steps as I approached the end of my stay. I believed I had finished my final exam. I would give a speech about that the next day on Christmas.

I paused, shaking with warm tears—good tears, tears of love. My breath came slowly as I swung my foot onto the final ledge. I became aware of another breath, another presence. There, opposite me on her own narrow ledge, stood Craney. I froze and closed my eyes a moment, visualizing all the stages and growth I had just witnessed in my mind's eye. I breathed deeply.

"And yes, here we are, dear Pina." Craney's voice was loud and strident.

Centering myself in my eyes and heart, in my mind, I tasted the herbs and drank the tea. They were in my blood. I called on the light.

"Hello, Miss Craney. I've been thinking about you." I wasn't lying. I thought I did understand her hatred, her need to destroy me.

"I'm sure you have." She jerked her head back and looked down her long bony nose at me. "Do you want to tell them down there?" She pointed her arthritic finger at the gathering.

"I can't look down; I think you know that. Please…I want to tell you I'm sorry. I've had everything you wanted for yourself. I know that now."

"Do go on." she said to me and then called down to Père Sablé and Mère Paul, "Hello!"

I heard a scream from down below and Doc's voice reassuring my mother I'd be okay. Père Sablé was saying something I couldn't make out, but I think he and Mère Paul were urging calm.

"I've had all these people show their love for me. You think it came easy to me. Like at birth, something I could just accept along with some smarts and okay looks. It was hard to open myself to them, to accept their love. I think I understand you. Miss Craney, it's not too late. I'm not mad at you. We can go down together."

"You'd like that, wouldn't you? Ha! You think I can go free now? You and your youthful hope."

I breathed deeply and took a step closer to her. "Please, I'm not angry. I understand you wanted what

I had, and I took it all away. I am sorry." I opened my hand, palm up. "Take my hand…"

From the ground, I heard Alda shouting, "She'll kill you, Pina!" And Dorotea screamed she would come up and get rid of Craney once and for all.

"No!" I screamed. "That's not the way. Miss Craney, here, I'll help, really. I forgive you."

Craney turned away a moment and, hiding her face, asked, "Why would you do that? You say you feel no hatred for me? Tell me," she all but whispered.

Steps echoed up the stairs. I yelled, "No. Stay down!" Then, to Craney, "I don't hate you. I learned not to hate myself, either. I can teach you. Mère Paul and Père Sablé will teach you. Please!" Again, I extended my hand.

Craney turned slowly. Her left eye seemed to glisten. Was it a tear?

"Miss Craney, please. Here, take my hand. We'll go down together, please."

Small convulsions ran up her body; her hand began to open. She extended it toward me.

Katie screamed, "Pina, I love you!" My eyes softened and started to close at the sound of Katie's voice.

I pushed across on the ledge as Miss Craney sprang. I grasped and failed, opening my eyes wide at the last minute to see Miss Craney pitch forward over the ledge, falling the fifty feet to the ground.

I screamed. Friends and family screamed as I charged down the tower stairs. On the terrace, Doc attempted to stop me. "She's gone, Pina. She must be."

Katie reached out to touch me as I pulled away from her grasp, still rushing toward Craney's body.

Lying in the rotting, moldy weeds, Miss Craney

moved her lips. I bent over to beg her to stay with me. "I can get help. Doc is here, please."

She was struggling to say something. I put my ear to her mouth and felt her warm breath as she formed her final words. "I forgive you, Pina."

I put my hand under her head as I watched the light in her eyes go flat and her head fall back.

Père Sablé was at my side. As he held his hand to the sky and mumbled something, I saw Miss Craney's face ease and soften. Père Sablé closed her eyes as a bolt of lightning lit up the sky.

I cried as my family and friends came down to surround me. Katie held me so tight, she almost wouldn't let my mother hug me. Alda and Dorotea hesitated an instant and asked if Craney was trying to pull me down at the very end. I wasn't sure, but I said, "No. She wanted me to help her get down." I had to believe that.

Mère Paul arrived out of breath. "*Mon enfant*, you have earned your place in the Panthéon!" She hugged me and kissed my forehead.

Giulia knelt before me and took my hand in hers. "You must eat something."

I asked to stay for a moment with Giulia, Mère Paul, and Père Sablé to do a silent mind prayer. I glanced over at Craney's corpse. Her face seemed at peace. I somehow felt at peace, too. A shooting star flew across the ancient fortress.

⁂

I moved off a few feet and stretched out on the hillside. A constellation seemed to circle the top of the tower. Occasional flashlight flickered from where Craney's corpse lay. I wrapped myself in a blanket someone had brought me. I waved them away.

Death stood close by. I glanced over at her crumpled body between short, staccato sobs. I had never been this close to someone else's death—and dying. To my own. I raked my fingers through the rocky clay soil. Cold stones.

I shook my head. I hadn't wanted it. Not this way. Not now. I sent a thought her way—in the direction of her body. "Sorry." I blew out a breath. Sorry?

Sirens, flashing blue lights, the breeze in the black night. Everything read cold, tragic, austere. Yet a warmth radiated from the hillside and up my back. How long did spirit linger in one's body?

My lips moved in my old church Latin. "*Pax vobiscum.*" I closed my eyes and smiled. "Peace be with you." And the response... "*Et cum spiritu tuo*—and with your spirit."

❧ ❧ ❧ ❧

My parents and Katie came along and took me by the arms to go eat something back on the terrace. Père Sablé and Doc stayed to deal with the police.

As I ate, surrounded by my friends, I felt layers of stress and sadness peel away from me. With each strand of spaghetti I twirled and each oyster I slurped, I grew progressively calmer and more convinced of the blessing of this fatality. For all of us and for Miss Craney.

After a while, I helped my father soothe my mother enough to get her to sleep. Katie and I had a few more glasses of wine with Alda, Gina, Dorotea, and Lorenzo. When I gazed into their kind, caring eyes, I had the sense my friends had grown older and calmer. They stayed to clean up, sending Katie and me back to the *pensione*.

As Katie and I walked to our room, we saw Père Sablé, Mère Paul, and Giulia, heads bowed and holding hands, in the flashing blue light of the withdrawing police car.

Katie stopped me, tears in her eyes. "Are you really okay? I mean, I think you're incredible. I, uh…"

I held Katie and wept. "Katie, I'm not freaked, really. Something happened up there. Something, the right thing."

"I was terrified for you."

I shook my head. "I think she died at peace. I think maybe she was ready."

Katie sighed. "I'm just so glad I have you."

We walked on another twenty feet or so, and then I stopped. "Katie…"

Katie brushed her lips against mine. "Shush. We're okay."

꧁꧂꧁꧂

Before we turned out the light, I snuggled with Katie, mumbling, "I know where I'm going."

She shut the light, laughing. "Yeah, to sleep."

"No. No. *Where…*"

"Huh?"

"Stan…"

"Sandman?"

My head still buried in Katie's pit, I managed to pull the sheet far enough away from my mouth to pronounce the whole word—"Stanford."

Although my mind drifted in and out of sleep and dreams, my body told me we had made mad, passionate love. I felt her move in me, and I came in her. I heard her say, "Not so far," and then, "Forty-four miles." Our lovemaking had never brought us so far!

Chapter Forty-three

Light on the Hill

Christmas morning had arrived. In honor of Paris and our plans to light the fire on the hilltop at dark, we called that day the Feast of Light.

We had decided not to exchange traditional gifts but gifts of our making. Père Sablé blessed our gathering at breakfast and reminded us of the day before. "The past is gone," he said, "but remember that in a way, Miss Craney did give Pina a hand, a hand into the future." He shrugged in his impish fashion and raised his coffee mug. "To hope!"

We toasted and tore off a piece of Mère Paul's king cake, which she said was too early for the Feast of the Three Kings, January 6, but that we were all royalty.

Giulia made us copies of the recipes she would serve at Gangivecchio when she opened the restaurant. Alda and Gina declared their engagement and plans to study at Le Cordon Bleu in the States. Lorenzo announced, with cow eyes aimed at Dorotea, that he would study medicine while Dorotea raved about doing a year of her medical studies at Stanford Medical School. With that, she threw me the hairy eyeball, and I just shrugged. Katie held up an envelope her father had handed to her. Berkeley had accepted her, awarding her a significant scholarship.

My father sheepishly said that he would play

Bach's Cantata 47 on his violin at the fire lighting, while my mother presented each of us with a small crocheted afghan.

Doc and Joe rose to their feet somewhat solemnly and raised a toast to Sarah Craney. At a loss, we stood just the same and raised our glasses. Joe announced that previously unknown to all, Miss Craney had an orphaned niece, Sarah, whom he and Doc would champion through four years of Albert, having seen to it that Craney's record was expunged.

When it was my turn, I apologized in advance for the length of my gift. My friends groaned as the adults tapped their glasses with their forks. I read my speech through my tears:

Resistance

Sometimes, we fight behind the scenes, not with guns but with love, and not by lurching forward but by holding up when appropriate, holding back when necessary, standing up when it's time, and inching forward in the nick of time.

Sometimes, we must open our arms to hold and offer love; sometimes to contain the ugliness and the evil.

Both actions are needed. We only know the right action when the light turns on to guide us—or to heal when we err and beg for grace and hope.

The Résistance in France, in Italy, in Germany has introduced me to freedom fighters, my peers and my elders, my friends and my one-time enemies. They have all taught me what they knew: to be alive, to be free!

My gift to all of you—and to myself: I choose the "wind of freedom."

I held up the red and white, redwood-tree-emblazoned crest and insignia of Stanford University, along with its motto, "The wind of freedom blows."

I paused a few seconds and added in a softer voice, "I'm ready for Stanford and ready for home."

As the applause died down and the hugs eased, my mother and Katie peeled themselves off me, the back doors sprung open, and Cassia and Sophie burst into the room. "*Mon Dieu*," cried Cassia. "You are alive!" Everyone laughed, especially after my long speech. "*Attendez!* My father got word from security that Craney was coming for you. Hurrah. You are safe?"

"Holy crap!" I shouted. "How did you get here?"

We all hugged Cassia and Sophie. As the bells on Cassia's shoes tinkled with the excitement, she explained that her father, who she indicated with a flick of her thumb, had taken them in the official municipal rescue boat from Bastia through the Mediterranean from Corsica to Palermo. We all cheered.

Sophie grabbed a glass to raise to all of us and to love. In her heavy French accent, she sang out, "Love will always find the way."

Cassia's father nodded politely and quickly spotted fellow *résisteurs* in Père Sablé, Mère Paul, and Giulia. Alda and Joe regretted that their fathers, *résisteurs* of sorts, were not there to celebrate since they had a previous date with the Madonna of Lourdes. Dorotea bowed her head, thinking of the FBI, I was sure.

Cassia and Sophie joined in the rest of the festivities and toasted many times to love and forgiveness.

❧❧❧❧

As the stars began to twinkle, the moving sounds of my father playing Bach welcomed us onto the crest of the old fortified hill. We assembled as Père Sablé spoke in French and Italian. "To the light, to rebirth!"

We all threw a lighted stick into the pile of dried branches, which soon rose to signal best wishes and joy in the new year to villages all around Giuliana.

We huddled close to one another as the wind picked up and then two shooting stars flew across the sky. We let out a cheer of "bravo" on the hilltop and all the way home as the fire on the hill died down, leaving the blaze in our hearts.

Our families were leaving for the States. Père Sablé and Mère Paul would leave by boat for Corsica with Cassia, Sophie, and Cassia's dad. Our families would see Katie and me at home in a few days. We extended invitations to the States to all the others.

Alda and Dorotea hung around a bit while Giulia, Gina, and Lorenzo prepared the car.

"I love you guys so much. You taught me everything I know about love." Alda was bawling.

"Everything?" I said.

Katie winked.

Dorotea melted as she tried to speak. She turned away a second to breathe deeply. "I am so proud of you, Pina. You're not a doofus anymore." We all laughed as Dorotea continued, "And you, Katie, never were." She hung on our necks, sobbing. "I can never say goodbye properly."

We toasted one last time. "To friendship and reunions in the States!"

Alda put on her devilish grin. "To Berkeley and Stanford."

Gina, Giulia, and Lorenzo came out and toasted with us as we exchanged goodbyes.

I put my arm around Katie as we watched them drive away. "It's just you and me now, Katie."

"Yup. And time for a delayed discussion."

"Oh, crap," I said, giggling.

"So, Stanford?"

"Yeah. And?" I slit my eyes at her.

She hooted and slapped me on the back. "Oh, Pina, I just love you. Oh, and by the way, I am so proud of what you tried to do for Craney."

"Tried…"

"Sweetheart, you offered her life."

"You know, maybe she took it. Maybe she did."

❧ ❧ ❧ ❧

We got to Raisi-Palermo Airport early and rushed to board the Alitalia propjet for Rome. Katie and I melted into each other's eyes, recalling our first propjet flight and orgasmic takeoff two years earlier on our trip to Albert. We sat back and waited as the engines revved up.

"I love you," Katie whispered in a breathy voice.

I smiled. "Me too!"

Katie began to tell the story of a hot air balloon in 1785 and a flying boat in 1916 where passengers found the lofty vessels conducive to sexual adventure en plein air.

We both rose to make our way to the lavatory to test out their theories and to begin our next adventures into the near and distant futures.

About the Author

Dolores grew up in Ozone Park, Queens, New York, where from the age of three she ventured away from this home on her own. While this first solo mission landed her in a nearby cathedral, her further ventures brought her to great physical and psychic distances from Ozone Park.

In addition to teaching foreign languages, and selling antiques, Dolores worked as a psychotherapist with children, teens, and couples and published reference books on lesbians and psychotherapy and child custody.

Dolores lives in Portland, OR and Borrego Springs, CA with her wife, Terrie, and Murphy, the rescue poodle, and Xander, the lynx point critic. She enjoys hiking and gardening with Terrie and Murphy and birding with Xander, from the safety of his indoor perch.

Other books by Dolores

Death and Love at the Old Summer Camp – ISBN – 978-1-943353-77-4

For Pina, summer 1959 started off a boring drag, just like every other summer with her folks at Owl Lake Lodge in Maine. The only good thing was seeing Katie and hanging out with her in the creepy cabins of the old boys' camp. But this summer, Katie seemed different, cuter. Pina didn't have a clue why. Katie just somehow made her nervous – and excited. Another thing rattling Pina's nerves were her dreams; well, not exactly sleep dreams, but awake dreams. All fine and good, but they came from her dead Sicilian grandmother, and they told her things, crazy things, love things, like her and Katie falling in love things. They also showed her dead stuff, dead like a long-time dead from the camp dead. So the summer heated up. And so did her feelings for Katie. Things got even hotter when Katie's dad, Doc, and his very, very close, old camp friend, Joe, started hiding camp secrets about dead stuff – and other stuff. How hot could Pina stand it?

If she didn't want to lose this one chance for a different kind of life, could she solve the murder – and clear Doc's name?

And would Katie have her and would Pina have herself?

Love and Lechery at Albert Hall: Pina and Katie and the Stalker of Albert Hall – ISBN – 978-1-948232-02-9

In September 1959 Pina's got only one thing on her

mind at the elite Albert Academy: four years of blissful rooming with her heartthrob Katie, pursuing their taboo relationship of the previous summer—only one thing until Pina stumbles over the lecherous Head Mistress Craney, lurking in the hall. Pina and Katie become obsessed with the blood-curdling game of cat and mouse Craney is craftily staging in every nook and cranny, from the fire escape to the bedclothes. Aided by quirky roommates, Pina struggles to elude Craney's clutches and her sinister machinations when Craney calls Pina's bluff in a salacious duel of wills. Must Pina submit?

Will the scorned and unrequited Head Mistress expose Pina to her parents, and the eventuality of shock therapy?

Who will banish whom?

Other books by Sapphire Authors

The Shower – ISBN – 978-1-948232-49-4

Alex Aoki, a talented and aspiring artist, has had an opportunity to paint full time for the last five years thanks to the very generous patronage of Lucia DelAlessio. In exchange for accompanying Lucia to events around the world and occasionally sharing Lucia's bed, Alex is able to focus on her art without worrying about day-to-day hassles and expenses.

Lauren O'Brien has left the rat race of a large Manhattan law firm to live a more peaceful life in rural New York. She meets the vivacious painter Alex at the small town's library, and it is clear that the attraction between the two extends beyond a love of books. Lauren dismisses Alex's interest as a schoolgirl crush because of their substantial age difference, but discovers that Alex is both persuasive and persistent. Lauren soon learns of a bigger issue that Alex has been hiding--the rich, jet-setting patroness whose financial support comes with sexual privileges.

While Lauren tackles her ideas of relationships and monogamy, Alex must face hard questions about what is really worth sacrificing for her painting. As they each search their souls for what is most important, they must sort out their feelings about age, passion, propriety, honesty, art, truth, and above all, love.

Silver Love – ISBN – 978-1-948232-51-7

Jill, Dory, Robby, and Charlene are a fantastic

foursome that embodies the varying experiences that come with being Lesbians of a Certain Age. They are vibrant and vulnerable, wise and foolish, introspective and outgoing. The close-knit friends fight aging at every turn--or just ignore it altogether. These four will never go quietly into the night, redefining life after fifty. They are the new mature woman.

But along with twenty-first-century attitudes come twenty-first-century problems. Public office candidate and retired judge Charlene is confronted by a wannabe blackmailer, Jill's passions threaten to swamp her common sense, Dory's best-selling book could turn out to be a national disaster, and Robby must confront the hard reality of learning that her wife may not be the woman she thought she was. Steadfast in their faith in themselves and each other, and bolstered by the rich history of their friendship, the four women struggle with twists and turns as they try to navigate a landscape generated by the actions of others as well as their own choices, proving that experience does not always pave a smooth road.

In a world where everything increasingly seems relative, these women remind us that some things don't change--like the bedrock of relationships. Silver Love is all about love; love among friends, love between lovers, and the unexpected role of love with acquaintances who may not always be what they seem. If you can keep up, join the ride and follow these ageless heroines as they pursue their adventures in the modern world.